TOROPO'S
SISTER, TAWA

Credits

David Hersman granted permission to quote his chapter on the *Wantok* System from his book, ***The True Course***.

Quotes from Ms. Hirsi Ali's book are used by permission.

Scripture quotations are taken from the ***Jewish New Testament***, copyright 1979 by David H. Stern. Published by Jewish New Testament Publications, Inc., 6120 Day Long Lane, Clarksville, Maryland 21029. www. messianicjewish.net/jntp. Used by permission.

Don Richardson granted permission to Linda Kelley to quote the Author's Epilogue from the new edition of ***Peace Child***.

Permission was granted by Christina Kewa to quote from her book.

Quotes from ***The Shack*** are used by permission of Wm. Paul Young and his daughter, Amy.

Linda Harvey Kelley has permission to quote the poetry of Melissa A. Kinnett, Florida Pugupia and Louise Kousa in her writings.

The songs "My God Is So Big" and "In His Time" are used by permission.

Quotes from the first chapter of Dr. Meg Meeker's book, ***Strong Fathers, Strong Daughters*** are used by permission.

Permission was granted to use David Barton's letter. Wallbuilders 1-800-873-2845

Testimonial

Your style will doubtlessly be well received and helpful in PNG…. At any rate, I think what you have will be helpful; God bless all of your efforts. I should like a copy for myself when the volume becomes available. Since I have PNG students in my classes, it will give me a flavor of their lifestyle and manner of worship, seeking the Lord, etc. Keep in touch.

God bless you, your family and your work!

Dr. Paul Kaufman

Published by
Whispering Pines Publishing
11013 Country Pines Road
Shoals, Indiana 47581, USA

Dedication

To all the girls and women in Papua New Guinea and in particular to Wameyambo Mann, Ellepe Nomi, Sarah Eme, Pauline Basua, Anna Mulu Davis, Helen Tua, Tawame Kewa Timba and her daughters, Ruth Awina, and Rebecca Mokanu Asi and her daughter.

To Pila Niningi's mother, who may be alive or deceased, who portrayed Bani-Ma for me.

Lastly to the memory of Waiye Aleka and the little bride who hung herself before she reached puberty and started me writing all this.

Photos On the Cover

Front cover: Susan Bonau

Back cover: top: Mala Mulu with her daughters,
Pauline Mulu Basua and baby Rahab

Back cover: middle: New Guinea Madonna (I don't know
her name. I met her on the trail one day, and wanted a photo
of the way she was carrying her baby.)

Back cover: bottom: Marilyn Lavy and Dianne Lytle
(having a sausage roast!)

Glossary of ImboUngu Words

ai!	hey!
ama	mother
ambo kunana	love chant, head-turning (tanim het)
ambo mopene	beautiful young girl, debutante
ambo	woman
aminienga glapa!	an exclamation (lit. "your mother's father!")
ango	brother, sibling of the same sex
ara	father
aya	sister
bagol	girl
balkangoma	children
ere!	exclamation olaman!
glanie (or lanie)	your father;
Gote	God; Ara Gote–Father God or Arai Gote
imbo	people, real, natural, real people
Imbo-Ungu	Real Talk, or Real People's Talk
iye	man
kambe ulke	isolation hut
kamukumu	for always
kango	boy
kangu	hug
kanguglembili	let's us two hug
kani	so, so there, etc
kapogla	all right
kariyapa	mirror
keri	bad
kogol	dear little, tiny, (a term of endearment)
koinje	(bamboo) tongs
komaglaiye	first born
kombu	place
komu tsindindu	I forgot
kondodle	red, red skins, light-skinned
konjo nowi	"eat-it-raw" – cucumber
konopu lteyo	I think
konopu maa tondoromo	I forgot

5

konopu mondoro	I love
konopu	friend, dearest (lit. thought, part of the verb "to love")
kuro kelkawe	the good spirit
ltemo	it's evident, or on evidence
magol	son
mendepogol	only, just
moglowiyo	good-bye (lit. you may stay)
moromo	he/she is
mundu	mound for planting kaukau
Na paa niyo	I'm telling the truth;
nu paa nino	you're telling the truth;
yu paa nimo	he/she's telling the truth
nagol	but
nanga	my, mine
-ndo	to
nopi	namesake or same-name
Nu tendo puni ?	Where are you going? (This is the ImboUngu greeting.)
nunge	your/yours
owa!	exclamation (lit. dog!)
owiyo	you may come
paaimbo	truly
paa-tsingo-we	very delicious
pamili	let's go
pendepende	show off Na pendepende teli iyemu – I am a show-off (male)
Peyamo-peli	where the spirit Peyamo sleeps
pumo	he went
puni	you want to go
puyo	good-bye (you may go)
tagol tsipe	second
te	where; tena – where at; tendo – where to
tendeku	one
tiro	I give
tsingo-we	delicious, sweet
tuku	inside; tukuna – inside
tukundo	into or inside
wayo	you all come
wenepo	young
wenopoma	teen-agers
yupoko	three

Glossary of Kewa or Kewapi Words

andaponda ande alinu	seers
erepere naki	last son
erepere nogo	last daughter
koma	dead
kone	thought
kone rugulaaru	I forgot
kundina	extinquished
lapo	two
naki	boy
nogo	girl

ora ta
   ora lalo
   ora lale
	he/she's telling the truth;
	 I'm telling the truth;
	 you're telling the truth

paitepaape	you all lie down/sleep
pogolasa	jump up
pu	liver
ramea	rotten
rende pia	is sweet
reka	stand up
repo	three
rero pi	is bitter
u patea	sleep
yarayowe	so sorry
yola	pull

Glossary of Pidgin Words

ai gris	"eye-grease," flirt
amamas	praise, joy, happiness
apinum	afternoon (a greeting)
askim	ask
bilum	net bag, or netting worn on the body
dia tumas	expensive, very dear
dispela	this

Em i gutpela.	He/she is good.
Em i taitim bun.	He/she tightened her bones, meaning he/she tried with all his/her might.
gen	again
go nating	"go nothing," shack up with someone, without marriage ceremony or brideprice
God i bekim prea.	God answers prayer.
God bai bekim prea.	God will answer prayer.
God i harim prea.	God hears prayer.
haus kapa	house with a metal roof, or "permanent house"
haus-sik	"house-sick," hospital
helpim	help
Jisas	Jesus
kalabus	jail
kapsaitim	pour out, spill, shed
kaukau	sweet potato
kiap	government officer
kotim	take to court, prosecute, sue
kunai	tall, sharp-edged grass (perhaps elephant grass)
laplap	length of cloth
lapun	old person
long	for, or most any preposition, at, on, to, etc.
meri	woman, female
mi	I, me
Mi amamas tumas.	I'm so happy.
Mi go wokabaut gen nau.	I'm going to go wandering again now.
Mi no save.	I don't know.
mumu	pit oven in the earth
na	and
olaman	"all the men," an exclamation without literal meaning

pitpit	a cane, similar to bamboo but much thinner, smaller (though 6-8 feet tall)
ples	place
purupuru	grass skirt
rabis meri	"rubbish woman," whore, prostitute
rausim	"rouse," send away, dismiss, discharge, take out or away
samting	something
singsing	dance
tainim	turn, translate, interpret
tingting	think, thought, cogitation
toea	penny, cent
tru tumas	Truth! or "That's very true!"
wanem	what
wantok	literally "one-talk," someone who speaks the same language
wasim	wash
yo, -eyo –iyo	la, la, la, la, la, in singing (no translatable meaning)
yumi	we /us (you & me)

Glossary of Wiru Words

angorai	my father
Kewa	someone from the Kewa language area; foreigner, stranger
kewaroa/kewarowa	foreign woman, strange woman, woman from the Kewa area
nimini	true, truth
nimini uku	I'm telling the truth;
nimini oko	you/he/she is telling the truth
wene	thought
wene kaiyapekou	I forgot; (literally: I spilled my thoughts)
yawaliyo	decorations (an exclamation in Wiru, also Angorai yawaliyo!)

The Palms Pelfreys planted at Pabrabuk

Acknowledgments

The author wishes to thank all her continuity readers and proofreaders who have helped her try to get this book in print: Lowell Lavy, Erin Duffy Hildebrand, Elizabeth Rivard, Kathryn Ghering Goodman, Melissa Kinnet, Rev. Norman Imbrock, Dr. Paul Kaufmann, Rev. Paul Wolfe, Rev. Steven Harvey, Ruth Blowers, and Elizabeth Werner.

I also wish to thank my husband, George Kelley, for allowing me to retire early, and work full time on writing and research for many months. I thank George and my children for all their help and blessing, and permission to quote them and tell their stories, as well as so many of my friends in PNG and USA. I want to especially thank Lowell Lavy and his family, and Connie Lavy and Jason and Joanna Sturtevant for helping me with the tribute to their sister and mother Marilyn Lavy Sturtevant and the photos; and Cheryl Mahan for the photos and story of her husband, Dale Mahan's life.

I thank my husband and children, Bob and Vicki, Dean and Pam, for all the meals they have cooked for us, and all the other duties they have done to free me to write. I want to thank my pastor, Rev. David G. Ward and his wife, Ruth, and their daughter, Abigail, for much help with my granddaughters, and for allowing me to spend seven weeks in PNG in 2008, while they stood in the gap here.

I want to thank David Hersman for permission to quote his chapter on the *Wantok* System from his book, ***The True Course***, Dr. Paul Kaufman for his sermons on holiness, Rev. Paul Wolfe and Rev. Steve Harvey for the sermon on forgiveness, and all my mentors, pastors, and men and women of God, including Dr. Philip Kereme, Paka Kili, and others who have influenced my belief system and endeavored to instill in me a Biblical worldview.

I appreciate each person who has allowed me to quote them.

On the Plane

Port Moresby

Stewardesses on Air Niugini

L. & Lily Tangawe & Dr. Peter

Pila, Maria & Vicki Niningi

Daphne Basua made friends all over the airport.

Danny Kanga; Pauline, Daphne & David Basua (M.P.); G+L; Pila, Steve Harvey & Dr. Philip Kereme

Esther Vele was very friendly and she made the tiring night pass quickly.

Maria & Vicki, Billy, Kathy, Tiye, Rosalie & Dr. Philip Kereme   April 14, 2000

Chapter One

Tawa ran the fingers of her left hand over the pleats of her meri-blouse as she slid into her seat for the last class of the day — eleventh grade English. What a delight! Mrs. Grace Bonau was a stimulating teacher. She loved reading and writing as much as Tawa did, and she loved sharing books with her students. Tawa couldn't wait to see what book or chapter they were taking up next.

Linda and Annie entered the classroom together and came to sit on either side of Tawa. Tawa's Trio, people called them, though they could have just as well said, "Linda's Trio" or "Annie's Trio," but maybe people liked the alliteration — two T's together.

"Tired?" Tawa asked Linda sympathetically.

"Yes, and starved!" returned Linda Stanley, "but this is our last class so I'll make it. Did you pass that test in socio-economics?"

"I think so," returned Tawa. "I'd have done better if it was just socio-stuff without the economics. I'm not much good in economics. I guess I'll have to let my husband manage the money, do the banking and everything!"

"Oh, no, Tawa," inserted Annie. "That's too traditional! You're a third-world woman. You want to make your own money and keep as much of it as the tribe will let you! You don't want to be handing it over to any man to take care of for you! If you get an education at all, you must get it in economics!"

"How about getting an education in law? My Dad doesn't allow my mother to own anything. Is there some law saying a woman owns what she earns? How about your father, Annie? What does Pastor Yakura do?"

"Dad and Mom don't have all that much money to worry about, but Dad handles what they do have. There have been a lot of us to put through school. It's all they can do to scrape enough together to pay our school fees. If Dad hadn't been able to build our own house, we would not be living in a *haus-kapa*. Our whole tribe went together to buy my brother's ticket to America. Jack had worked hard and saved up money of his own too. I don't know what's going to happen when Jack wants to get married. I don't know how Dad can canvass the tribe for one son two times!"

The last of the latecomers entered the classroom and took seats.

"Let's ask Mrs. Bonau if she's a traditional woman in money matters, or if she handles her own money," said Linda.

"Maybe sometime outside the classroom. That's too personal to ask in front of a whole class."

"Yes, I guess you're right," agreed Linda, just as Mrs. Bonau began speaking.

"I've got some poems to share with you today, class. How many of you have heard of Louise Kousa, otherwise known as Louijah M. Salote Kousa?"

A third of the class raised their hands.

"Her book, **A Sense of Interest**," and Mrs. Bonau held the slim volume aloft, displaying the artwork on both front and back covers, "was copyrighted under PNG Teachers' Association: Occasional Publications Number One. It was probably published in 1978 or 1979.

"The first poem in here is my favorite of hers. I did meet her once at a high school near Ukarumpa. She impressed me as much by her speech as she did by her poems. We didn't talk about the weather or any other silly, polite, superficial talk. She cut right to the quick, mentally. She faced issues and she expressed emotion freely.

"My creative writing students, if you want your creative writing to be read, allow some emotion into it.

"Just listen to the emotion in her first poem:

Nothing

I talked
    Nobody listened
I laughed,
    Nobody cared
I cried,
    Nobody heard
I was nothing.

Were people so deaf
So dumb
So blind
Had they no hearts
Couldn't they see
That I was in need?

Mrs. Bonau lowered the book and looked at her class.

"What is your response? How do her questions make you feel?"

No one raised a hand and after a few seconds Mrs. Bonau continued, "Take a piece of paper and write out your response. Write for five minutes and then pass them forward. Don't forget to write your name on the paper."

For five minutes there was no sound except for the scratch of pen or pencil on paper. When Mrs. Bonau had collected all the papers she asked who wanted to share their response with the class.

A young man raised his hand.

"Yes, David?"

"She began by talking. When no one listened she proceeded to laugh. My experience is that laughter usually draws attention. But when she laughed, she felt nobody cared. That's so sad. And so she cried, but still no one heard or responded."

"That's a very good observation, David, and you showed that she went through a very logical sequence. Anyone else?"

A hand in the middle of the room went up.

"Yes, Pilipo?"

"And then, being a girl, she cried," said Pilipo.

Laughter followed his response, but it was subdued laughter.

Mrs. Bonau smiled, "Be careful. You don't want to sound chauvinistic. Remember Lord Byron's poem asking for a tear? A man wrote that. Have you never seen boys cry?"

Tawa looked around the room. Some girls were nodding their heads, and even one or two boys.

"Do you think PNG girls might have more to cry about than boys, Pilipo?"

"Yes, I imagine they do," answered the honest boy. "I know I wouldn't want to be a girl!"

"Nor I!" said several boys.

"Me neither," responded a few more.

"Do you know," said Mrs. Bonau, "in sixty-nine countries of the world, there are more men committing suicide than women? Do you suppose maybe men ought to cry more, instead of holding their emotions in check outwardly, until they are desperate?"

"Yes," agreed several muted voices.

One hand went up.

"Yes, Thomas?"

"How do you know that? I don't know of a single man who has committed suicide, but I do know of more than one woman."

"You're right, Thomas," said Mrs. Bonau. "PNG is not one of those sixty-nine countries. Four countries in the world have more female suicides than male, and PNG is first of those four."

"How do you know?" asked Thomas again, without raising his hand.

"Go to Mt. Hagen to Internet Café or Six-Story Telecom. Pay your fee to use the internet and google 'Worldwide Suicide Rates.'"

"What will that tell me?"

"It will list the number of male and female suicides for most countries and the year of the statistics. Unfortunately PNG isn't even listed. You have to look for PNG's statistics elsewhere. But you will see that in most other countries more men commit suicide than women.

"In my quote box here I have some statistics for Papua New Guinea and India. In 1979 Healey completed a paper saying, 'Regional studies also find that among the Mareng people of PNG, only females commit suicide.' Also a person named Banerji and his group, referred to in doctoral dissertations as Banerji et al, wrote in 1990 that in the Daganga region of India, women constitute more than two-thirds of all suicides. Robert A King and Alan Apter wrote a paper on *Suicide in Children and Adolescents* in 2003 and these are some of their compiled facts.

"Maybe we can get back to that later, but now I want to read you another poem. This one isn't as well known as Louise Kousa's, but it too shows a lot of emotion. Unfortunately, this one isn't even published yet. This one is written by Florida Pugupia and it's titled

The Court Case

The hour of judgment
The moment of truth
Has dawned on all I hold dear.
This child I bear, The man I do care
Will he acknowledge us both?
I just do not know.

There sit the women called wives
Preening with pride and self-righteousness,
Around stand the men, and him in no-care fashion
Showing to one and all, their place in society.

Magistrate nods and fabricates
Man steps forward and elaborates
Verdict reached and I retreat,
My child and I abjectly dismissed.

Is there a society with monogamy rules?
A place where woman can defend herself?
Or a court with a just judge?
Is this all there is to life?
Male tyranny, polygamy and bribes?"

Wow, thought Tawa. What a list! "Male tyranny, polygamy and bribes." She realized her eyes were filled with tears. Mrs. Bonau was blurred in front of her, as well as the front rows of students. These were the sort of sentiments Tawa had heard women voice all her life. She had heard her own mother say things like this. Her mother just hadn't expressed it in poetic form. She had heard Bani-Ma, Mombo-Ma and Mindili-Ma all say similar things.

Aminienga glapa! "Male tyranny, polygamy and bribes." Where could a girl go to escape?

"The picture she paints is very dark indeed," said Mrs. Bonau. "Do you know any pictures this dark in the world around you?"

Several students nodded their heads.

"Does anyone want to talk about it?"

"My dad has two wives and they fight a lot," said one girl.

"I've seen my dad beat my mum," said a boy.

Several more students depicted equally black scenarios.

"Do you know of any happy marriages?" asked their teacher.

"Yes," assented a few.

Tawa thought. She tried to think of married couples in her village. Many a morning, many an evening, the sound of escalated arguments brought onlookers. Many times it ended with the man beating the woman. But she was sure she had seen happy couples too. Mostly at church, she realized. Always where there was only one wife for each husband.

"Christina Kewa from Mount Hagen has a book on the market titled *Being A Woman in Papua New Guinea: From Grass Skirts and Ashes to Education and Global Changes*. Mrs. Bonau held the green book aloft to show her class.

"She titles Chapter Six "Woman in PNG" and the sub-title is "A Man's Property – Bought for a Price." She feels bride-price means the man owns the woman and can treat her how he likes. Do you agree?"

"Maybe," nodded several boys.

"Maybe not," offered David, "but the thing is, a bloke has to wait until he's almost an old man before his tribe is willing to get the bride-wealth together for him. So many older men keep wanting more wives that all the pigs and kina shells go for them."

"I'm sure that's true, David. Do you agree?" Her eyes roved around the class, and she decided everyone agreed. It was unanimous.

"Christina Kewa thinks women don't even object to being beaten because they too believe the man has paid for them, and they feel he has a right to beat them. They believe they have to take his abuse."

Tawa raised her hand.

"Yes, Tawa?"

"You don't think so?"

"No, I don't. Nobody has to take abuse. I don't think brideprice gives the man the right to misuse a woman."

The students looked at her unbelievingly. What reasons could she give?

She looked them in the eye and said, "Violence is always wrong. We should never be violent toward one another. Violence occurs when people lose control. It may lead to murder. Murder is wrong. 'Thou shalt not kill.' God says.

"Let's get back to bride-price: let me give you some more facts. These are from Africa.

"In 2006 Sister Namibia wrote a brief 177-word article titled: *Bride Price Leads to Abuse of Women*.

"The Tanzania Media Women Association (TAMWA) conducted a study in ten of Tanzania's twenty-one mainland regions between January and March 2006, and came to this conclusion: the practice of paying bride price is one of the factors contributing to women in Tanzania suffering sexual abuse, battery and denial of their right to own property.

"On April 18, 2005, an Anonymous Author wrote in Zimbabwe: *Bride Price and Violence*. '*Lobola* (brideprice) is steeped in tradition. On an apparent level, the man makes payments to the woman's family as part of the marriage process. But in reality, say critics, *lobola* condemns women to marital enslavement and denies them control over decision-making, marital resources, their children and their own sexuality.' This is from Women's Feature Service, provided by ProQuest LLC.

"Another article is titled *Bride Price* by Sandra A. Mushi and it begins, 'I bought you, woman!' he bellowed as he kicked her. 'You are my property! You hear me? Mine!'

"'*Vermilia*. Get used to it. That's marriage,' her mother and aunts told her whenever she could sneak to them in tears.

"This short story tells how he beat her so she couldn't bear children, burned her, partially blinded one eye and scarred her forehead. She determined to work day and night to get enough goats, rice, beer and a blanket to pay back her brideprice.

"She was so happy when she had it all together that she cooked her husband's supper with a light heart, then went to invite her parents. When she returned her husband had thrown a party with the bride-price payments, he had commanded women to kill the goats and was drinking the beer with his friends.

19

"Yes, she had indeed been bought. Only a sign on her forehead saying 'Once bought, can't be returned,' was missing.

"You can read about all these three stories from African countries on the internet," continued Mrs. Bonau.

"I wish we had a Six-Story Telecom in Ialibu," said Pilipo.

"So do I," assented others.

"And here is one more I also got from the internet, but it hits closer home. It is from *The New International*, Issue 270, which came out in 1995, I believe. It is written by Christine Bradley, a social anthropologist, who is now in Canada, but who spent eleven years in PNG. Five of those years she was running the Law Reform Commission's programme on violence against women. The article is titled "Disarming the Fist" and it is subtitled 'We pay for our wives, so we own them and can belt them any time we like,' said the Government minister in Papua New Guinea in 1987.

"Three paragraphs later, I am reading again, 'In the villages a husband's right to chastise his wife physically was accepted, with some tribes even recognizing this by presenting a stick to the bridegroom in return for the payment of brideprice. The payment of brideprice by a man's extended family is marked in most parts of the country. In the eyes of many Papua New Guineans it is also what gives a man the right to beat his wife if she displeases him.' Then it quotes again, the Government member's statement, 'We pay for our wives, so we own them and can belt them any time we like.'

"This article also brings in another component, and then uses the fact that a man has beaten a woman as proof that he owns her! Listen. 'In a famous court case involving a minister accused of rape, the fact that he had previously beaten the girl on several occasions was offered as a defense: the beatings "proved" that he regarded the girl as his wife and therefore could not be accused of raping her. (Papua New Guinea wives have no right to refuse sex with their husbands.)

"Obviously, other countries believe that a woman can refuse even her husband, when she wants.

"There is a chart with this article saying that 97 percent of patients treated for domestic violence injuries are female. Three percent are male. Reasons men give for hitting are: 1. Sexual jealousy, 2. Drunkenness, 3. Money problems or 4. 'the wife failed in duties.' There is only one reason women give and that is self-defense.

"I am told in the USA women are encouraged to leave their husbands, if they have beaten them, in order to protect themselves and save their own lives and those of their children. If a man can lose control enough to be violent, who knows if he will stop before he kills?

"Muslim men believe they have the right to kill their wives or their children. And according to the law in many Muslim countries, they are given that right. Sometimes they even try it in non-Muslim countries. For instance I heard in Denton, Texas, in the USA a man killed his two teenage daughters recently, supposedly because they were 'too American.' He has disappeared without being arrested.

"On the 13th of February 2009, in Orchard Park, New York State, USA, a Muslim man named Muzzammil Hassan killed his wife, Aasiya, by beheading her. She had filed for divorce because he was beating her and abusing her. Muslims call these three murders honor killings and say in their culture it is allowed. If a woman or girl brings shame to her husband or father, they may kill her to protect their honor. But that is wrong. Beating a wife is not acceptable. Beheading a wife is never acceptable for any reason whatsoever.

"Well, we are going to continue this topic for the next several weeks, so I want you to be thinking, brainstorming. Maybe we will even stage a debate on brideprice. Would you like to debate it?"

Several nodded.

Tawa worked alone in one section of the school garden that afternoon picking beans. Brideprice, she pondered. It's called *lobola* in Zimbabwe. I must learn more about Zimbabwe.

Brideprice, she mused. A girl is supposed to bring in a good price or she has to live in shame the rest of her life. Either way, her husband has to pay more, each time she bears another child, or the mother's tribe might say, "*Mipela les.* We're disgusted with you!" and the child might even be named "*Tiye*" in my language or "*Giame*" in the Kewa language. Tawa thought of the girl named Giame who had tattooed on her leg, in English, "Born to be hated" when she was a teenager. Imagine growing up with a name like Tiye or Giame. Oh, how sad! We learned about self-esteem in psychology class. How could anyone grow up having any self-esteem, being called Tiye or Giame all their lives? She mentally listed all the possible meanings of those two names:

1. Disgusted
2. Tired of me
3. They left me
4. Deserted
5. Abandoned

If *lobola* might be a sign on one's forehead, "Sold. Unreturnable," then naming a child Tiye or Giame or Bagol Keri or Meku is even worse. What would that do to self-esteem?

I will never name my child Tiye, Tawa promised herself then and there, between the sixth and seventh rows of beans in the Ialibu high school garden. Even if my husband has angered my tribe, by not paying more brideprice at the birth of this child, I will choose the best name I can from the Bible, maybe King David, maybe Solomon, or maybe the priest, Melchizedek.

Mrs. Bonau says brideprice results in wife abuse. She doesn't think a wife has to take being beaten. I've seen my dad beat Mindili-Ma, but she aggravated him. I thought she deserved to be punished, but now I wonder if Mrs. Bonau is right.

I want to marry a man I love, and I don't think I could go on loving him if he beat me. That would be like I was his slave, and he was a slave owner. How could you love someone who beats you?

I hope I can marry for love. I hope I can marry a young man who is educated and tall and handsome and who wears nice clothes.

I hope I don't have to be like my mother. She had to marry a man who already had four wives, even though she had been to a Primary T School and finished grade six. She was a Catholic and they did not preach against polygamy. Her tribe sold her to my dad in 1990. I was born on the 24th of June 1991. Mum wrote it down. She put it in plastic and kept it all these years. I'm seventeen years old! I'm the youngest one in my class of those who know their birthdays. Annie is eighteen and Linda is nineteen.

I'm so thankful my dad hasn't talked about me marrying yet. Toropo says he sold her in marriage when she was about fourteen. Mombo was fourteen or fifteen, they guess. I am the third daughter of Boss Boy Pombo, and I'm seventeen, and he hasn't pulled me out of school to get married yet. I wonder how long my good fortune can last. I hope he lets me go all the way through grade twelve! And maybe even beyond — to University at Goroka! How I would love to be a high school English teacher like Mrs. Bonau and open new worlds to my students through books, like she has opened to me. I wonder what will happen in my life....

"Oh, God," she prayed aloud, "don't let me have to marry an old man with many wives like both my older sisters had to do! Oh, God, save me!

"You saved me from my sins, God. You took away all my guilt and shame for my wrongdoing. You have helped me hold up my head like Mrs Bonau does. Now, please, God, save me from marriage to an old man and a polygamist. Oh, how I wish my daddy was a Christian and would listen to the preachers at PNG Bible Church. They preach against polygamy — and that's the very reason probably that he won't go. He has five wives.

"God, does it matter to You how a young girl feels? Do You only care about our souls and our eternal salvation, or do You care about our earthly life too, and our fears, and our desires? Oh, how I wish I knew! I wish there were somebody I could ask!"

Samane teaches Wall Weaving 101 to Deran Stalder and the Kelley Kids

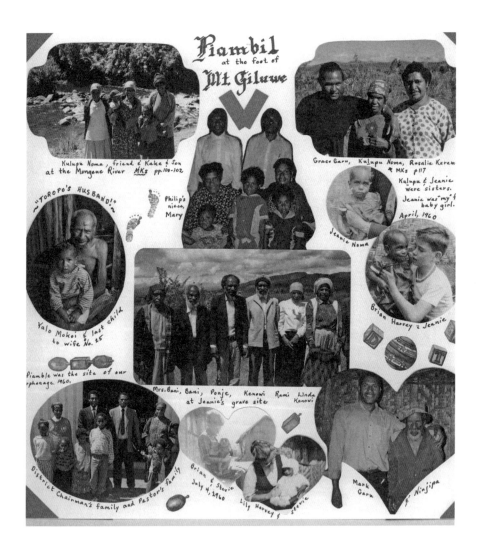

Piambil
at the foot of
Mt. Giluwe

Kulupu Noma , friend & Kake & Son
at the Mongene River _MKs_ pp. 100-102

Grace Garu, Kulupu Noma, Rosalie Kerem
& MKs p117

Kulupu & Jeanie
were sisters.

Jeanie was "my" baby girl.

April, 1960

"TOROPO'S HUSBAND!"

Philip's niece, Mary

Jeanie Noma

Yalo Mokoi & last child
to wife No. 15

Brian Harvey & Jeanie

Piamble was the site of our
rphanage. 1960.

Mrs. Bani, Bani, Ponje,   Kenowi Rami Linda
at Jeanie's grave site   Kenowi

District Chairman's family and Pastor's family

Brian & Stevie
July 4, 1960

Lily Harvey & Stevie

Mark
Garu

& Ninjipa

24

Chapter Two

That evening Tawa's Trio was walking together to the Nazarene Church at Ialibu where the movie, "Peace Child" was to be shown.

"Is this all there is to life? Male tyranny, polygamy and bribes?" quoted Tawa as they walked together, down the stony road. "I wish I could know Florida Pugupia and Louise Kousa, don't you?"

"Yes," agreed Linda Stanley. "It would be fun to meet a poet in real life. Mrs. Bonau said Louise's conversation even was different than that of most people.

"But she didn't tell us anything about Florida Pugupia, did she?"

"No, she didn't," agreed Tawa. "I wonder where she got her poem, and who she is."

"We will have to be sure to ask her next class. I can't wait to go on with the topic, can you?"

"I felt like she opened a whole new world to us, a world that I thought before had to stay hidden, and was only talked about by old men. I feel like I learned so much, in just one class," said Annie Yakura.

"Same here," agreed Linda.

The trio entered the Nazarene Church and sat down quietly about two-thirds of the way forward. Pastor Paul Bali was behind them and walked on up to the platform where two guitarists were playing, "Nothing but the Blood of Jesus." A white woman was playing a keyboard, accompanying the guitarists.

"That's Pamela Houck playing the keyboard. She is the one I told you I met at the Health Sub-Centre, remember?"

Tawa and Annie nodded their assent to Linda as they watched her fingers on the keys. Annie and Linda were soon looking around, taking everyone in, but Tawa could not take her eyes from Pamela's fingers. She watched with hungry, thirsty eyes, drinking in the music. She saw Pamela nod to her sons, sitting on the platform, and two little boys stood up, left their father's side and came to center front where Pastor Bali handed them each a microphone.

> "Wanem samting wasim mi?
> Blut bilong Jisas, em tasol.
> Wanem samting wasim mi?
> Blut bilong Jisas, em tasol.
> Jisas i dai long mi.
> Long Maunten Kalvari.
> Wanem ken rausim sin?
> Blut bilong Jisas, em tasol."

"Aren't they cute?" said Annie. "I wonder how old they are."

When the boys completed the chorus the three instrumentalists played the verse and chorus through again.

"The smaller one has to be at least three years old," said Tawa. "Did you hear him say bwut for blut? And I guess the firstborn to be seven years. What do you say?"

"Six," said Linda.

"Eight," said Annie.

Just then their mother nodded to the boys again and they repeated the words they had just sung. This time their mother sang along with them, harmonizing. They both came on stronger with the melody as their mother sang the alto.

"Look at that little one's blue eyes flash when he looks at his mother!" said Tawa.

"And the older one has brown eyes like us, and he is Mr. Serious, doing everything right," commented Annie. "Aren't they adorable? It makes me want to get married and have two sons who can sing!"

"It makes me want to learn to play the keyboard, so I could teach my sons to sing," said Tawa.

Crowds flocked in to hear the music and the little boys' singing. Soon the church was packed.

"I'm glad we got here when we did! We got seats!" Throngs of children filled the center aisle and the space between the platform and the front seats. When there was standing room only at the very back of the large building, Pastor Paul Bali accepted the microphones from the two little boys and said, "It's time to begin our service." The two boys turned and walked to their father with smiles. The smaller boy crawled into his father's lap.

"Look how their daddy loves them," whispered Tawa to her friends as the tall thin man wrapped his right arm around his firstborn, *Kango Komoglaiye*, while settling *Tagol Tsipe* on his lap.

"Turn in your songbooks to page 100," said Pastor Paul. The keyboard led out with the first strains of *"Askim Jisas Long Helpim Yumi"* to the tune of "Jesus Lover of My Soul" and the guitarists joined in.

When the lights were turned out and scenes of Don Richardson and his wife in the canoes with the Sawi tribesmen came on the screen, the crowd gasped at the sight of the ocean, and men who looked like themselves, paddling the canoes so effortlessly, seemingly. Every eye was riveted on the screen. Every other sound was shushed; adults wanted to hear the sound track. Babies were quickly soothed.

What a story!

How those coastal tribes in Dutch New Guinea had fought! All of the older people in the congregation were suddenly remembering fights they had witnessed; battles in which they themselves had fought. There seemed to be no end to the fighting in Dutch New Guinea. Treachery was thought to be the highest and best performance by these tribes. Tawa's Trio gasped like the rest of the congregation and made clicking sounds in their throats when the Sawi let the missionaries know that Judas Iscariot was their hero, not Jesus Christ! How sad!

What were the missionaries to do? How could they reach a culture who valued treachery and fighting over everything else? Tawa agreed silently with the Richardsons that they would have to leave. The fighting was not going to stop.

But no, what was this? A cultural custom of giving a child to another tribe to make peace? And this couple with only one child, one son, was giving him up to their enemies, so there would be peace, so the missionaries could stay? *Aminienga glapa!* How could anyone do such a thing?

And then Don Richardson told the people, "Jesus Christ was **God's** Peace Child!"

"Oh, no! Oh, no! No one dare harm the Peace Child! But Judas Iscariot betrayed Him! Oh, no! How could he do such a thing?" And the same people who had recently thought Judas was great because of his treachery, now thought him a fiend to have harmed the Heavenly Father's Peace Child.

Tawa's trio thrilled to the Story with all their hearts and souls! All three girls had been to the altar in the Papua New Guinea Bible Church. All three had given their hearts to Christ. How it thrilled them to see the whole Sawi tribe turn to their Savior!

Would to God my Tona Tribe would turn to God this way, thought Tawa. Then she wondered if some men had to be fighters like the Sawi before they could realize their sinfulness and feel their need of God. She wished her father could have seen this film tonight. "Oh, God, let him see it somewhere, sometime," she prayed silently.

Pastor Paul Bali was announcing that, due to the crush of crowds, there was no way anyone could come forward for prayer. People should pray right where they were standing, sitting or kneeling, and lift their hearts to God. Pastor himself led them in prayer.

What a volume of prayer ascended from that building heavenward! Tawa, Annie and Linda lifted their voices with the crowd. They recommitted their own lives to Christ. Tawa prayed for her father and her uncles to turn to God as the Sawi men had done.

Annie prayed that her father and mother might see this film and understand how God had reached through to the Sawi Tribe on the other side of their very own island of New Guinea! Oh, that they might see, and have their faith increased, as hers had been tonight!

Linda Stanley prayed for her uncles, that they might turn from sin to the Savior, just as the Sawi men did, even though none of them had been fighters like the Sawi. She thanked God for her father, Stanley Unda, her mother, Nogo, her grandfather, Unda, who had accepted Christ long ago, near the time of the Great Awakening at Mele, in the Wiru Valley. His picture was in the book, ***Out of the Shadows in New Guinea***, by Lily Harvey. How her family cherished their copy of that book! Linda loved looking at that picture of her grandfather and realizing that she was a third-generation Christian.

Robert and Lily Harvey with their graduating class from Pauline Kelley Memorial Bible School: Pako, Rakuna, Stephen Napia, & Paul

The volume of prayer lessened gradually until it finally came down to one last person praying alone and thanking God for eternal salvation. When the crowd said, "Amen" Pastor Bali arose and announced that Mrs. Houck had something more to share with them from Don Richardson's book, *Peace Child*.

Pamela Kelley Houck stood.

"I have here the fourth edition of Missionary Don Richardson's *Peace Child*, put out in 2005. At the back of this edition he gives an epilogue he titles:

Thirty Years Later
An Update on the Sawi Tribe

"He tells us the Sawi have more than doubled in size or population. In 1974 he and his wife estimated there were 2,600 Sawi. In 2005 there were 6,000.

"The two "peace children" grew to adulthood among peace-keeping sub-clans. Biakadon died as a young man. Yohannes (first called Mani) was such a good student in the mission primary school that the Richardsons' successors, John and Esther Mills, arranged for him to go to middle school and high school at Agats, forty air miles away, on a government outpost in the Asmat region. Following high school, this boy who had never even seen a hill in all his life, went up into mountains 'soaring even higher than clouds' and graduated from a

Christian teacher-training college established by Lillian Dickson's Mustard Seed International foundation, in a famous mountain-ringed valley called the Balim.

"Yohannes is now the principal or headmaster of a primary school among the Sawi. He married and is the father of several children," continued Pam. "My brother, Bob Kelley, saw Don Richardson at Bob's church in Lansing, Michigan, and Don told Bob that Yohannes is a good Christian man.

"National missionary couples from a mountain tribe known as the Dani came to work and teach in the Sawi villages. Don and his people built a house and a schoolhouse in Sawi villages that said they would like a Dani couple to come and teach them. Now the Sawi churches belong to a family of nearly one thousand churches in several cultures including Dani, Sawi and Yali. Don Richardson also wrote of the Yali in his book *Lords of the Earth*.

"As soon as John and Esther Mills deemed Sawi church leaders sufficiently mature, their mission ceded all its houses, schools and clinics to the church and withdrew all Western personnel.

"All over West Papua, formerly Irian Jaya, and before that Dutch New Guinea or Netherlands New Guinea, wherever the Sawi go, people have read the book *Peace Child*, in the Indonesian translations or seen the film, and these people invite the Sawis to dinner or to talk to assemblies of people about God.

"'Much to the Indonesian government's dismay, fanatic Wahhabi Islamists from Saudi Arabia are injecting extremism into the thinking of a growing number of Indonesian Muslims,'" read Pamela, then said, "This is complicated. Let me translate into Pidgin.

"*Dispela i had na mi laik tainim long Tok Pisin. Gavman bilong Indonisia ol Muslim tu tasol ol suruk taim wanpela lain Muslim bilong Saudi Arabia i kam na kirapim ol long i go moa, o i pait moa. Dispela lain ol i kolim Wahabi Muslim.*

"'Wealthy Wahhabis provide oil money and weaponry for an eventual imposition of Islam's ultra radical Sharia law everywhere in the world's most populous Muslim nation.' *Dispela Wahabi Muslim ol i gat plenty mani bilong oil o wel long Saudi na ol i givim dispela moni na maskit bilong ol lain bilong Indonisia bilong kirapim wanpela Sharia lo gavman nabaut*

nabaut. Namba bilong ol Muslim manmeri long Indonisia i winim ol namba bilong Muslim manmeri long narapela kantri. Planti Muslim tru i pulapim Indonisia na ol i painim graun bilong narapela kantri long oli ken i kisim," explained Pamela.

"Dispela Sharia lo mi bin ritim long kompyuta i tok olsem, i gat 3-pela kain lo long dispela graun, na olgeta lain bilong Muslim i mas kam ananit long dispela Sharia lo long olgeta ples. Ol i save katim han bilong ol stilman, na rausim het bilong planti hambak manmeri. Ol i no suruk, olsem man bilong pait tru.

"'Repeatedly over the last 1400 years Sharia law has led to genocide.' *Gen na gen long 1400 yia dispela Sharia lo i save kilim i dai olgeta lain ol i save bosim; kilim i dai pinis olgeta. Long narapela narapela kantri Sharia lo-gavman i kilim ol kainkain lain na ol Muslim kisim gruun bilong ol.*

"Don Richardson wrote a fourth book called **Secrets of the Koran**," said Pamela. "You can read much more about this subject in that book.

"'A threat of genocide now hovers over Christians in several parts of Indonesia. *Dispela pramis bilong kilim ol man, kilim i dai sampela lain olgeta, em olsem wanpela klaut i pairap, i stap antap long ol lain Kristen long hap ples nabaut long Indonisia. Klaut I save pramisim ren, yu save,"* explained Pamela, *"tasol dispela klaut i gat narapela pramis. Pramis bilong rausim lain Kristen olgeta; pramis bilong kilim ol i dai pinis, pramis bilong pinisim ol lain Kristen olgeta.*

"'Omens of that grim menace take several forms. *Sain o mak bilong dispela nogut pramis i soim mipela long kainkain we.* In the last decade close to 1,000 Christian churches have been destroyed by Muslim arsonists across Indonesia, sometimes with loss of life. *Long 10-pela yia i go pinis nau olsem 1995 i go long 2005, inap long wan tausen lotu bilong Kristen, olsem 10-pela 10, 10-pela taims, mekim 1,000 lotu ol Muslim i bin kukim long paia, na sampela dispela lotu i gat mameri insait na ol i kukim manmeri tu.*

"'Laskar Jihad (Holy War Force) after afflicting Christian areas of a large Indonesian island called Sulawesi with terrorist violence, is now infiltrating the domain of West Papuan tribes. *Dispela em hatwok long tainim, na ol i putim tokples long ol Sodi Arabia tu insait. Laska Jihad ol i kolim holi pait o pait bilong God o Allah. Tasol yumi save dispela i no stret long ya bilong yumi. Holi na pait, tupela i narakain, narakain long tingting bilong yumi Kristen, tasol ol Muslim i save bungim tupela wod na kolim holi pait. Ol i kolim nem bilong God Allah, o yu ken spelim Ala, tasol ol i puttim tupela l na h baksait. Ol man bilong pait long dispela holi pait ol i sakarapim bikpela graun Sulawesi bilong Indonisia pinis taim ol i kam nau insait long graun bilong Niugini o West Papua.*

"'Although the Indonesian government officially decries Laskar Jihad, elements of the Indonesian armed forces seem at times to favor its policies. *Ol Gavman bilong Indonisia ol i save tok ol i no laikim dispela pasin bilong holi pait o Laskar Jihad tasol sampela ami na sampela polisman insait long Indonisia ol i soim ol i laikim; sampela ol i givim bel tru long ol pait bilong Allah.*

"'Let a few Papuans disaffected with Indonesian control act up in a community and strangely, paramilitary armed men may appear and inflict havoc. *Sapos sampela man bilong Papua i kamap les long pasin bilong Indonisia, na soim narapela long viles ol i les, ol ami i save kam wantaim ol maskit na hamarim ol nogut.*

"'Yet violence is only one weapon that hate-filled people may use in a campaign of genocide against people of a different race and/or religion. AIDS is another. *Paitim na kilim man em wanpela we bilong rausim arapela lain. Narapela we em HIV/AIDS.*

"'Nefarious businessmen in collusion with elements of Indonesian armed forces gather prostitutes known to be infected with AIDS as migrants from other parts of Indonesia to West Papua. *Sampela nogut man i wok bisnis, sampela ami sapotim na halivim dispela nogut man, ol i bin i go kisim ol pamuk meri i gat HIV/AIDS long narapela hap bilong Indonisia na bringim ol i kam insait long West Papua.*

"'Naïve Papua men, especially if primed first with offering of beer or marijuana, are induced to infect themselves and then their families back home by consorting with tragically infected women. *Dispela nogut bisnisman ol bai painim ol busman i nogat save, na ol bai givim bia o meriwana pastaim, na bihain bai bringim insait wantaim ol pamuk meri i gat HIV/AIDS.*

"'Olsem na ol dispela man i nogat save, ol i kisim bagarap long ol pamuk meri, na bihain ol i go bek long ples na bagarapim ol meri na ol lain bilong ol yet.

"'Such activity portends a possible undercover genocide of eastern Indonesia's Papuan population - a genocide that expends no bullet or bombs. *Dispela pasin em i wanpela hait we bilong kilim olgeta lain bilong Papua na i no nitim maskit o bom.*

"*O Fren bilong mi, yupela mas lukaut,*" pled Pamela. "My Friends, take care, but do not be cast down, and do not give up hope. Before I sit down I just must tell you one story my pastor told me in America, after the great tsunami here in the South Pacific a few years ago.

"He said in one Indonesian village there were four hundred Christians who wanted to celebrate Christmas, and they asked their leaders, since the village was Muslim, if they could celebrate Christmas in their homes. They were told that they could not. 'If you want to celebrate the Christian way you have to go up on that mountain there to celebrate. No way would we allow it here in our village.'

"So all the Christians climbed the mountain on Christmas Eve and celebrated Christ's birth together on the mountain top. They were still all there on the mountain when the great tidal wave washed their village away, and nearly ninety per cent of the Muslims with it. Not one Christian perished, but almost all the Muslims drowned.

"My mother was telling this story to her Australian friend, Joy Hall. Joy told her the same thing happened to them. They were having their annual meeting on an island near Asia, and they were not able to rent their usual building for the meeting. So they had to go to higher ground to rent a place to have their annual meeting. While they were meeting on this higher site, the tsunami came and flooded the building they normally rented. They saw God's Hand in their inability to rent the usual building.

"God has His ways of taking care of His children, my Friends, so do not despair! Just take care," she said as she nodded to Pastor Paul and sat down.

Pastor Paul exhorted them in both ImboUngu and Kewa, and sometimes in Melanesian Pidgin, to live lives of purity and

Wyatt and Brody

godliness. He had sat under Dr. Irwin and Dr. Radcliffe as they lectured at Kudjip, and he had seen and heard of the terrible destruction of AIDS.

When Pastor Paul dismissed them, the crowd flocked out. The Trio sat still, watching.

"I want to go talk to that mother of those two boys," said Tawa.

"Great!" agreed her friends. "Me too," they exclaimed simultaneously.

As soon as they could push their way through the crowd to the front, they did. Tawa reached her hand out to *Kango Tagol Tsipe* (second son), and he took it and shook it quickly and let go instantly, flashing a big smile, as his eyes twinkled.

"Wow!" thought Tawa. "So much male charm in one so young! He is all but flirting, but he probably isn't even weaned yet, so it is all innocent.

Kango Komoglaiye (firstborn son) offered his hand to Tawa, keeping a big-brotherly eye on his little brother.

"You truly are *Kango Komoglaiye*, aren't you?" smiled Tawa.

"Yes," agreed the serious little man, "and he is *Kango Tagol Tsipe*."

"Good for you for speaking ImboUngu," complimented Tawa.

"Everybody says it all the time, so I couldn't help but learn it."

"Yes," agreed Tawa. "Birth order is important to us Imbo Imboma."

"Do you know how to say 'last son' in Kewapi?" asked Linda.

"No."

"It's *Ere Pere Naki*," she coached.

"*Ere Pere Naki*," echoed the boy. "I like that! It rhymes! Hey, Brody, you're *Ere Pere Naki* in Kewapi!"

"Ere Pere Naki," echoed Brody, and ran to his mother where she was talking with Pastor Paul. "Hey, Mommy, I'm *Ere Pere Naki* in Kewapi!"

Pamela turned to the Trio, laughing with her son. "I know, Brody. I was *Ere Pere Nogo* all my childhood at Katiloma."

"You lived at Katiloma?" asked Linda astounded.

"Yes, do you know Katiloma?"

"I sure do! My mom used to work there before she married my dad, and she named me Linda after the missionary she worked for."

"My mother's name is Linda. What is your mother's name?"

"How amazing! Wait until I tell Mom and Dad! My mother's name is Nogo."

"Nogo, is it? I remember Mom talking of a lady named Nogo. She worked for Mom when my older brother was a baby."

"And his name was Bobby George, wasn't it?"

"Yes, it was. He goes by Bob or George now, not both.

"So you are Linda. And what are your two friends' names?"

"This is Tawa Pombo and this is Annie Yakura."

"I'm Pamela and my friends call me Pam for short. Hi, Tawa. Hi, Annie," said the young woman, shaking both of their hands in turn. "You three are the most beautiful Trio I have seen in a long time!"

"And you are beautiful too! You make me think of Princess Diana!" returned Tawa.

"Oh, come on! That has to be flattery! What do you know of Princess Diana?"

"I've seen more than one book of pictures of her, and I've also seen movie clips."

"Aren't you worldly wise? How did you become so educated? Tell me about yourselves."

"We are all three in the eleventh grade here at Ialibu High School, and we are all three from different language areas. I speak ImboUngu. Annie speaks Wiru, and Linda speaks Kewapi and Mendi."

"And you all three also speak very good English, but what else do you have in common besides your good looks?"

"In common?" asked Tawa, wondering what that meant, and turning to the other two to see if they knew. Both girls shrugged their shoulders.

Tawa turned back to Pam. "I guess I don't understand what you mean by 'in common.'"

"I mean, what brought you together besides being in the same class?"

"Oh, I guess we met at church. We had seen each other in class among many other students, but when we saw each other in church, we just started sticking together."

"What church is that?" asked Pam.

"PNGBC. Papua New Guinea Bible Church."

"Oh, I know that church. I grew up in it at Katiloma."

"Where did you learn to play the keyboard?" asked Tawa.

"Well, it's a long story, but I started on a piano in Pennsylvania when I was four years old." She paused, not sure how much the girl wanted to hear.

"How old are your two little boys?" asked Annie.

"Brody is three, and Wyatt is six."

"I was right," exclaimed Linda. "I have the most little brothers and sisters. Tawa guessed seven and Annie guessed eight."

Tawa had to bring the conversation back to her all-consuming topic. "Is it hard to play the keyboard?"

"Come to my house on Saturday afternoon and I will give you a lesson on my piano. I would like to get to know all three of you better."

"How much do you charge to teach piano?" asked Tawa.

"The first lesson will be free, and we will see after that. Maybe you could help me sometime if you decided you wanted another lesson."

"*Yawaliyo!* Our Tawa will be a pianist!" exclaimed Annie to Linda. "Won't we be proud?"

"My friends play lots of instruments," said Linda. "Angelos was given a music scholarship at UPNG, but he chose to do computer engineering at Queensland University instead. He and his brother, Joel, play trombone and saxophone and any other instrument they can get their hands on."

"Where did they have the opportunity to learn?" asked Pam.

"I don't really know. Their mother is from Ialibu here, but their father is Filipino. He went back to the Philippines and the mother was raising them alone until her sister married Jacob Mambi. He became like a father to them."

"I know Jacob Mambi," said Pam. "He went to America with us when I was four years old. I remember he babysat us once while Mom and Dad went muzzleloader hunting."

"Hunting for what? And what's a muzzleloader?" asked several people standing around listening.

"Dad was hunting for deer, and Mom was taking pictures of him. A muzzleloader is an old fashioned gun that you have to load with powder."

"My mom and dad go to the same church as Jacob Mambi in Mendi," continued Linda. "It is the Assemblies of God Church."

"I'd like to see Jacob and his family and his nephews. Next time you see him, tell him I am here in Ialibu, and I'm inviting him to come see us."

"He went to America with you?" asked Tawa. "That sounds like a dream. I used to think America was 'heaven-on-earth!'"

"I remember when I thought America was up in the air like heaven," laughed Pam. "I was four months old when my parents brought me to PNG, the year PNG gained its independence. As a toddler, I knew you had to get in a plane and go up in the air to go to America, so I thought America and heaven were both up there in the sky somewhere...."

Linda Kelley and Jacob Mambi reading proof

"How cute!" the girls laughed.

"Mom and Dad tell me I couldn't pronounce America correctly. Back then I said, 'A-bear-a-cwa.' Daddy was always talking about hunting so I used to say, 'I'm gonna hunt bears in Abearacwa!'"

As soon as the laughter subsided Tawa asked, "And did you ever get to hunt bears?"

"No, I hunted deer but never bear."

"Imagine carrying a gun and shooting a deer!" The girls looked at one another in consternation.

"Well, can I plan on seeing you on Saturday?"

"Yes! We will probably all three come if that's all right. We like to hang out together even on weekends. Thanks so much for showing *Peace Child* here tonight!"

"You are welcome. My father showed it at Katiloma when I was a little girl. It is one of my favorite stories."

"I was wishing my unsaved father could see it," said Tawa.

"Your dad is not a Christian?"

"No. He has five wives, and he won't go to church."

"My father is a PNGBC pastor, and I wish he could see it," said Annie. "It increased my faith, and I know it would increase Mom and Dad's faith too! And what you said about the Muslims is something more people need to hear, as well. Did you know they are at Lama Sawmill now?"

"Yes, I've heard. When you come Saturday, if we have time after the piano lesson," she winked at Tawa, "I will show you some books and a CD of two Somalian women who speak out against Muslim customs."

"Somalian. That's African?"

"Yes. Somalia is a country on the east coast of Africa."

"Okay. We will look forward to Saturday!"

They all exited the church together, with Wyatt and Brody calling "Good night, girls!"

"Good night, *kango tagol*."

"Good night, *bagol yupoko*."

"*Paitapape, naki lapo*."

"Say '*Paitapape, nogo repo*," said Pam.

"*Paitapape, nogo repo*," echoed the boys.

"Good night! Good night, you adorable boys!"

Pam and Brody

39

Dorcas Howard & Pamela Kelley

Two-story house George Kelley built.

1979

PNG

Pila Niningi wa at the Universi of P.N.G., Port M He came to Katiloma to

Pila Niningi & the Kelley Ki

Chapter Three

"Dindi, would you pass out these books? I think we have enough for everyone in the class to have one," said Mrs. Bonau.

"Toropo: Tenth Wife," whispered Tawa. "Toropo is my sister's name."

"And look! There's my name on the cover too! Linda Harvey Kelley," read Linda Stanley.

"She is your *Nopi*, Linda. I think I have heard of this book," continued Tawa. "The last time I went to Piamble to see my sister, I heard some men talking about it. Somebody said it has all the names of the Piamble people in it."

"Goody!" exclaimed Annie in a low voice. "We will get to read about your sister!"

"Look! There's an ImboUngu word! Oh, my! A whole page of them!" exclaimed Tawa.

"*Ai! Ama, ambo, ambo kunana,*" Tawa broke into laughter. "I never thought I would see the words *ambo kunana* in print!"

"Why? What does it mean?" asked Linda trying to see over Tawa's shoulder.

"*Tanim het,*" answered Tawa, "or as it says here, 'love chant, head turning.'"

"*Yawaliyo!*" exclaimed Annie.

"Woman-song might be another translation," mused Tawa.

"So *ambo mopene* means beautiful young girl," read Linda, having found the page Tawa was reading.

"Won't this be fun?" injected Tawa. "Imagine reading a book that has my own language in it. No wonder those Piamble men were excited about it."

"Let's get quiet, class," said Mrs. Bonau. "Thank you, Dindi. Does everyone have a book?"

"There was a murmur of assent.

"We'll skip over the pre-pages and go straight to page one. There are some ImboUngu words in this so I want an ImboUngu girl to come up here and read Toropo's words.

Tawa raised her hand. "Let me, please."

"Thank you, Tawa. There's another female ImboUngu speaker named Keri, Bagol Keri. Who wants to play her part? Mondi? Great! Come up to the front. Now we need a narrator to read the non-conversational parts. Let's have a man for a narrator."

Several boys raised their hands.

"Samuel, you may do the first three pages. Then we will let someone else have a chance. Let's begin with you three," the teacher continued as Samuel walked to the front, "and when someone else appears in the story with a speaking part we will enlist some more.

"Go ahead, Samuel."

"Toropo heard the distant call of her best friend," read Samuel. "She stopped her digging to yodel an answer."

Samuel stopped for Tawa to yodel.

"Keri-yo-iyo-iyo!" yodeled Tawa.

"Oh, come on! You can do better than that!" exclaimed several boys.

"No, I can't!" said Tawa. "My father says girls don't know how to yodel."

"Have you ever tried?" asked Mrs. Bonau.

"Not really," admitted Tawa.

"Well, it's probably just lack of practice then. Girls' throats are exactly like boys' throats. There is no anatomical difference. Boys begin practicing yodeling when they are toddlers, as soon as they can talk. Girls are always told they can't, so they don't try. You may not be able to be a good yodeler by starting now at your age. But again you may. Practice makes perfect. I'd like all of you girls to try it out of class. You do have to realize that you do not have the lung capacity of a man, so you may not make the sounds as deeply, or with as much volume. Now, go ahead, Samuel."

Mondi and Tawa conversed back and forth like Keri and Toropo in the book. The class became caught up in their conversation and enjoyed it thoroughly. They squealed with delight when Ialibu was mentioned at the top of page two.

When the narrator finished the fourth paragraph on page two Mrs. Bonau asked, "Who wants to be Ama?"

"I do," answered Kuglupu.

Kuglupu joined the other three at the front of the class and read the next two paragraphs. On page three, Temambo took Teni's part.

At the top of page four Samuel sat down and Kewa became the narrator. Mrs. Bonau chose Kipugul to play the part of Pombo, Toropo's father.

At the bottom of page four she told Kewa's sister, Kewaroa, to play the part of the second wife, from her seat.

When Kewa read, "the voice of his second wife sounded through the partition," Kewaroa yelled, "Yapa! You stupid boy! You nearly pushed your little brother into the fire! Will you learn to sit still when you are inside the house?"

Half the class began laughing aloud. Kewaroa was such a natural actor, like Tawa and Mondi, and they had been yelled at by their own mothers the same way. It brought back memories to so many minds.

Tiye played the part of Turi on page five and they finished chapter one. When Mrs. Bonau said they wouldn't read any more today, half of the class groaned aloud.

"Can we take the books home?" asked several students.

"No, I want them all here for class tomorrow.

"Let's discuss some questions from the Study Guide. What are 'old wives' tales?'"

"You can't catch a man with skin like a frog," quoted Tawa.

"How many of you have heard that one?"

More than half the class raised their hands.

"Yes, Wameyambo?"

"My mom always bathed me and let me try to swim in the river whenever she took the clothes to the river to wash them, but she always quoted that saying and said her mom always said it to her when she was a little girl."

"Is Toropo right about the purpose of the saying? Is it true that our culture tries to make girls work more than boys?"

"Yes, that is true," answered several girls.

"What do you say, boys?"

"No," answered Samuel. "I get firewood two or three times a week."

"Does that take as much time as making a garden?" asked his teacher.

"No, I guess not."

"Taking *kaukau* to the pigs has to be done every day," said Mondi, "rain or shine. Mum never asks my brothers to do it. It's always me or my sister, or Mum herself. It's the chore I hate most, and I have never seen any boy in any family do it."

"Yes," agreed their teacher. "Let's consider the teenaged boys who aren't in high school. Do you think they have too much time on their hands? Is that why they go into rascal activity?"

"Probably," agreed several.

"I think there is an English saying or two for that, though probably not ImboUngu. 'Satan finds work for idle hands to do.' And 'Idle hands are the devil's workshop.'"

"What are idle hands?"

"Hands that aren't busy?" suggested Kewa.

"Yes. Exactly!" responded his teacher. "Now, enough on that. Let's look at this word *konopu* in ImboUngu.

"The Study Guide says *konopu lteyo* means I'm thinking, whereas *konopu mondoro* means I love.

"*Lteyo* means I put for something that is not alive, and *mondoro* means I put for something that is living. So ImboUngu speakers are making a differentiation between two kinds of thoughts for these two phrases. Isn't that interesting? What other verbs do you put with *konopu*, you ImboUngu speakers?"

"*Konopu maa tondoromo* is one way to say, 'I forgot,'" said Tawa, "although you can also say *Komu tsindindu*."

"Yes. Annie?" said Mrs. Bonau.

"*Wene* is the word for thought in Wiru, and to say 'I forgot' you say, *wene kaiyapekou. Mi kapsaitim tingting*, or 'I spilled my thoughts' or 'I poured out my thoughts.'"

The class chuckled in delight.

"I like that!" said Dindi and Mrs. Bonau in unison. "*Wene kaiyapekou. Mi kapsaitim tingting*. Aren't languages interesting?"

"In my language, to say, 'I forgot' we say, *Kone rugulaar*u which literally means, 'I tore my thoughts,'" said a girl named Kewanu.

"Oh, another and different idiom! We can spill them or pour them out or we can tear them. Each of these different idioms represents a different way of looking at things. We could try to pick the word 'forgot' apart in English, to see why they put

44

those two small words – for and got – together in English to make one with an entirely different meaning."

"Words are fun!" exclaimed Dindi.

"Now, back to love," continued their teacher, "the Study Guide says there are four verbs for love in Greek. Where is Greek spoken, class?"

"In Greece," answered several.

"What famous books were written in Greek originally?"

"The **Bible**?" suggested Samuel.

"Part of the **Bible**. The **Old Testament** was written in Hebrew."

"The **New Testament** then?" asked Roger.

"Yes. Do you know any others?"

No one knew others.

The Iliad and **The Odessy** are two famous Greek stories," said Mrs. Bonau. She wrote the titles on the blackboard.

And here are the four words for love in Greek: *storge*, or in Greek letters, στοργη; *philia*, φιλια; *eros* ερος; and *agape*, αγαπη. Before we talk about the variation of meaning in Greek, let's see how many ways to say love there are in Pidgin English.

"*Laikim*," said one student.

"*Laikim tumas*," suggested another.

"*Givim bel long narapela*."

"Right, all three are right," agreed the teacher.

"One translation of 'Jesus Loves Me' is '*Em Man bilong Sori*.'"

"Excellent observation," said Mrs. Bonau.

"*Lewa bilong mi kirap taim mi tingting long yu*," suggested Kewanu.

"Excellent, and it is probably a literal translation from one of PNG's 700 languages, or perhaps from many of them! Most of us feel that the liver is the seat of affection, whereas English-speaking people feel it is the heart.

"Since I lived at Katiloma and taught there many years and had the privilege of reading some of Dr. Karl Franklin's writings on the language, I can tell you that the word in Kewa for liver is *pu*. *Pu kundina* means 'liver is extingquished' meaning 'dead.' *Pu koma* literally means 'liver dead' but idiomatically it means 'disappointed.' *Pu ramea* literally means 'liver rotten' but idiomatically it means 'full of pity.' *Pu reka* means 'liver

45

stand up' but to the Kewa it means 'excited.' *Pu u patea* or 'liver sleep lies' means to 'be lazy.' *Pu yola* means 'liver pull' or 'to entice someone.' *Pu rero pia* means 'liver-bitter-it is' or to 'be hard-hearted.' *Pu rende pia* is 'liver-sweet-it is' which means to 'be happy.' *Pu pogolasa* means 'liver-jump up' or to 'be excited,' and it just goes on and on. Any emotion is the liver doing, feeling or being in one state or another, much as the English speak of heart-broken, rending the heart, and other things happening to the heart. Their physical heart is not broken, any more than the Kewa's liver is dead, or standing up, or jumping or what have you.

"English speakers speak of like and love. They may use like more for inanimate things and love for animals or people, or they may not. Children especially use them interchangeably, and so do some adults.

"However the Greeks use their four different words for love in four different situations.

"*Storge* (στοργη) means familial love, the love of a parent for his or her child especially, but also the love of a child for its parents. C. S. Lewis calls στοργη 'affection.'

"*Philia* (φιλια) is the next kind of love. C. S. Lewis calls it friendship. In the USA they have the city of Philadelphia, Pennsylvania. Philadelphia means the city of brotherly love from φιλια and αδελφοs. I think we might call it *wantok* love or the feeling of camaraderie within a group, a team, a class, a club, or some such. C. S. Lewis says, 'Without *Eros* none of us would have been begotten, and without Affection none of us would have been reared, but we can live and breed without Friendship.' On the other hand, in PNG we might say our feeling for our *wantoks* is the all-consuming passion of our lives, and the foundation upon which we build our tribes and villages. That is doubtless because, as some people say, our culture is based on the brother-brother dyad instead of the man and wife dyad. In the *wantok* system a man puts the other members of his tribe ahead of his own wife. And that may be because he has many wives, so he can treat them as sub-human, or it may be because he bought them, so they are just possessions. Anyway, C. S. Lewis thinks Friendship is one type of love most people can live without. He just did not know Papua New Guineans.

"Eros (ερos) is the third type of love, and English takes its words, erotic, eroticism, and so on from this Greek word. What does erotic mean to you, class?"

Grace Bonau paused and looked around the classroom. Not a single hand was raised. Several students were looking through their dictionaries.

"Page 130 of this condensed edition of Webster's says 'Eros (Myth.) the Greek god of love…erotica n. literature dealing with sexual love."

The class turned to the page in their dictionaries and studied each word that began with ero-.

"And the fourth word for love is *agape, (αγαπη).*"

A hand went up and Mrs. Bonau looked to see, and then called on Pilipo. "Yes, Pilipo?"

"I have heard of αγαπη at church. Isn't that God's love, or divine love?"

"Yes, it is usually thought of that way, though the internet tells us that it is used much in ancient literature to denote 'feelings for a good meal; one's children and a spouse; about being content and also having a high regard' or respect for someone. C. S. Lewis calls it charity, and says it is first decency and common sense, but it is later revealed as goodness, and then the whole Christian life. It is the attitude of God toward man, and the attitude that God wants us to have toward our fellow man.

"I remember Linda Harvey Kelley, author of **Toropo**, telling us that in John 21 after Peter had denied Jesus three times, Jesus asked him, 'Peter, do you love me?' or in Greek, '*Agapes me?* Αγαπεs με?' Peter answered, '*Philo se.* Φιλω σε.' What word for love was Peter using, class?"

"*Philia,*" answered several voices in unison, and then a couple more echoed, "Philia."

"And what kind of love is that?"

"Brotherly love or *wantok* love."

"Right.

"So Jesus asked him a second time, '*Agapes me,* Αγαπεs με, Peter?' and again Peter answered, '*Philo se,* Φιλω σε.'"

The class groaned.

"What would you have said?"

Hands went up all over the classroom.

"Yes, Kenny?"

"*Agapes se?*"

"You have the pronoun right. Anyone else with an idea?"

"*Agapo se?*" queried two girls in unison.

"Very close, it is *agapao se,* Αγαπαω σε. The omega on the end of the verb signifies first person. By the way, what do you think omega means?"

No one raised a hand.

"Have you ever heard the adjective mega or the prefix mega-?"

"I read about the megaton in science," answered David.

"And what's that?"

"A unit for measuring the power of thermonuclear weapons."

"Here it is!" exclaimed two boys at once, dictionaries in hand.

"A Greek prefix meaning great or mighty."

"Well done. So what does omega mean?"

"Great o? Big o?" suggested one.

"Mighty o?" queried another.

"Exactly," agreed their teacher. "There is also omicron in the Greek alphabet."

"Little o?" asked Tawa.

"Yes! You've got it! Some teachers say omicron is pronounced as a short o while omega is long, but others pronounce them both long, Linda said."

"*Agapao se,* Αγαπαω σε," murmured several. "*Philo se,* Φιλω σε," added others.

"Do you remember conjugations from English grammar: I love, you love, he, she, it loves; we love, you love, they love?"

Heads nodded all around. Eyebrows were raised in the affirmative.

"Well, here it is in Greek," and she wrote on the board:

Agapao Αγαπαω   *agapomen* αγαπομεν

Agapes Αγαπεs   *agapete* αγαπετε

Agapei Αγαπει   *agapousi* αγαπουσι

"Some letters are written the same in Greek and English, but some are different. Capital A and capital alpha are the same. Small a and small alpha are the same. The next letter in this word, g, is different. It is called gamma in Greek, and a gamma looks a little bit like an italicized y in English *y.* Gamma is γ. You all know the math symbol called pi, π. Well, that is the letter p in Greek. Long o, or big o is called what, class?"

"Omega," chorused the class.

"And omega is written almost as a w, ω. Maybe you could say a w with its raised arms turned inward. Thus we have αγαπαω! And we love is αγαπομεν. The only letter different there is what, class.

"N."

"Yes, N is called nu in Greek, and looks a little like an italicized v."

The class copied it quickly into their notebooks, happy to be learning a Greek conjugation.

"Who wants to try conjugating *philo*?"

The teacher looked around the room at very alert students, but all seemed reluctant to risk it.

"Come on, Kewa, you try it," she said. "Here is something interesting. This is the letter phi. It is an o with a line through it. It is pronounced like an f, but it is transliterated ph in English. Now you know why the word Pharoah is spelled with Ph instead of Faroah!"

Kewa did it:
Philo	φιλω	*philomen*	φιλομεν
Philes	φιλες	*philete*	φιλετε
Philei	φιλει	*philousi.*	φιλουσι

He looked at the conjugation of αγαπαω a few times, and he did it perfectly!

"Very good, Kewa. Excellent, in fact!

"Listen, my students, one of the most prestigious universities in the world is Harvard, and one of the first three rules of Harvard University's **Rules and Precepts of 1642** was 'decline nouns and verbs in Greek.' So there, you are on your way to a good education. You can decline or conjugate a Greek Verb!"

The class very carefully copied the conjugation of *wantok*-love into their notebooks.

"Let me give you another exerpt from C. S. Lewis' book, **The Four Loves**," continued their teacher. "C. S. Lewis himself says that he thinks there are two or three main classifications of love, as he sees it in the world. First there is Need-love, which all babies have. They need their parents. We all have Need-love

49

throughout our lives, he says. And we all have Need-love for God. And that will always be. We will always need God.

"Then there is Gift-love. Need-love we have out of our poverty. Gift-love longs to serve. Gift-love longs to give the recipient happiness. We need to be needed, and some unfulfilled individuals make the lives of others miserable because their need to be needed is so great they will not let their children grow up. Perhaps we do not see that in PNG like Clive Staples Lewis saw it in his world. But it is great when we can go beyond Need-love to Gift-Love.

"Then the third type of love according to this Oxford professor's classification is Appreciation-love. I would like you to read this paragraph of his that I have photocopied for you, and write me your thoughts on it, for the remainder of our class time."

NG Madonna

The Kelleys: George and Linda holding Deanie on the left,
George Sr. and Pauline holding Bobby in the center,
Larry Smith and Judy holding Miriam on the right.
April, 1974

Ellepe Nomi and my Mother, Lily Harvey, at Translyvania Bible School
in PA about 1995 or 1996

PABRABUK

Yuon, Regina & Hilary
Tainapel

Holiness unto the Lord

ping
aste
or
EX!

Tonya
Rebekah
Joseph
James

Tom & Denise Raish
Sandy   Melinda, Velma, Wayne, Kinza & Michelle

Holiness unto the Lord

Kinza & Kids

Chapter Four

Tawa's Trio knocked timidly on the Houck's door Saturday morning. Of the three, only Linda Stanley had visited the home of an expatriate before that morning.

"Are you scared?" Annie asked Tawa.

"Yes, I suppose I am, but I want so badly to learn to play the keyboard that my longing for one overpowers my fear of the other."

"Let's just hope Pam opens the door, and not Mr. Houck."

Wyatt opened the door.

"Hello, *Nogo Repo!*" he squealed.

"Hi, *Kango tendeku! Kango tagol tsipe tena moromo?*"

"*Tukuna moromo. Tukundo waiyo.*"

"Hey, translate, somebody," said someone.

"Wyatt said, 'Hello, three girls,' and I said, 'Hi, one boy. Where is Second Son?'" translated Tawa. "Then Wyatt said, 'He's inside. Come on in.'"

"Way to go!" said Annie, as she entered, laughing.

Their laughter soon brought Pam and Brody into the room.

"Hi, Girls," exclaimed Pam. "We have been hoping you would get here soon. Make yourselves to home. Sit where you like."

Annie and Linda found stuffed chairs, but Tawa went straight to the wooden piano bench and laid one long index finger on the gleaming keys.

"*Lanie tena moromo?*" she asked Wyatt.

"*Kewa kombundo pumo.*"

'What did you say, Wyatt?" asked Annie.

"She asked me where Dad is, and I told her he went to 'ples Kewa.'"

Tawa gently touched one key after another letting the soft notes linger in the air.

"Why does your husband shave his head?" Annie asked Pam.

"He likes it that way, I guess."

"Has he always done it?"

"No. He had hair at our wedding. Here, I'll show you our wedding pictures." She withdrew a picture album from their bookshelves. "See here, my Prince Charming."

"You both are gorgeous!"

"Soon after we were married he started shaving his head. He stayed that way for months, and then he let it grow again. But for the last few years he has shaved it consistently and just changes his facial hair. I'm okay with the shaved head if he lets his beard grow. Quite a few men in America shave their heads; more African Americans than Caucasians, I suppose."

"That's interesting. Papua New Guinea men hate to shave their heads. Traditionally they added hair instead of cutting it off, you know."

"Bigwigs were popular all the time in the olden days," inserted Tawa. "My dad has his bigwig in safekeeping. He still gets it out for singsings and such."

"Yes," agreed Pam. "I remember seeing bigwigs when I was a little girl. Sometimes they frightened me a bit."

"Really? Truly?"

"Yes, I was almost kidnapped by a crazy man in Lae once when I was two years old. It made me fearful of any man I didn't know, for a while."

"How long were you afraid of them? And how did you get over your fear?" asked Linda.

"Wiwa Korowi came to Kagua when he was a Member of Parliament, before he became Governor General. He picked me up and talked to me in English about his own children. When he set me down I ran to my mother and said, 'Wiwa Korowi's my friend. He didn't take me away!' Here," and Pam withdrew another book from her shelves. "Mom wrote the story in this book."

Linda was soon absorbed in **MKs — Missionary Kids and their Playmates** while Annie looked at a photo album. Pam went to the piano bench and showed Tawa middle C on the piano and middle C on the book. For an hour the two played notes, and finally little tunes. Wyatt answered Annie's questions about photos, and Brody alternated between the photo albums and his picture books, occasionally asking Linda to read him a story.

Pam slipped out of the room while Tawa practiced and made some tea. She called them to the dining room for tea and passed around a plate of pineapple and papaya.

"Pam, may I ask a question?" asked Tawa.

"Sure. Go ahead."

"Do you think God cares about a girl's happiness?"

"I am sure He does! 'Casting every care upon Him for He careth for you.'"

"I mean, can I ask God not to allow my father to sell me to a polygamist? Can I expect God to answer such a prayer, or is it too selfish?"

"No, it is not too selfish. Yes, you can ask God for this, and you should. God's plan way back in Genesis when He created the world was for a man and a woman to leave their parents and cling to each other, and 'be one flesh.' One man and one woman, God said."

"My father has five wives. He has mostly sons, but I have two older sisters and they've both been sold to polygamists. Dad's a boss boy, and he always says, 'As the leader of my tribe I must get the most I can for my daughters,' and of course, the older men can amass more bridewealth than the younger men.

"When I think on this for long the future is so bleak I can't face it. Mrs. Bonau read us a poem this week by Florida Pugupia, which ended, 'Is this all there is to life, Male tyranny, polygamy and bribes?'"

"No, no, dear, that is not all there is to life."

"But that is almost all my mother and her fellow wives have known."

"My heart breaks for these women and the ones who have it even worse."

"Someone has it worse than PNG women who are sold to polygamists?"

"Yes, many Muslim women have it worse."

"How so? Because they have to cover their whole head, face and body with those dark clothes?"

"Yes, that and even worse. In twenty-eight countries of Africa six thousand little girls or women are cut and mutilated every day. Many of them die."

"Cut and mutilated?" gasped Tawa. "How? Why?"

"A witch doctor or a bush butcher cuts their genitals. It's called FGM – female genital mutilation, or FGC – female genital cutting. Most Muslim men call it circumcision and say the **Bible** and the **Koran** command it, but that's a lie and a misnomer."

"A lie and a misnomer?"

"Yes. The **Bible** doesn't command any such thing. It only makes male circumcision the sign of the covenant between God and Abraham, or God and the Jews. And by the way, girls, they told us on the news years ago in America that males who are circumcised have six times less chance of getting HIV/AIDS. But back to girls, circumcision is a misnomer or false name because they don't cut around as 'circum' implies, on these little girls; instead, they cut parts **out**. The word should include the suffix: -ectomy, as in appendectomy – cutting the appendix out of the body. Or tonsillectomy – cutting the tonsils out of the throat."

"Why do they mutilate their little girls?"

"So they will stay pure. So their fathers can guarantee that their daughters are virgins. Now they say it's a tradition, and a girl can't get a good husband unless she has been cut, and sewn shut, or almost shut."

"God, have mercy!" whispered Tawa. "I never dreamed of such a thing."

"Or had such a nightmare," added Linda.

"Right," agreed Pam and the Trio, shaking their heads in consternation.

"Twenty-eight countries, you say?" Annie asked.

"Yes, I once heard Paul Harvey News say that the months of October and November were the worst for the women of Egypt. 97.8 percent of Egyptian women endure FGM. Up until I heard that I had thought Egypt was a civilized country, not a third-world country like so much of the rest of Africa, where over two million women and girls are mutilated each year.

"But that's not the only way Muslims hurt women. They say in many places that women should always stay inside their own homes unless they have a male escort.

"They say even rape is a woman's fault."

"How could rape be the woman's fault?" asked the Trio.

"They find some way to lay the blame on the woman, saying she wasn't dressed right, or she was in the wrong place. Just this month a thirteen-year-old girl was gang raped by three men in Somalia, the news said. The Muslim militia said, 'That's adultery. She has to be stoned to death.' They took this thirteen-year-old who was named Aisha Ibrahim Duhulow and buried her legs and arms in the earth, then fifty men stoned her to death. Aisha kept saying, 'I don't agree. I don't agree,' when they were burying her limbs.

The girls covered their faces with their hands and cried. Tears were running down Pam's cheeks also, as she talked.

"It's not fair, girls. It's so unfair! I was a SANE nurse in Michigan. That stands for Sexual Assault Nurse Examiner. A man of any race can be beastly when he goes far from God, but what is so hopeless is when a culture or supposedly a **religion** supports this bestiality, this selfish, cruel behavior.

"In South Africa a few years ago, the news told us, six men raped a baby girl to death and went unpunished because no one would witness against them. There is a false rumor being propagated around Africa that if a man with HIV/AIDS has sex with a baby girl, it will cure him of AIDS. So men are destroying more little girls this way! It's probably a rumor a perverted man made up, so he and other men could supposedly justify the desires of pedophiles. That means men who rape children.

"A man named William Paul Young said in his book, 'I have always wondered why men have been in charge....Males seem to be the cause of so much pain in the world. They account for most of the crime and many of those are perpetrated against women...and children.' He was a small boy on the other side of your own island of New Guinea. His parents were missionaries in Dutch New Guinea, and the local men abused him.

"And think about Steven Tari; I heard about him on the news when I was in America. Have you girls heard about him?" Linda Stanley had, but the other two hadn't.

"He calls himself Black Jesus, and is notorious for alleged human sacrifices, rape, murder and even cannibalism of the 'flower-girl' virgins that he has raped and killed."

"Oh, my, where is he from?"

"He is from Manus, but he went to a Lutheran Bible School in Madang called Amron Bible College, and either ran away or was expelled from there, and went into the mountains of Matepi where he began to form a personality cult around himself as the

Messiah. It is another horrible story. You wouldn't think people would follow him, but he had a following of six thousand!

"Let me show you these two books," and Pam went to her bookshelves again.

"This one is **Desert Flower** by Waris Dirie. Look, isn't she beautiful?"

"Oh, yes she is!" exclaimed the Trio together.

"And this is **Infidel**, by Ayaan Hirsi Ali, another beautiful Somalian woman. They both tell the story of how they were cut and mutilated as little girls and how terribly they were treated until they made their break for freedom."

Ayaan Hirsi Ali

The girls were leafing through the books, looking at the photos.

"How did they make their break to freedom?" asked Tawa.

"Waris Dirie was going to be sold to an older man for many goats or camels, I forget which, so she asked her mom to waken her early, and she ran away over the sand dunes of Somalia. She had been a goatherd out in the desert. She was good at running, and even though she had hours of headstart, she heard her father calling her name, and looked back to see him cresting a dune. *Em i taitim bun* and she ran for all she was worth, into the next night. She said it was like she and her dad were surfing waves; they were surfing dunes or waves of sand.

"She finally outran her father and collapsed at noon or *big-sun* up against a tree and fell asleep. She awakened to see a lion pacing back and forth in front of her. She was too exhausted and weak to stand, let alone run away, so she just leaned against the tree and stared the lion in the eye. It finally turned and left her. She prayed and said to God, right then, 'You must have a reason for me to live.'

"She went to her sister in the capitol city of Mogadishu and later to her aunt. From her aunt's she went to London with a relative who was an ambassador to Great Britain. Four years she slaved in his household, without learning English. When she was taking the ambassador's niece to school one day a man approached her. She could not understand him, but he gave her his business card. He was a photographer. She buried her passport when the ambassador's family left London, so they left her behind. Eventually she became a model for that photographer, and climbed from pinnacle to pinnacle of success. She enjoys freedom but has never left Islam, the last I heard. However she does speak out against FGM, and she tries to help her countrywomen.

"Ayaan Hirsi Ali's story is quite different. She has been called a major hero or heroine and a political superstar! She shines in politics whereas Waris Dirie shines in the world of fashion and modeling. Hirsi Ali's father was a freedom fighter, so was in hiding for much of his children's childhood. Her mother was taking him food when the grandmother had all three children 'circumcised,' as she termed it. Ayaan's brother was six years; Ayaan was five, and her sister, four. The sister fought like a crazy girl, and so she was cut much worse. The stitches pulled out a week or so later, if I remember the story correctly, and she had to be re-sewn. This double or triple trauma changed her personality for life, her sister said, and she lost her mind during her teens or early twenties. She died a few years later, before her thirtieth birthday.

"Ayaan lived in Somalia, Sudan, Saudi Arabia, and Ethiopia as a child. You need to read this book. It is incredibly interesting. She tried to obey Allah and her imam in her teens, covering her whole body and making her ink from charcoal and every other load they laid on her. Once she rebelled over the ink-making, and her imam beat her and gave her a fractured skull. She would have died but for the intervention of an auntie who took her to the best hospital.

"Her father betrothed her to a Canadian Muslim, and while in Germany, en route to Canada, she decided to 'disappear.' She took a bus or train to Amsterdam, changed her name from Ayaan Hirsi Magan to Ayaan Hirsi Ali, and filed for asylum, lying about her age also. Though her mother considered Ayaan's brain inferior to that of her siblings, Ayaan soon learned Dutch, went to university to study government, and became a member of the Dutch parliament. After 9/11 Ayaan left Islam and began to speak out openly against terrorism and abuse of women. She and Theo Van Gogh made an eleven-minute film against Islam, and a Muslim killed him and promised to kill Ayaan next. She fled to the USA, began to work for the American Enterprise Institute in Washington D. C. and wrote the book *Infidel*.

"Let me read you something that came out in the news which she wrote before the 2008 presidential election in America. I clipped it and inserted it in this book. Well, this is what she has to say about it:

"'About the most vital interest of the day, however, one hears virtually nothing from either candidate. Neither mentions radical Islam. Thus they do not define the ideology of terrorism. Instead, they maintain the vocabulary of the Bush administration: "terror is the enemy; Islam is a religion of peace." But terror is a tactic, and you cannot wage war against a tactic. Political Islam must be addressed as an ideology, as a set of ideas that can be countered only with another set of ideas, much as Communism was contested during the Cold War. This will be the most important task for the next president, and for the American people. In this struggle the US has numerous assets it can deploy. The emancipation of Muslim women, human rights in countries like Saudi Arabia and Egypt, not coddling regimes that provide the resources for this ideology (the Saudis first and foremost) – although both candidates avoid the subject of Islam, promoting these goals would be a start. Whether it is Obama or McCain who squares off against radical Islam, neither will escape it, or any other challenge that requires an American response.'

"Doesn't that little piece of writing show you what an incredible mind she has? She can think logically. She can put her finger on precisely what she feels is the problem. She mentions the emancipation of Muslim women, and we need to be thinking about freeing our PNG women from superstitions and traditions that bind them.

"You have heard how, right here in our own capital city of Port Moresby, a nurse was injured in a car accident, and then a rascal gang came upon the accident, pulled her out, and gang raped her.

"I fear traditional customs of brideprice and polygamy fit too well into the Muslim ideology of male supremacy. Someone said even polygamy used to be more workable when men protected their harems and went off in tribal fights regularly, and many were killed off. In times of peace there just aren't twenty-six wives for every man, or even ten wives for each man; so we have these hordes of young men, fearful they are never going to have their own wife, going out in gangs and raping every girl they can kidnap, spreading HIV/AIDS and even descending like animals on a car accident, pulling an injured nurse from the wreckage and gang-raping her.

"Besides all that evil, polygamy leads to overpopulation of our earth. Muslims allow men to have four wives and some, like Osama Bin Ladin's father, apparently keep replacing the fourth one with a younger wife until he had sixty-five children!"

"Sixty five?" gasped the girls in shock.

"Yes, Osama bin Ladin has sixty-four siblings!"

"*Angorai Yawaliyo*!" said Annie.

"*Aminienga glapa*!" said Tawa.

"*Aiya, mi prêt*!" said Linda.

"I am afraid, too," agreed Pam. "You know how children of polygamists here in PNG are sometimes treated. I know a little boy who seldom sees his father, and his mother has left his dad. The other wives don't want to be bothered with his care, so he is growing up almost an orphan, ridiculed by his half-siblings who have mothers to dote on them. This can cause so much anger in a child. You can imagine how they might erupt in blind fury striking out at the whole world. In fact this is exactly what happened in Osama Bin Ladin's childhood, from what I have read. It's like the gorillas in Congo's Djeke Triangle of Africa. One male gorilla has as many females as he can gather and care for, or mistreat, however you view it, because he never allows them to eat the food they find until he has eaten all he wants, or has all he wants. The January 2008 issue of **National Geographic** tells how one "child" or offspring is "the lowest ranking female" because her mother ran off after another male, (p. 100) The child of the 'most loved female' is called Ekendy in the BaAka language evidently meaning just that—child of the most-loved wife.

"Why should men live like gorillas? Men have minds which can be educated. Men can learn that women are human too, and can have the same feelings, emotions and thoughts a man can have. There is no need for them to behave like animals.

"It scares me because they are not just over-populating the world, when one man can father sixty-five children, but they are raising angry alpha-males who will take their anger out on the whole world, or as much of it as they can reach, as Osama bin Ladin has done in Pakistan, Afghanistan and Sudan, and other countries by sending trained emissaries to wreak havoc elsewhere.

"They can take over the whole world by populating it and not have to worry about terrorism to do the trick. But aside from that, they are raising monsters without fathers to train their children in gentleness, kindness, and all the traits the world needs.

"When I was in universities in America we were taught to control the world population by having only two children per couple."

"Is that why you have only two sons?" asked Annie.

"Yes, and my brother, Bob, and his wife Vicki at Katiloma, have only two children. My other brother, in America, Dean, also has two children, two daughters. However, that is only a recommendation, by people we respect. There is no law against having more children if you want them. You just need to take into account the fact of how much it costs to clothe, feed and educate each child, and not have more than you can care for, in that manner. In China each family is allowed one child only, and so often that has led to baby girls being thrown out or abandoned.

"Just recently it was on BBC that tens of thousands of children in China are being kidnapped and sold."

"Boys?"

"Boys *and* girls. Boys, because some couples are too afraid to have their own child, in case it is female, and they would rather just buy a boy. Girls, because wives are needed for all these boys who have been thriving while girls were unwanted. Some families buy a girl and continue raising her, so she can be a wife for their son when he is ready."

"Oh, my! Oh, it is too much," said Tawa, sobbing again. "I can't stand it. What can we do, Pam? What can we do?"

"Let's pray," said Pam.

"The four women knelt by the dining room chairs and poured their hearts out to God as sounds of the little boys at play came from the playroom, reassuring their mother that all was well with her sons' little world, at least.

Pam led out in prayer for the six thousand girls suffering mutilation in Africa that very day. The Trio raised their voices in their own languages until they drowned out Pam's voice, crying and pleading to God in behalf of their sisters in other lands, other cultures.

As they were crying their hearts out and interceding on behalf of others, an assurance of the Presence of God stole over their whole beings—bodies, souls and spirits. "God hears us!" was the thought uppermost in each mind.

"God is touched with the feeling of our infirmities," murmured Pam. She began humming and then singing the words: *God I harim prea* (x3), *Em i gutpela*." She sang the second verse, "*God bai bekim prea* (x3), *Em i gutpela*." The little boys came out of the playroom to join the singing.

Pam led the way into the living room, pulled Tawa to the piano bench with her and showed her how to play the simple chorus. After they had played it together on different octaves, with Pam adding extra accompaniment, she turned to the three girls and said, "Do you girls know what poise means?"

"Not really," said Annie as the other two half raised their eyebrows hesitantly.

"You all three have such poise. That is the biggest source of your beauty. Psalm 3:3 says God is the Lifter of your heads. You walk and talk with your heads up! Thank God, He is 'your Shield, and your Glory, and the Lifter of your heads!' May He continue to keep you pure and virginal. May He be your shield from polygamists and even from boyfriends who would not cherish and honor your purity. You know, being a virgin is worth more than gold! It is worth more than money can buy, even though one crazy girl auctioned her virginity off on the internet once and got bids into the millions! Your virginity may be the greatest gift you can give to your Prince Charming, to the man whom you love enough to marry. So I say again, may God protect all three of you from both polygamists and thieving boyfriends!"

"Amen," agreed the girls as a knock sounded on the Houck's door.

Pam gasped when she opened the door. A battered woman stood there. One of her eyes had come out of its socket and was hanging on her cheekbone.

"Her husband beat her," said an older woman who stood off to the right and back a little.

"We must get her immediately to the hospital! Why did you come here?" asked Pam.

"Because you're a woman," answered the old one again. We hoped you would be sympathetic. We weren't sure the medical men would be.

"Wyatt, Brody, come here. Girls, would you come with us and watch my boys until I see that this little lady gets all the help she needs?"

"Yes, we will come," agreed the girls.

Pam got her keys, locked her doors, and went out to the gathering crowd. She led the way toward the health sub-centre, after assuring herself of the safety of her sons. She saw Tawa had each little boy by the hand, and Annie and Linda had the boys' other hands and were walking five abreast. People thronged them so that their pace was slowed.

"Girls, something else Muslim men do is kill their daughters if they talk to boys or flirt with them. They call it honor killings. One teen-aged girl was brought to my Emergency Room DOA; that means dead on arrival. Her father had told her two brothers to hold her while he slashed her stomach with a knife."

The girls gasped.

"The three young people had grown up in the United States of America, and gone to school there in Lansing, the capitol city of Michigan. Their parents were from a Middle Eastern Arabic-speaking country, but they knew the English language and the American culture. They knew that honor killings were illegal in our country. One of the boys lost his mind. He became unable to talk. He could only make animal sounds and had to be confined in a psych ward, or a mental hospital after that.

"What did American policemen do to the father?"

"They went looking for him in his own home. When they did not find him there, they went next door and found him with the knife still in his hands and blood all over himself. They arrested him and put him in jail, but before he could stand trial his own country demanded he be given back to them. What he had done was not a crime in his country, so his country wanted to protect him."

"And his sons?"

"I suppose they went too. I never heard any more about them."

"Could they come back to your country later?"

"I doubt it. I doubt if the USA would ever allow the father at least to return."

"I would like to tell you about Jesus' protection for my mother when she was a young girl in Port Moresby, but we are almost to the health sub-centre now. If I forget to tell you sometime, you remind me. Remember, God can protect you and will if you ask Him and follow His commands and if You walk close enough to Him to mind His checks, I truly believe. I have heard a South African man say since the end of apartheid in his country, no white girl is safe on the streets. I hope PNG doesn't ever come to that for girls of any race! Okay?"

"Okay," agreed the Trio.

"Oikay," echoed some of the crowd who did not understand English, but wanted to be included. They nodded their heads and said "Oikay" again.

"Kapogla," said Tawa, nodding to them with a wide smile.

"Kapogla, oikay, kapogla," they smiled back.

"And remember, girls, Psalm 3:3. God is our Shield against all evil; our Glory, (sometime I want to share more of that special word with you) and the Lifter of our heads. Hold your heads high, girls, and keep praying."

The Stephen Mann family in 2000. Bottom center: Wameyambo reads the pages about herself in my doctoral dissertation, *Parents as Teachers*, 2008. Wameyambo was a great teacher of her own children as well as others. She was called "Mama bilong Wakwak School."

Chapter Five

Tawa's Trio surrounded the teacher's desk to talk to Mrs. Bonau.

"Are we going to read another chapter of **Toropo — Tenth Wife** today?" asked Tawa.

"Yes, most definitely. Maybe two or three chapters. Do you like the book?"

"Yes," answered the Trio with one voice.

"Mrs. Bonau, Toropo is my half-sister. Boss Boy Pombo is my father. Turi and Bani are my half-brothers."

"Really?" Mrs. Bonau stopped all motion and looked Tawa in the eye.

"Really? Truly?"

"Yes, Mrs. Bonau. Really! Truly!"

"Oh, my! I don't know what to say."

"Why?"

"It's too preposterous! It's too amazing!"

"Why?"

"I've been teaching for forty years! I know the lady who wrote this book. And now to think that I should meet Toropo's sister, it's almost too startling to be true! Toropo married Kedle of Peyamo-Peli, or Piamble."

"Yes, Toropo married a polygamist at Peyambele named Yalo Mokoi. He's dead now. He died last year. He had twenty-six wives when he died."

"*Angorai yawaliyo*!" exclaimed Annie. "I don't know any man with twenty-six wives! Did he have sixty-five children like Osama bin Ladin's father?"

"I don't know how many children he has. I'm not sure he has kept track of how many daughters he has sold in marriage." Tawa said, "He has far more daughters than sons."

"Where's Toropo now, if Kedle's dead?"

"She is still alive and still at Peyambele."

"Thank God they don't burn a man's widows with him when he dies like they have done in India!"

67

The Trio and others gasped. "Truly? In India they burned a man's widow when he died? You mean burned her alive?"

"Yes, burned her alive on the funeral pyre."

"*Aminienga Glapa*! Thank God this isn't India!"

"You can say that again for more than one reason!"

"Maybe Pam Houck is right about some women in other countries having it worse than we do here in PNG," said Tawa to Annie and Linda.

"Could you get Toropo to come to speak to our class here, Tawa?"

"I don't know."

"Let's think about it."

"I'm afraid it would be impossible. I haven't seen her for six months."

"Where is her brother, Bani? Your brother, I should say."

"He is a teacher at Kagua High School.

"Do you have a cell phone?"

"No."

"I do. Do you know his number?"

"I have it at the dormitory."

"Let's try giving him a call to see if he would consider helping us find a way to get Toropo here to our English class."

"Oh, my! Wouldn't that be exciting?"

"It's past time to begin our class. Let's sit down and go on with our story.

"Class, may I introduce to you Toropo's sister, Tawa? This brings the story so much closer home! How many wives does your father have, Tawa?"

"Five."

"Boss Boy Pombo of Tona now has five wives, class. Toropo was the daughter of his first wife. Right, Tawa? Bani-Ma?"

"Mmm," assented Tawa, raising her eyebrows.

"Are you the daughter of his fifth wife, Tawa?

"Yes, madam."

"Does your father have children younger than you?"

"Yes. My mom has three children younger than I. Mindili-Ma has two children younger than I. Lkoraiye-Ma also has two children younger than I. The other two wives have stopped having babies."

"Tawa must play the part of Toropo again today."

Tawa did. She entered into the part of going to Kauapena, entering the classroom there and wow-ing Mr. Kasi with all of her creative ability. She became a true actor that day.

In Chapter Three when her father was brow-beating her publicly she felt Toropo's humiliation clear to the marrow of her bones. Toropo's tears ran down Tawa's cheeks.

The part of Turi was played by a boy named Maurice this time. When he was called to the front on page 8 he said, "May I say something, Mrs. Bonau?"

The teacher nodded.

"Some of you know I am from the Baruya Tribe in the Eastern Highlands District. Traditionally we don't sell our sisters or daughters in marriage. This story makes me glad of it. Sometimes the sister-exchanges we arrange might not be as happy as they should be, but I think we avoid a lot of the problems the ImboUngus have."

"That is very interesting, Maurice! We will want you to take part in this debate if we do stage one. So you get your thinking cap on!"

Maurice, alias Turi, proudly showed off his sister to his dorm parents and Mr. Kasi.

On page 14 he truly did become the solicitous brother who said, "I like to see you happy, *Aya*. You should always be happy."

Maurice entered into Toropo's sorrows to such evident extent that his teacher said, "Thank God for brothers!" as the students returned to their seats. "Toropo looked to her older brother, Bani, for help, and he was certainly supportive and sympathetic even though he didn't know how to help. Linda Kelley's original intent in writing this book was for it to be read by politicians, people who might change the laws. She felt men almost looked at women as sub-human creatures, and she thought if they could read about a girl's emotions and thoughts and heart, maybe they would realize that females are as human as they, with the same needs, desires, and rights. She was hoping educated men would be different than bushmen, perceive the world differently and change some laws. So far not many changes have been made legally, but there is a female lawyer in Mt. Hagen. Rebecca Kalepo has her own office. I have been to it.

"Christina Kewa's case was revolutionary and she won, so that has set a precedent other lawyers can refer to and remember.

"Christina filed for divorce, full custody of her children, and child maintenance. The lawyers who helped her win her case were Paulus Dawa, Danny Godol and Peter Kak. Christina pays tribute to them and to the judge also, and to a "shining PNG woman" named Maria Kunjil, a National Court Registrar, who kept pushing her case to the forefront, keeping her files in evidence, and not letting them be shelved until they could be forgotten. Her second husband, who is not a PNGn has now adopted her first two children, Queenie and Britain, and she says he is a wonderful father to those two children as well as to the two sons they have had together.

"But back to brothers, sometimes our brothers care more for us and our difficulties than anyone else in our lives. Consequently, I appeal to you young men in this class. Remember your sisters. Share with them in their heartaches. Stand up for them to your fathers. Help your fathers to see that education has broadened your mind and you now know that women have just as much brainpower as men. Perhaps our country can never be a force in the world until it raises its women and frees the creative energy in them or us, to lift us as a nation. Remember, women are the mothers of the boys as well as the girls. Researchers and educators know now that ninety percent of a child's brain develops in the first five years of his life. Who is he with during the first five years of his life? His mother. He is watching her, learning her reactions, learning how to look at life. If she is happy she can center more of her thoughts on her child and his development. If she is being beaten and battered, her child's development may be stunted and thwarted.

"I remember watching the author of **Toropo: Tenth Wife**, as a mother. Our children played constantly together. Her elder son came to my first grade after he finished his home schooling each day. I remember what a gentle, caring little lad he was. All the kids loved him.

"Then my own son did pre-school with her second son and her daughter. I remember how excited Roland was when he learned that G was the letter that started my name. It was as though he had made the greatest discovery in the world! He

Grace and Pam with cake

came home shouting, 'I know Mommy's name! I can write Mommy's name!' My husband burst his bubble when he showed us he could only write the G, but Linda Harvey Kelley never burst any child's bubble. She just loved learning and loved teaching, and blew the children to great heights of knowledge. I have tried to be like her. Most of my life I too taught the beginners, preparatory or first grade, the youngest possible age.

"Linda's daughter, Pamela, when she found two wooden blocks in her toy box with the letter R on them, came running to her mother, saying, 'Me found it! Me found it!' When her mother asked her what she had found she said, 'Reuben and Roland! Me found it!' and she showed her mother the two R's that started my husband's name and my son's name. Linda bragged her to high heaven and acted like it was as big of a discovery as the two-year-old thought it was. Later when Pamela was three years old she baked me a cake for my birthday. At three years of age she had read the directions on the cake mix box herself and baked that cake under her mother's supervision."

Some of the students clicked their thumbnails on their teeth. Most of them had not yet baked a cake. Pilipo raised his hand.

"Is it the same Pamela who now lives here in Ialibu?"

"It is. She married Chad Houck. Her name is now Pamela Houck."

"It is nearly time for class to be dismissed. I hear there is a special speaker for Religious Instruction class today. David Hersman comes from Goroka Evangelical Bible Mission, and he is here in Ialibu to give a seminar on Christian Education. This afternoon however he is going to be speaking at the Gospel Tidings Church. You are free to go hear him now. I hear he is going to speak on the '**Wantok** System.' It sounds like a very interesting and relative topic for us! He has been a co-ordinator for Accelerated Christian Education in PNG until Southern Cross Educational Enterprises eliminated that post in 1999. They have some wonderful ideas and methods of teaching in ACE. When Pamela Kelley was four years old, she was doing ACE paces. Her brother, Bob, did ACE paces as well as a second curriculum before he came to my class each day and entered into our activities in simple English and Melanesian Pidgin. David Hersman is also a pilot and a pilot instructor. I hear he has taught several PNG girls to fly a plane."

"Girls?" questioned the startled students.

"Yes, girls!"

"*Olaman!* We want to go hear him then, don't we, girls?" Annie asked of her friends.

"Absolutely, positively!" they agreed.

"Are you coming, Mrs. Bonau?" asked Julie John.

"Yes, I hope to. I have a few matters to attend to first, but I plan on making it to as much of his session as possible."

When the trio entered Gospel Tidings Church they saw Pam and Brody Houck there.

"Why, you're here, Pam! How nice!"

"Yes, my mother eulogizes this man's writing, so I wouldn't miss a chance to hear him speak.

"And how are you, Brody?" asked Tawa.

He held up one miniature thumb and said, "I'm bweeding."

Tawa examined the little thumb closely and saw a pinpoint of blood.

"Is that from a hangnail?"

"No, a pwicker poked me."

"I guess he needs a band-aid to make it all right," said his mother, searching in her *bilum*, and producing one.

"That's a wittle one," said Brody.

"A wittle band-aid for a wittle thumb," teased Tawa.

"It's not a wittle fumb! It's a big fumb," said Brody raising his thumb as high in the air as he could reach.

"Okay, Big Stuff. Look! There's the American who is going to speak."

All heads faced forward as David Hersman said, "Join with me if you know 'At Calvary,'" and led out with a beautiful singing voice. A few joined, and when it ended, he led in a short prayer asking God's "help and Presence as we endeavor to adapt our hearts and cultures to a Christ-centered culture, pleasing to our Triune Godhead."

After his "Amen" heads were raised and people gave him their full attention.

"You realize your island country has over 800 languages and almost as many cultures and sub-cultures. Accordingly, someone who speaks your language is your *wantok* (one-talk) and you feel a special kinship with him if you're away from home, especially, even if you have never met him before in your life.

"Let's consider how the *wantok* system should work in the 21st century, how it is a good thing if used properly but can become very burdensome if abused.

"Many times I hear Papua New Guinea people refer to the *wantok* system in such a way as to give the impression that it is all bad. Such is not the case. We are told in God's Word to love one another, care for those who cannot care for themselves, provide work opportunities for the poor, share with those in need, and not be too proud to accept assistance from others when needed. The principles of God's Word would produce a perfectly balanced *wantok* system! Of course some people are not Christians and are not even remotely interested in what God has to say.

"It is the abuse of the *wantok* system that creates the problems that frustrate so many people. I have used the following illustrations from *The True Course:*

THE TRUE COURSE

Traditionally, in the village environment everyone had responsibilities, and everyone reaped the benefits of the collective efforts of the village. I assume that men had daily responsibilities, and survival required quite a bit of cooperation—or interdependence. I also believe that, even though it was a tribal society, there was still respect for the property of others. I do not believe it was accepted to simply go into another person's bush house and take or demand whatever a person wanted. The picture here shows the interaction between the households of the village. The small arrows on the right illustrate the fact that trade outside of the village, or group of villages, was very limited.

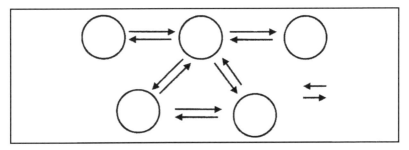

Most of what was needed for survival was produced locally. There was not much dependency on outside trade, although there was some. If someone was sick or had another special need, the other people of the village took care of that need. Probably every culture, even today, has some form of "wantok system"—people helping people in the community. Whatever can be handled on the local level will save a tremendous amount of bureaucratic red tape and governmental expense (your tax money).

Almost every need was met locally. Since there was little interaction and trade with other distant areas, there was not much need for cash as we know it today. Not so long ago, cash did not even exist in the highlands. The local village could pretty well support itself by sharing the work and benefits—sort of passing the blessings around and around in the village.

This simple little remote world had a lot of good points, but it was not perfect. Life was often a matter of mere survival, doing everything by hand: carrying water, food, and firewood by hand over great distances. Their spades were bones and stones. Many things taken for granted today, such as a simple steel spade, were unknown to your ancestors just a few decades ago. Diseases were prevalent, and often epidemics destroyed hundreds of lives. Many superstitions about spirits, sickness, and death persist even today—causing scores of needless deaths. Tribal fighting and fear were part of everyday life, and worst of all, they did not know the "peace of God, which surpasses all understanding" (Philippians 4:7).

The "outside world" does exist out there, and it's not all bad either. Actually, it has some real advantages, and one day a fellow—let's name him Jake—in the little inter-dependent village decides to go for an education in a large town. He needs money for school fees, and his wantoks all contribute. He goes away to school. Suddenly (see second illustration) instead of a balanced interdependence between the houses, we see a big flow in one direction, and a lot of it flows right out of the village to the school where Jake is going for his training. Instead of being interdependent, he has become dependent, and the support is flowing in only one direction.

Ah, but you say, "No worries! This fellow is going to get an education, a job, and he is coming back 'bringing his sheaves [harvest of money] with him!'" And he does eventually. Jake finishes school, gets a good job, comes back, and builds a permanent house in the edge of the village.

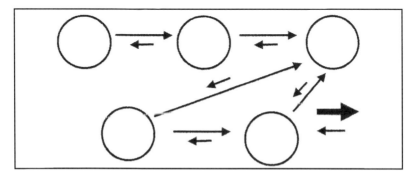

Should Jake be generous and sharing with the people of the village? Absolutely! They helped him, and now he is helping them. That is good. It should work that way. He should remember his roots, his parents, his grandparents, and his friends, and he does.

But then some problems pop up! One of Jake's uncles says, "It is not fair for you to have a permanent house with a metal roof while the rest of us, who paid your school fees, are still living under our kunai [grass] roofs!"

Others start neglecting their responsibilities, saying, "We worked hard, paid your school fees, and now you can take care of us." Don't forget—while Jake was away at school the rest of these folks were at home having babies. There are a lot more mouths to feed than there were before, nearly 6 million in Papua New Guinea now—four times as many as in 1948.

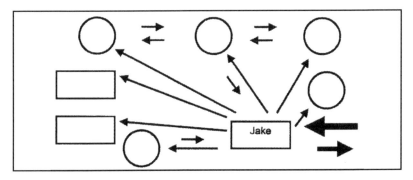

But Jake is generous. He builds a permanent house for Uncle Gimi and later one for his parents. By now, some young men are asking for help on their bride prices, and several others are wanting help on their school fees. All the time the village has become more populated—but less productive. They have become dependent instead of inter-dependent.

If these people were still content with the same standard of living that they had in the original village, things might work a little better, but they say, "Why should we live that way with all this money Jake is making?" even in the villages people want more than they used to. They want "kappa" roofs, permanent houses, electricity, gas cooking stoves, television and video equipment, radios and compact disc players, refrigerators, cars (or at least rides on PMVs), and metal tools, such as axes, bush knives, and spades.

All these things require some cash flow. Common sense, or mathematical calculations, would show us that there needs to be a corresponding increase in productivity and earning power. Everyone seems to agree that the present abuse of the wantok system has produced *an economic disaster in which many unproductive people are dependent on the productivity of a few!*

Papua New Guinea is not really a poor country. We have almost unlimited natural resources. Through the wantok system everybody is taken care of—at least their minimum needs. We do not have many people starving to death. We usually have sufficient rain, plenty of water, abundant gardens, fruits, and vegetables. I have heard Papua New Guinea nationals make reports after visiting India, Africa, and other places of extreme poverty. They all say the same thing: "We are so blessed with abundance in Papua New Guinea!"

Most of the poverty in Papua New Guinea is probably the result of dependency and mismanagement.

Dependence—Independence—Interdependence

Let's take a deeper look at the words "dependence," "independence," and "interdependence." The root word of all these is "depend." Who are you depending on?

One of the best examples I can think of to help us understand these principles is the Declaration of Independence of the United States. This was the document in which the American colonies of Great Britain declared themselves to be "absolved from all allegiance to the British Crown."

This document of independence was also a document of total *dependence* on God—referred to as "nature's God," "Creator," "divine Providence," and "the supreme Judge of the world."

It is also a declaration of *interdependence*: "We mutually pledge to each other our lives, our fortunes, and our sacred honor."

The dictionary defines "independent" as "needing, wishing, or getting no help from others." "Independence" means "condition of being independent; freedom from the control, influence, support, or help of others."

We say a person is independent if he or she is productive, self-motivated, and not easily controlled by the opinions of others. In reality, none of us is totally independent. We are the products of many influences, experiences, and opportunities that others helped to influence. When the American colonists declared their *independence* from England, they realized they would not be able to rely on England for help in the future! They stated that they would have to be aware of their *dependence* on divine providence, and they would have to be *interdependent* on each other.

Interdependence is real life! Nobody has the right to be totally dependent on others unless he or she is severely handicapped, mentally or physically. Ironically, these who we should be supporting are often the most neglected ones in society, while able-bodied, unproductive people often demand support they do not deserve!

Your own personal economic stability, or that of any business, ministry, or nation, depends largely on an understanding of these principles. We are all interdependent on each other. We buy food from stores and markets because we are dependent on other people for part of our sustenance. The women selling in the market places are dependent on the buyers for the cash they need for other purchases. This interdependence gives all of us a better standard of living than we would be able to provide if we were totally independent. *This interdependence helps make life more comfortable, more productive, less burdensome, and more healthy.*

People are often worried about poverty, and they compare their own income or possessions with that of those who have more. Then they become dissatisfied, jealous, and critical of those who are more productive or more fortunate. Quit thinking about whether or not you are in poverty, and start thinking about productivity as opposed to dependency. *The opposite of dependence is productivity.*

If you are not productive, you are a slave to somebody, and the bottom line is that you have to do what that controlling person says in order to survive—or else become demanding and corrupt. This attitude of dependency is the root of the crime problem in Papua New Guinea.

Another Problem with Dependency

A person who is dependent on the productivity of somebody else has to appear quite generous to his or her wantoks. This gives the person a feeling of "giving" when he or she actually might be doing it to receive something in return—maybe way out in the future. This necessity to appear generous causes many people to be generous with other people's goods! If you are not the rightful owner of something, you do not have the right to give it away or even to lend it to somebody else.

For instance, an employee has no right to be generous with the merchandise or time that belongs to his employer unless the employer (owner of the goods) has authorized the employee to distribute the stock in such a way. I will not even lend something that belongs to my children unless I have their permission. Why? Because God requires us to teach absolute respect for the property rights of others.

When king David wanted to offer an offering to the Lord in one case, Araunah offered to give everything that was needed— land, wood, and oxen for the sacrifice. David refused this offer, saying, "No, but I will surely buy it from you for a price; nor will I offer burnt offerings to the Lord my God with that which costs me nothing" (2 Samuel 24:24). So David bought the threshing floor and the oxen for fifty shekels of silver (2 Samuel 24; 1 Chronicles 21).

By the same principle, why would a person want to appear very generous when he or she is actually a thief? We should give generously to those who are in need, but biblical principles of ownership, stewardship, and honesty are always required. You are not really giving if you give what rightfully belongs to someone else—you are stealing!

If something has been entrusted to your care, you do not have the right to give it or lend it to somebody else. "Love your neighbor as yourself." Respect your neighbor's right of ownership.

God has ordained that everyone should be productive. The Bible strongly condemns laziness and lack of productivity. Please carefully read the following Bible story.

In Matthew 25 we find the parable of the talents. A parable is "an earthly story with a heavenly meaning." In this story, beginning with verse 14, Jesus said,

> The kingdom of heaven is like a man traveling to a far country, who called his own servants and delivered his goods to them. And to one he gave five talents, to another two, and to another one, to each according to his own ability; and immediately he went on a journey. Then he who had received the

five talents went and traded with them, and made another five talents. And likewise he who had received two gained two more also. But he who had received one went and dug in the ground, and hid his lord's money.

After a long time the lord of those servants came and settled accounts with them. So he who had received five talents came and brought five other talents, saying, "Lord, you delivered to me five talents; look, I have gained five more talents besides them." His lord said to him, "Well done, good and faithful servant; you were faithful over a few things, I will make you ruler over many things. Enter into the joy of your lord." He also who had received two talents came and said, "Lord, you delivered to me two talents; look, I have gained two more talents besides them." His lord said to him, "Well done, good and faithful servant; you have been faithful over a few things, I will make you ruler over many things. Enter into the joy of your lord.

Then he who had received the one talent came and said, "Lord, I knew you to be a hard man, reaping where you have not sown, and gathering where you have not scattered seed. And I was afraid, and went and hid your talent in the ground. Look, there you have what is yours."

But his lord answered and said to him, "You wicked and lazy servant, you knew that I reap where I have not sown, and gather where I have not scattered seed. So you ought to have deposited my money with the bankers, and at my coming I would have received back my own with interest. So take the talent from him, and give it to him who has ten talents. For to everyone who has, more will be given, and he will have abundance; but from him who does not have, even what he has will be taken away. And cast the unprofitable servant into the outer darkness. There will be weeping and gnashing of teeth."

—Matthew 25:14-30

By this world's socialistic economic philosophies, this employer would be considered very unfair, but by God's standard of righteousness, the lazy servant was stripped of what he had because he was not faithful.

Consider some facts and observations from this story.

1. *Each servant was entrusted with something with which to work*, and make profit. God has entrusted to you some time, talents, skills, or interests, for you to work with. To deny this, and cry about what you don't have is sin, laziness, and dishonest. God has given you something!
2. *The master trusted each one "according to his ability."* He knew which ones could be trusted with more. If you feel like God has not entrusted much to you, maybe you have not been faithful with "that which is least." If you are faithful, in the future He will entrust more to your care and control.
3. *The master did not expect the same performance and productivity from everyone, but he did require each one to be faithful and profitable.*

In another place, Jesus said, "He who is faithful in what is least is faithful also in much; and he who is unjust in what is least is unjust also in much" (Luke 16:10).

Many times people are jealous of those who have more, are demanding handouts from them, or even do them bodily harm. The real problem is their own love of dependency and lack of productivity. Productive people should never be expected to support those who choose to be unproductive!

In my own country we have a similar problem in our welfare system. Government programs, which were probably started by people with good motives, have become tremendous drains on the taxpayers. Several years ago New York City, one of the world's economic control points, had a million people on welfare. At one point that city actually went bankrupt and had to be bailed out by the United States taxpayers! In reality any system that pays people who are unproductive will produce more and more dependency and more and more unproductive people.

Socialists often cry out about the "unequal distribution of wealth" in a free market society. Under their economic philosophies poverty always escalates, nearly everyone becomes poor except a few fat cats running the tremendous bureaucracy. Nothing succeeds like freedom!

Many people are neither bothered nor ashamed of their dependency at all. Being lazy, unproductive, and totally dependent is fine with them, but we should know two major things about this attitude.

1. *It is sin!* God ordained and commanded us to be productive, and take care of our families. God inspired Paul to write, "If anyone does not provide for his own, and especially for those of his household, he has *denied the faith* and is worse than an unbeliever" (1 Timothy 5:8, emphasis added). The King James Version uses the word "infidel."

2. *It will hold you down economically.* Consider a vertical scale of numbers from 1 to 10. Let's say that a very poor person, just barely surviving, is on the first level, number 1. In the middle numbers, 4 through 8, we have the average working people, living comfortably yet not really "rich." Numbers 9 and 10 represent those who are very well off financially—maybe rich. Where do you consider yourself to be on this scale?

We know that not every "dependent" comes out at the same level, of course, but for this illustration let's say that by depending on the wantok system, or the welfare system, a family can live on level 3. If that is what you are content with, you will be stuck right there!

However, if you choose to be productive, if you develop your talents and skills, learn new skills, learn to earn, you can move up to level four. Eventually you can move up to level 5, 6, or 7. There is really no limit on how high you can go if you ask God to

10	Rich
9	Well to do
8	
7	More Productive
6	Productive
5	Improving Skills
4	Low Skills
3	Wontok Dependency
2	
1	Very Poor

help you, use your skills for His glory, use your resources to honor Him, and be wisely generous with others.

Am I promising that you will become rich—level 10? No, but I am assuring you that in a free country such as Papua New Guinea, you can improve your own standard of living significantly. You can become a blessing to others instead of a discontented dependent on level 2 or 3. God's will is for you to be productive, and He will give you something to do.

I heard a fellow once complaining about the Asian people running businesses in Papua New Guinea. He sounded very resentful—almost hateful. I said, "Hey—don't hate these people. Learn something from them." That seemed to be a new thought for him, and he took it to heart. Soon his productivity had increased, and the last time I saw him he had a car of his own.

I am not saying we should emulate all the business practices of every Asian. I understand that some of them pay very low wages for extremely long hours of work. That is a violation of Christ's command to "love your neighbor as yourself." We should always pay our helpers a fair wage, and God will bless us if we do (Colossians 4:1).

When your productivity increases, you will have more than you do now. You're probably thinking. "If my productivity increases and I start to get ahead, the number of wantoks on my doorstep will increase also, and I might be worse off than I am now." Funny you should mention that, because the Bible speaks of that very thing. "When goods increase, they are increased that eat them: and what good is there to the owners thereof, saving the beholding of them with their eyes?" (Ecclesiastes 5:11, KJV).

As your productivity improves, you will also have the added responsibility to help others more. Does this mean that you will have to pass out money to all your unproductive wantoks? No, you must try to help them in ways that do not make them more dependent. You may provide employment, share a little to help them get started toward a profitable business venture or otherwise improve their own productivity.

Of course, there are emergency situations in which you do give outright contributions toward someone's needs. Jesus said not to expect something in return Your Heavenly Father will take care of you.

One day while I was working on this very chapter, I was informed about three different abuses of the wantok system.

In the first one, a fellow told me that twenty-some (evidently close to thirty) years ago, his papa died, and the people of the village "gave" to help this widow and her children. Now after all these years demands were made, supposedly to honor this

83

woman, but each son had to come up with a large sum of money to repay these wantoks who had helped their mother a quarter of a century ago.

This might not seem at all unusual to you and may seem very proper, but what does the Bible say about helping those in need?

Jesus himself spoke these Words: "Just as you want men to do to you, you also do to them likewise" (Luke 6:31). This is often called the "Golden Rule."

But if you love those who love you, what credit is that to you? For even sinners love those who love them. And if you do good to those who do good to you, what credit is that to you? For even sinners do the same. And if you lend to those from whom you hope to receive back, what credit is that to you? For even sinners lend to sinners to receive as much back. But love your enemies, do good, and lend, hoping for nothing in return; and your reward will be great, and you will be sons of the Most High. For He is kind to the unthankful and evil. Therefore be merciful, just as your Father also is merciful.

—Luke 6:32-36, emphasis added

This is really a strange idea to the wantok system. Would you like to have God's blessing? Or would you settle for the rewards of the wantok system? Jesus taught that you aren't really giving if you are sharing "to receive as much again." Did these people help this widow out of a heart of love or out of a heart of greed? Probably some were in each category, but if you are expecting God to bless you, reward you, and provide for you, you will have to accept His concept of love and giving. I can assure you that it will work for you.

We should help those in need because of their need, because we are blessed enough to have something to share, and because God has promised to provide for us if we care for others. Give it! Let it go! Forget it! Trust in God!

Some people give to impress others. Evidently the Pharisees in the time of Christ actually blew a trumpet to call attention to their "giving" to the poor. Can you imagine the embarrassment this probably was to the poor people? The Pharisees didn't really care about them—they were exalting themselves. Here's what Jesus said: "When you do a charitable deed, do not sound a trumpet before you as the hypocrites do in the synagogues and in the streets, that they may have glory from men. Assuredly, I say to you, they have their reward" (Matthew 6:2, 5).

This phrase "they have their reward" is used three times in Luke 6. Don't expect any reward or blessing from God for your selfishness!

Jesus also said, *"When you give a dinner or a supper,* do not ask your friends, your brothers, your relatives, nor rich neighbors, lest they also invite you back, and you be repaid. But when you give a feast, *invite the poor, the maimed, the lame, the blind. And you will be blessed,* because they cannot repay you; for you shall be repaid at the resurrection of the just" (Luke 14:12-14, emphasis added).

When I have preached about this application of love in action, many simply smile as if to say, "That's not how we do it here." Maybe not, but it is the command of the Lord Jesus Christ. Would anyone claim that the Papua New Guinea wantok system has produced a better standard of living than God has bestowed on countries that have taken this command seriously?

A young lady told me that when her papa was sick, a fellow came with a chicken and prepared chicken broth for him. He recovered, and later the guy tried to demand K500 for his help. Are you willing to give to someone in need—"expecting nothing in return?" If not, you are cheating yourself out of God's blessing.

In the third situation, a young father has died, and his widow is expecting a baby. Since his "bride price" was not paid, her house line is threatening to take her baby when it is born. Here again, this fellow's dependency on the wantok system has created a trap for his wife and child—even after his death. In all these situations, Christian people should be asking themselves, "How can we settle this in the light of God's Word? How can we free ourselves and our children from what is essentially slavery? Does the Bible support the radical idea that anyone has a right to take this woman's child? Who is right—God or the wantok system?"

Let's summarize a few points from this chapter:

1. The original wantok system probably worked quite well to provide a minimum standard of living in a mostly closed culture.

2. Today people want a higher standard of living, and there must be a corresponding increase in productivity to meet these needs.

3. Everyone should be productive. God will give you something to do.

4. God has given every one of us something that can be developed to meet our needs and enable us to share with those in need.

5. Everyone should be taught to be inter-dependent rather than dependent.

6. We should help those in need through a heart of love—expecting nothing in return.

7. When someone has shared with us, we should not be indebted to them, but we should be free and happy to pass that blessing on to someone else. God told Abraham that He would bless him and make him a blessing.

8. We do not have right to expect or demand to live from the productivity of others. That is covetousness and leads to stealing. Both coveting and stealing are sin, condemned by the Ten Commandments.

9. Greed and mismanagement will hold our country down economically and otherwise.

10. Do unto others as you would have others to do unto you (the Golden Rule).

* * * * *

With a short prayer Mr. David Hersman dismissed the Religious Instruction class.

Annie turned to her classmates and Pam and said, "*Yawaliyo!* That's a lot of information to take in at one time! I'm familiar with those passages from the Bible, but I hadn't heard anyone interpret them quite like that before."

"My heart says 'Amen,'" said Pam.

"Mine too, inasmuch of it as I understand," said Tawa. But I think if we followed it here in PNG a lot of things would really be different."

"I can see how debts and obligations could hold people back from yielding their hearts and lives to God," said Linda. "My daddy always said, 'It's often easier to live for God away from the village than in it!'"

"But wantoks probably seek your father out wherever he goes, don't they?" asked Pam.

"Yes," agreed the tallest of the Trio, "but not as many as in the village."

"So the wantok system could actually tear down extended family life and make people not want to go back to their village, could it?'

"Yes, I know that's true."

"I know PNG men who have married American girls and just stayed in America. Maybe they can't face the demands of the tribe back here."

"Are they being selfish to stay away?"

"No," said Pam. "I wouldn't call it selfish. They have demanding jobs which require their presence in order to provide for their family. In three places in the Bible God says a man is supposed to leave his parents and cling to his wife. They are to be fruitful and multiply and replenish the earth. And if a man doesn't take care of his own family he is worse than an infidel as Mr. Hersman has just told us. Besides, the tribe didn't help him pay brideprice for that American girl, so he doesn't owe the tribe for that."

"Say, Sister, you're right about that. Some of our best, most spiritual young men are going to Bible colleges in America. If they can get free brides there and stay there, we have lost them to our country."

"Meanwhile fathers here in PNG may be making their daughters marry non-Christians who have big brideprices. This is a serious situation. We need to be praying about this!"

"Yes, please, my Pam, my sister. Please help me pray. Sometimes when I think of my sisters, Toropo and Mombo, both married to polygamists, I think, how can my fate be any different? And I get so depressed I don't know how to go on."

"We need to pray that your dad will give his heart to God," said Annie.

"Right, but will that stop him from taking a large brideprice from a polygamist for me?"

"It should. My dad is a Christian, and he would never sell me to a polygamist! I was at Kumiyane Revival in July 2008. Pastor Poria pastors there, and he reminds me of photos I have seen of holy men in India. He walks so close to God that he seems to almost exude the Presence of God. I wish you three could have seen him hug each man and boy who prayed at the altar in that Sunday morning service. Then he presented each new convert to the congregation in such a stately way I felt like I was seeing Jesus, the Son, present this person to the Father. I felt almost caught up into the heavenlies like Paul said in the Bible.

"But then later in that same service Ricks Levongo called seven men to stand in front facing the congregation. They then called seven younger men, some of them new converts, to come and sit at the feet of these seven mature Christians. They too faced the congregation. Then they committed to these fourteen men the task of keeping Kumiyane Village pure for God. These fourteen were to 'keep out alcohol, marijuana, card playing, promiscuity, and second wives!'"

"Really? Second wives?" asked Pam.

"Really, truly! Isn't that wonderful?"

"It is!" exclaimed Pam and Tawa together. Tawa continued, "It makes me want to marry a Wiru man from Kumiyane Village! But how and where is my father ever going to meet a Wiru man with brideprice already accumulated for his son?"

"Invite your dad to come to the holiness camp meeting at Pabrabuk in January," urged Annie.

"Pabrabuk? In the Western Highlands?"

Stanley Unda, son of Boss Boy Unda
at Mele, and father of Linda Stanley

88

Lovedy Kupaloma 7, Bob Kelley 5 in back row; Aisapame Kupaloma 6, Deanie Kelley 18 months, Lytle Semane, 6. This was taken upon our return from furlough in 1975. We tried to save Lytle, feeding him and doctoring him but we were too late; he died.

Timba and Liriame and children, Kewa and Alu in the back, Konga and Mark center front, with Timba holding Daryl

Lily at 2 years of age with her father Tanguwe, mother Wingi-Mae and sister "Jessica Jiau" Mele June 1966

Mele 1963
Linda Harvey with her teen-age girls class. Lily's mother Wingi-Mae, is in the back row.

I was with Wingi-Mae at Meles in 1964 when Lily was born. I was at Katiloma in March 1971 when Peter was born and his father called him Second Peter.

Peter's mother died when he was born. He is specializing in gynaecology to save other women from dying. He calls us Mom + Dad because of the bottles we fed him.

Dr. Peter Yama of Katiloma & Lily Tanguwe of Mele Doctor & Nurse in Port Moresby.

90

Chapter Six

"Students, look here. Look whom I have here!" said Mrs. Bonau. "This is Toropo! This is Tawa's sister, Toropo, the protagonist of our book, **Toropo: Tenth Wife**.

"We are ready to read Chapter Ten of our book together, but first we want to hear an update on Toropo's life from the woman herself. Even though she understands English well, she says she's more comfortable speaking Pidgin, though you'll see, her Pidgin is full of English phrases because she reads English. Go ahead, Toropo. Tell us about yourself."

"Good afternoon, class. I'm happy to be here with you today because my sister, Tawa, has told me a lot about you and your interest in my story.

"I am the mother of two children and the grandmother of two. I am a widow now because 'Kedle,' as you know him, died two years ago. But the most important thing I need to tell you is that Kedle became a Christian before he died. Rev. Wane Ninjipa won him to the Lord. So my husband is in heaven now.

"My daughter, whom I named Tamara after my friend, Tamara Talbot, went through primary school and high school. She is an accountant with MAF, Missionary Aviation Fellowship, in Mt. Hagen now and married to a fine Christian man there. They have two lovely sons and attend PNGBC in Mt. Hagen.

"My son is in grade six at Peyambele, or Peyambettle as one government officer said it should be spelled. I named him Benjamin Banneker, after the grandson of Banncky, an African prince who was kidnapped by a slaver and taken to America on a slave ship. There he was bought and freed by Molly Walsh, and later they married. They had four daughters, and they bought slaves straight off slave ships from Africa for their daughters' husbands, and gave them their freedom. One of these couples had Benjamin, who became the author of many almanacs and helped survey Washington D. C. You should read about him and his parents and grandparents. It's a wonderful story. My friend, Tamara, told me about this family from the history of her country, the USA.

"But back to my own story, life hasn't been easy for me, but it has been a lot better than I ever dreamed it could be in the first two years after my marriage. Back in those years I wanted to commit suicide more than once, but I learned that God says 'Thou shalt not kill,' not even one's self. God is the Giver of life, and He is the only one who can take away life. Suicide is wrong. Abortion is wrong. I have preached that to my little sister all her life, haven't I, Tawa?" Toropo paused, looking at Tawa. Tawa nodded her head and raised her eyebrows.

"Promiscuity is wrong. I am so glad God kept me from that sin before I knew much about Him. Our old tribal customs taught us sex before marriage was wrong for a girl, and many enforced it by killing a girl if she messed up before marriage. But now we know sex before marriage is wrong for both the man and the woman, class.

"May I read you a little of Proverbs 7 from my little Gideon New Testament that I carry everywhere with me?

"'My son, keep my words, keep my laws. Verse 3. Wrap them around your fingers, write them on the table or page of your heart. Verse 4. Say to wisdom, "You are my sister," and call understanding your kinswoman. Girls, see what a compliment the writer of Proverbs was giving us women in calling wisdom "Sister" and understanding, "a female relative"? PNG men would have us think women can't or shouldn't learn. At least that was the way it was when I was a girl of school age, and I know it still is for some girls. Now it's different for many girls, and I am so thankful. My own father would not let me go to school, but he has allowed my half-sister Tawa to go, partly because of all of us pleading for her, most of all her own mother, and partly because my dad wants to keep up with the times, in some ways.

"You remember Jesus' parable of the talents? To some of His workers, the Master gave five talents, to some two, and to some one. It doesn't say He gave none to any. So girls, even if we only have one talent we have to use it. We dare not bury it in the dirt. We must use it or lose it. The Master will take it and give it to the one who has five if we don't develop it. Toropo began to sing in a clear contralto voice:

> 'One talent have I To take to the sky
> While others are blest, With ten of the best.
> Why should I complain, Or from duty to refrain?
> I'll never, no never. Not I.

"Sing with me, class:
> *'Mi amamas tumas, Mi amamas tumas*
> *Insait long Kraist, Mi amamas tumas.*
> *Em i rausim olgeta sin bilong mi;*
> *Olsem na mi amamas tumas.'*

"And back to Proverbs 7: 'Call understanding your relative. So that they can keep you from unknown or strange women, from loose women with their seductive talk, with their *aigris* and *mausgris*.* *Yu mas abrusim*,** you young men. Likewise you girls, when it's the boys who *aigris* and *mausgris*, the boys who flirt and flatter just to get you into bed with them. Girls, you must keep your virginity. It's the most precious gift God gave, the most desirable talent of all! You want to save it to give to your Prince Charming, a man who has also kept himself pure for you. In this way you can both avoid HIV/AIDS and your children can be strong and healthy."

"Girls and boys, you must learn all you can here in school and in every classroom of life, so you can be the best parents on earth as God planned. Pattern yourself after the heavenly Father. Polygamists are not good fathers. I speak from experience. I know firsthand. I had to be both mother and father to my children. They got very little attention from their father. He was always taken up with his newest wife, right down to his deathbed. He could never be a father to his children. Even in the old way, with the manhouse, his sons at puberty went to live with him, but he had no time to teach them, to train them. Thank God my children had the Pastor at Piamble that they could look up to. He was a wonderful role model and father figure to them, just as Mr. Talbot was to me, showing us how a

---

*Aigris – literally eye-grease, meaning "flirt"
*Mausgris – literally mouth-grease, meaning "flatter"
**Yu mas abrusim - you have to avoid (them)

93

man can live with one woman and put God first in his life. Also my children both knew Dr. Philip Kereme, one of the noblest of men, one of the kindest, most loving fathers this land has ever seen. And he is from Piamble. His first teacher was Mr. Talbot. He went to the Wiru Valley with the Talbots. He has told me that the people of Talipiko and Mele still speak of 'Wane, Tene' as though those two boys started a new tribe, a new breed of men who live and work for God. For you who don't know them, Dr. Philip Kereme's ImboUngu name is Tene, and my friend Tamara used to call him Alfred, Lord Tennyson. He has been Director General of Higher Education in Port Moresby. And Wane Ninjipa has been the president of Pacific Bible College and is now vice chairman of PNGBC. He won my husband to the Lord. Wane went to Kentucky Mountain Bible Institute for his tertiary education and Tene went to London, England, to university. Tene taught briefly at the University of Hawaii and at length at UPNG in Port Moresby. And as I mentioned earlier, he has held the highest education job in our country, Director General of Higher Education. Both of these Piamble boys, Southern Highlands men have married only one woman and been true to her all their lives. From outward appearances at least, they have taken their enjoyment from the wife of their youth, as the Bible says. Look to them, boys, for edification, as role models. Dream of careers like theirs for God. God has given you special talents. Don't chase women all your lives like my husband did. Use your talents for God.

"One more thing, before I sit down and we read Chapter Ten," and she glanced apologetically at Mrs. Bonau, "if you do mess up, boys and girls, take ownership of your wrongdoing. Accept the consequences of your behavior and take responsibility like an adult. Boys, if you have fathered a child, brought life into being, pay child support. Girls, if you have conceived a child, given birth to a person, admit it. Don't hide it. Of course, I don't want you to brag about it, but be truthful to the man you later marry. If he won't marry you because of the child, so be it. That is your consequence. But be the best mother you can be to that child. You may need your parents' help, or some woman's help until you finish your education, but when you have finished it, take responsibility for that child. Don't make your parents raise it.

"Jesus said in John 14, 'I am the Way, the Truth, and the Life.' If you want Life, you have to follow Truth. If you want to walk in the Way to eternal Life, you have to keep Truth, live Truth, be Truthful all the Way. To be Christians we need and want to be like Christ, and Christ is Truth."

With that, Toropo sat down. Mrs. Bonau stood up and said, "That is some of the best teaching I ever heard. You are a born teacher, Toropo."

"Thank you. I like being a teacher's aide to an elementary teacher at Piamble. I take her class and keep it going when she goes to get her salary, or if she's sick."

"Do you really? And what else do you do?"

"I teach Sunday School and women's classes. Sometimes I go to the outstations around Piamble and have women's classes."

"Wonderful! I like what you said about Jesus being Truth. You know when He was with Pontius Pilate He said, 'For this cause came I into the world, that I should bear witness unto the Truth. Everyone that is of the Truth hears My voice.'

"One of my favorite writers, a British woman, Elizabeth Goudge, wrote the book titled *God So Loved the World*. I often quote her to my class. Talking about Jesus, she wrote, 'This one Man made man, was man, saved man, and is Man to all eternity, and apart from Him no other man has any manhood at all.'"

Mrs. Bonau wrote the quotation on the blackboard.

"I have the students save a section in their journals for "Quotes" and I am asking them to copy this into their quotes if they haven't already," she explained to Toropo as she handed her a new exercise book and pen to copy the quotation for her own keeping.

Mrs. Bonau repeated the quote as they were writing and said, "It is true for women too. Apart from Christ, no woman has real womanhood. Apart from Truth, no person has true personhood. The more we believe in Truth, the more we practice Truth in every area of our lives, the more REAL we are. Let's be real, class. Let's be open. Let's be truthful. Let us be sincere. Then this one Man Who made man can continue to make us all He wants us to be.

"Toropo was telling you about talents. As you practice Truth and use your talents in Truth, for Truth, God increases those talents. He helps them grow and develop, and makes you into the great person He had in mind when He first made you.

"George MacDonald, another of my favorite writers said, 'God meant every child to be a queen bee,' or words to that effect." As she was talking she picked up her Quote Box and pulled out a card. "Here it is: It's from his book *The Curate's Awakening*. 'So her present condition was like that of the common bees. Nature fits everyone for a queen but its nurses prevent it from growing into one by providing for it a cell too narrow for the unrolling of royalty, and supplying it with food not potent enough for the nurturing of the ideal. As a result, the cramped and stinted thing which comes out is a working bee. And Helen, who might be both, was as yet, neither.'

"You know about bees. You know how there are worker bees and drones and a queen bee. Well, George MacDonald, or G. Mac as I call him for short, is saying here, Nature means for everyone, or equips everyone to be a queen bee; every person born into this world, but its nurses — its mother, its father, its teachers, all of its nurses push it into a tiny little cell, so it can't grow as big as God wants it to be.

"Toropo said to you girls, 'Be the best mother you can be.' She asked you boys to 'be the best father you can be.' Parents are the child's main nurses and teachers. With God's help you can cause your children to climb higher in God's world than you are able to climb, because you have educated them in wisdom and truth earlier than your parents taught you. You see how terribly important it is for girls to have a good education and to start teaching their children before they send them off to school? If a child learns the greatest percentage of his learning during his first five years, a mother's job is the greatest job there is. She is training, molding future leaders. She is enlarging the cell so that the child can grow into a queen bee. She is setting the emotional stage for the child's later learning. Of course, other teachers need to take over from her in primary school and later secondary, and tertiary, and keep challenging the child, the young person, all along the way. They too are its nurses, providing larger cells, enlarging the child's cell, so he can grow bigger physically, mentally and emotionally and even spiritually. God means for each of us to be a great big queen bee in life's careers and callings. There is so much to do out there! So much to learn!

"Think of what a narrow cell Toropo's nurses provided for her. Her father did not even allow her any schooling at all, and he was a polygamist, more interested in gaining other wives than training his children. Her mother had never had a chance for education either. She could have been a nothing, so to speak, but God...! God intervened in her life. She listened to Him and did not commit suicide, and now she appears to be a happy fulfilled woman, a mother, a grandmother, and a teacher's aide, a Sunday School teacher, and a women's classleader!

"So many more people could do great things in God. When they turn their lives over to Him, He helps them do just that. But according to G. Mac, He wants us to have these opportunities sooner in life. He wants our nurses to provide a larger cell for us from birth with more challenges, more opportunities, and the discipline needed to help us excel.

"Cause your children to climb higher than you can climb because you have educated them in wisdom and truth earlier than your parents may have taught you. However, again, as Toropo mentioned, HIV/AIDS and other things like alcohol and marijuana are killing off our young people before they even begin climbing the career ladder.

"Teach your child the word 'No' before he is a year old. When he wants to touch a sharp knife or a hot potato, say 'No.' When he's two and wants to wander out onto the highway say 'No' and set him in time out if he doesn't listen. When he is a teenager then, maybe he will say 'No' to drugs, alcohol, free sex, if you have taught him well enough.

"Now..." Mrs. Bonau paused, looked around at her class to see if she had everyone's attention. "Let's open our book to page 52, Chapter Ten. She handed a book to Toropo.

"Tawa, you play the part of Toropo for two pages, and then maybe the real Toropo will oblige us by playing herself."

Mrs. Bonau winked at Toropo. Toropo smiled.

"Who wants to be Rami today?"

All the girls raised their hands. They were into this story and loving it.

"Toropo, you choose one."

Toropo chose Annie Yakura.

"And Rami's mother-in-law?"

Annie and Tawa walked to the front with their books.

"Will you choose again, Toropo? I know they want your attention as much as they want to read."

Toropo chose Linda Stanley.

"And who will be Mrs. Talbot?" The boys laughed as every girl still seated, raised her hand. Mrs. Bonau looked at Toropo.

Toropo pointed at Kuglupu saying, "I don't know your name."

"Kuglupu," responded three people at once.

"Jinx," laughed Mrs. Bonau.

"What does that mean?" asked Toropo.

"When people say the same thing at the same time, we say 'Jinx.' I don't know why. I guess I learned it from others.

"Who will be Rami's husband, Unjo?"

Six boys put up their hands. Mrs. Bonau looked at Toropo. Toropo chose Pilipo.

"And who will be the narrator for these two pages? That's a long part."

Toropo chose David and they began to read.

When they finished page 53 and Mrs. Bonau had seen that Toropo was following well, she asked Toropo to go to the front. "Stand beside your sister, and she can help you with any words you don't know."

Toropo complied and stood beside Tawa.

"Would you like to be the narrator for a while?" Mrs. Bonau asked Glaimi.

Glaimi smiled and nodded and went to the front as David took his seat.

"Who will be the driver?"

Mrs. Bonau called on Timothy, and he went to the front, revving his engine and pretending his book was a steering wheel.

"Mondi, would you play the part of the Mondi in the book?"

Mondi nodded with a smile and followed the driver to the front.

"Toropo, you choose Tamara. Is there any girl here who reminds you of your friend, Tamara, or your daughter, Tamara?"

Toropo chose Kewaroa.

Mrs. Bonau appointed Kewa to be Ronald and Tundumbo to be Ronald's wife. They finished the chapter in no time. At the end Mrs. Bonau asked Toropo and Tawa to say together, "I wonder what a bear is," and Glaimi said, "thought Toropo."

The cast sat down laughing, and Mrs. Bonau asked, "Do you know what a bear is now, Toropo?"

Toropo raised her eyebrows in the affirmative. "Rev. Bruce Blowers once showed us a picture of bears coming after boys who had teased the prophet, Elisha, about his bald head, so I learned what bears are."

"Good for you!"

"Let's look at the study guide questions. Dindi, will you read number one?"

"Do you know anyone who has died in childbirth?" read Dindi. Half the class raised their hands. "Can you understand Rami's fear?" Everyone said, "Yes," or nodded their heads.

"Read number two, Anjo," said Mrs. Bonau.

"Unjo means wood or tree. What does your name mean?"

"Can you answer it?" asked Mrs. Bonau.

Anjo said, "My name means back or away. 'Anjo pa' means 'Move back,' or 'Go back,' or 'Go away.'"

"Interesting," said Mrs. Bonau and looked around the room at all the raised hands.

"Glaimi, what does your name mean?"

"Cassowary," said the lad with a laugh.

"Kewa?"

"Foreigner or stranger," answered Kewa.

"Kewaroa?"

"Foreign woman, or strange woman," answered Kewaroa.

"Pilipo?"

"My name is a gerund meaning understanding in the first person, or 'I, understanding."

"Good for you! I'm glad you know what a gerund is. Maybe we can continue this next time. We have to end the class now."

Dr. Philip has even taught at the University of Hawaii.

Ellape with the Kereme Family

... in the office of ...

Dr. Philip Kerew

The Director General of Commission for Higher Ed

After many years of lecturing and having a full professorship at U.P.N.G. Dr. Kereme now has a desk job.

Dr. Philip Kathy Linda Billy Rosalie Scott (18)
          Fiona Tiye   was absent

Chapter Seven

"I've heard about Seven-Corner-Mountain," said Annie Yakura. "I can't wait to see it!"

"We will be there in just a few more kilometers," said Chad Houck. Chad was driving a ten-seater Toyota, former police vehicle to Kagua. His wife and two sons were in the front seat beside him. Behind him sat Tawa, Toropo, Annie, Linda, Pastor Bali and his brother, Yomagae.

"Oh, isn't it beautiful?" squealed Annie, as they descended the gorge on the other side of the river from Seven-Corner-Mountain.

"*Angorai, yawaliyo!*" she exclaimed again and again, as they reached the bridge, crossed it and began the assent toward the first hairpin bend or "corner" as some liked to call it.

"Your brother is coming to Kagua to meet you and be in the weekend services, is he?" Tawa asked Pam.

"Yes, Bob will be there, along with his wife, Vicki, and their children, Cody and Brianna."

"Cody's my best friend!" said Brody as he twisted his head around to see Tawa, and flashed his big blue eyes at her.

"Oh, Cody is your best friend, is he?"

"Yes, we've been best friends a lon-n-n-ng time!"

"And how old are you?" asked Toropo.

Brody held up three fingers and said, "Fee," for double confirmation of sight and sound, visable and audible.

"So you have been friends for three lon-n-n-ng years — your whole life?" asked Tawa.

"Yes, fee lon-n-n-ng years," affirmed Brody.

The whole Toyota Land Cruiser was full of laughter.

"*Ora ta,*" laughed Pam. "At Brody's birth Cody held him and loved him like a brother. In America they lived next to each other on adjoining property, so Wyatt and Brody thought neighbor meant cousin."

"*Nimini oko,*" said Annie to Brody.

"*Nimin'oko,*" parroted Brody.

"Can you say '*Nimini uku?*'"

"*Nimin'uku,*" echoed Brody.

"*Nimini uku* means I am telling the truth. And *nimini oko* means she is telling the truth, or you are telling the truth," instructed Annie.

"Like *ora lale,* and *ora ta* in Kewa," said Pam, "and *nimini uku* is *ora lalo.*"

"*Na paa niyo, nu paa nino, yu paa nimo,* in ImboUngu," instructed Toropo.

Wyatt and Brody echoed, "*Na paa niyo, nu paa nino, yu paa nimo.*"

"Those are some of the most common phrases in these three languages. The frequency of their use shows that truth is important to Papua New Guineans, just like it is to our Heavenly Father in the Bible, and His Son, Jesus Christ.

"'I am the Way, the Truth, and the Life,' said Jesus in John 14:6," continued Pam, "and in the Old Testament the Psalmist said, 'Mercy and truth have met together, righteousness and peace have kissed each other,' in Psalm 85:10."

"Isn't that beautiful? That's poetry!" exclaimed Tawa.

"'Mercy and truth have met together, righteousness and peace have kissed each other.' What do you suppose that really means? I like the sound of it even though I don't really understand the meaning."

"That verse has intrigued me too, Tawa, so I have studied into it in Greek and Hebrew in the commentary."

"Commentary," interrupted Pam's little Echo.

"Yes, Adam Clarke's commentary, and I have even memorized it in Hebrew.

Psalm 85:10 reads in Hebrew: 'Chesed ve'emeth niphgashu, Tsedek veshalom nashaku."

"Veshalom nashaku," repeated Mama's Little Echo.

"Yes, Honey, shalom means peace in Hebrew and veshalom means 'and peace.'"

"Veshalom means and peace," said Brody again, emphasizing *and.*

"Adam Clarke says it would be better to say, 'Mercy and truth have met on the way, righteousness and peace have embraced,' or righteousness and peace have hugged each other.

Adam Clarke says mercy and peace are on one side; truth and righteousness are on the other. Truth requires righteousness; mercy calls for peace, and doubtless peace calls for mercy. He pictures these four meeting together on the way, one going to make inquisition for sin, or *'kotim sin'* as we say in Pidgin, and the other to plead for reconciliation or forgiveness. They meet, their differences are adjusted and righteousness and peace immediately hug, or *"kangu"* as my mother used to say from ImboUngu, because righteousness has been given to truth, and peace to mercy. Then he asks, 'Where did they meet?' and he answers, 'In Jesus Christ.' 'When were they reconciled?' 'When Jesus poured out His life on Calvary.' Then the next verse says, 'Truth shall spring out of the earth, and righteousness shall look down from heaven.' Adam Clarke says after Jesus died on Calvary the apostles went out to preach with great boldness and the Truth of the Gospel was spread all over the known world."

"And," said Pastor Bali, when Pam stopped, "righteousness looking down from heaven is, of course, Jesus, after He ascended, looking down on the Truth springing out of the earth?"

No one answered Bali and a few kilometers later Toropo asked in Pidgin, "Pam, do you feel Truth is springing out of the earth in our country now?"

"I feel it is, more than it was seventy years ago, here in the Highlands."

"What about in your country?"

"No, less than seventy years ago, I'm afraid. The media conceals so much and only talks about what it wants. A while back I heard on Paul Harvey News on Voice of America that journalists say they might as well not go to news conferences with President Elect, Barack Obama, because he won't call on them when they put up their hands to ask a question. He has a list of the ones he is going to ask, whom he pre-notified. I wonder if he even told them what to ask."

"It sounds like he cannot think on his feet and doesn't want any surprises," said Chad.

"And in the church in your country?" asked Toropo again.

"There are so many denominations within Christianity and so many cults. And Islam is trying to take over my country and the whole world."

"What's Islam?" asked Toropo.

"It's the Ishmaelites' version of Jewish history," said Pastor Bali. "Abraham fathered Ishmael and Isaac, and Christ came in Isaac's line or lineage. Mohammed came 700 years later in Ishmael's lineage and Muslims put him higher than Christ. They say Christ was just another prophet, but Mohammed is the author of the *Koran* and The PROPHET. The *Koran* is their holy book."

"So they don't have the New Testament in their holy book?" asked Toropo.

"Right."

"Oh, my! What would we do without Jesus' Words? Where would we be without the Way, the Truth and the Life?"

"We would be lost in the dark, in untruth and death! And without love!"

"It sounds terrible!"

"Yes. I heard Ekrom Goksu, a converted Muslim, preach and he said the *Koran* is full of hate and revenge. He was reading the New Testament with the intent to burn it after reading it, but Love got to him! By the time he got into the Gospel of John, he gave his heart to Christ and became a Christian."

"And according to Don Richardson, author of *Peace Child*," continued Pastor Bali, "the *Koran* is very repetitive, because Muhammad didn't read or write, so people wrote down what he said. He often did not tell the same Biblical story the same way twice in a row. Mr. Richardson said the *Koran* is so repetitive it wearies the brain, and it contradicts itself over and over. So the Bible is a more accurate picture of Israeli history, and pre-Israelite history."

"But another one of the worst things about Islam and Muslims is the way the men put women down, Toropo," continued Pam. "They treat women even worse than traditional PNG men did. Many Muslims don't want girls going to school. They make their wives stay in their houses, or enclosed yards. They make them dress in burkahs, and even cover their faces, in some countries.

"My mother has an Israeli friend named Dina Crees. Dina and her husband, Jim, were living on a kibbutz in Israel and prisoners were brought in to work on the kibbutz during the day, to help in the fields, right alongside the Israelis. An hour before the bus picked them up to take them back to the prison, each family would take a prisoner into their home for fellowship. The man who stayed with the Crees had killed his wife. He told Jim and Dina that it was a shame; she was a beautiful woman, but she wanted to go to the university. He told her she shouldn't, but she did, so his uncles said to him, 'Who is going to kill her, you or us?' So he met her on the way home from university, beheaded her, and carried her head to the police station saying, 'Put me in jail; I just killed my wife.'"

"*Amineinga glapa!*" said Toropo, remembering her own longing for education.

"They must have multiple wives if they are as bad as traditional PNG men?"

"Yes, they say they can have four wives each, but some men want more, so they keep divorcing the fourth wife and marrying many in fourth place, one at a time. Mohammed had eleven wives, and the youngest was only six years old in her wedding ceremony. History says she was nine years old when Mohammed consummated the marriage, but I heard Dan Glick say, 'Who knows how many times he might have tried before that?' He won some of his wives in battle just like the traditional PNG polygamist, but he limited his followers to four wives each.

"In the news recently they said, 'Any man who lets women or girls in his household go to school must be beheaded.' Under sharia law they behead people for a lot of acts they say are wrong."

Several made the velar clicks in their throats while others clicked their thumbnails off their teeth.

"Here's Kagua," said Chad, changing the atmosphere instantly.

"And there is Uncle Bob and Aunt Vicki," said Wyatt, as they pulled into the Papua New Guinea Bible Church yard, but I can't see Cody."

"He is here, somewhere in this huge crowd," Chad assured his son. Toropo and Tawa found Bani first, and hugged him, his wife, and children whom they could catch before they ran off to play with others.

The meetings between American brother and sister and PNG brother and sisters, cousins and in-laws were delightful.

Bob & Vicki, Cody & Brianna

Brody would not let go of Cody's hand for a minute, and Wyatt likewise, grabbed his cousin's other hand.

Tawa's Trio was in awe of Brianna's long thick hair swinging around her little body like a grass purupuru.

"I can hardly take my eyes off her to watch the trio of boys," said Tawa.

It was good they had some time to visit before service because Brianna and Brody were talking non-stop. Tawa's Trio was torn between wanting to listen to the children and wanting to listen to the adults. Again they were divided when they turned to the adults, between listening to the men, or to Vicki and Pam with pastors' wives and friends, Dani's wife and other teachers.

Soon their conundrum was solved for them when Bob Kelley introduced them to Pastor Rapea and his wife, Evangelist Timothy Asi Wambulu, and Rebecca-Mokanu, his wife, and Jeremiah, his son. Jeremiah ran off to follow Brody and the others, as he noticed Tracy Basua was sticking close to Cody.

Just then a Land Rover pulled up beside Bob. Norm Imbrock got out of the driver's side and said, "The Kelley Kids! What do you know?" A load of passengers climbed down from the back including two Caucasians.

"Hello, Norm, how are you?" rejoined Bob. "How good to see you and how right it seems to see you here in Kagua!"

"This is Philip Joel Martin, a friend of mine I am taking to visit Wabi, and his new wife, Hannah."

"Glad to meet you, Philip. Is this your first time in PNG?" asked Bob as he shook hands with the young man.

"No, actually, I was here as a teen. My parents were support missionaries at Ukarumpa, and I went to high school there."

"Oh, really?" said Bob. "About fifteen years before you would have been there I had asked my parents to let me go there to school. They said no, and I had a hard time with that for years."

"They probably could not bear to part with you," said Philip. "My parents said they could not understand how so many missionaries were able to do that. It's a sacrifice they said they were not willing to make."

Pam shook hands with Philip and Hannah and then walked over to the other side of the car to talk to Bernie Imbrock. Toropo and the Trio went with her.

"I have a question for you about the Yaa Mu. I am trying to find a photo of it. Have you heard of the Yaa Mu?" asked Norm, loud enough for the ladies to hear.

"No," said several, and others shook their heads in the negative.

"The Yaa Mu was a bird that came to Wabi valley in 1959 and 1960 when we were there. It was evidently a migratory bird because the Kewas said it came infrequently. Evidently one type of bamboo called the aria bamboo, flowers and goes to seed. These seeds are so heavy they crack the bamboo stalks and make a sound like a shotgun or rifle shot. The people say the sound attracts the Yaa Mu."

"I don't think I have ever seen that type of aria bamboo, or heard it, or if I did, I didn't know it," said Bob.

"They say if you eat the Yaa Mu as a young person, you just might get to eat it once again when you are old. It wasn't quite in the order of the *andaponda ande alinu* (the seers) but it was a mantra they said to us over and over in those early years.

"I am beginning to think like a Kewa national and wonder if the Yaa Mu is on its way again, myself! Maybe our meeting here is an unusual once-in-a-lifetime experience like eating Yaa Mu."

"How interesting!" exclaimed the girls.

"Yes, they valued them for eating and trading and even using in the brideprice exchange, strung in clusters on small bamboo stalks."

"Really?"

"I've heard of a cassowary bird being part of brideprice but not Yaa Mu," said Pam. "How big are they?"

"Small, like starlings, but with shiny rainbow-colored feathers."

"My, my."

"In other words, it sure is like old times to be together again in Kagua. I remember taking our daughters to your parents' wedding at Katiloma in 1970. Now my granddaughter, Naomi's daughter, Keziah is a university student in Australia! How time flies!"

"Norm and Bernie," said Pam, "this is Toropo, the protagonist of my mom's book. And this is her sister, Tawa. And this is Annie and Linda, Tawa's friends from Ialibu High School." She continued making introductions all around.

"How great to meet you," said the Imbrocks to Toropo. "We have read your story with interest. In fact, I remember back when Pam's mother, Linda, had me proofread it for her, and I encouraged her to send it to the Lutheran Mission Press, hoping they would publish it," added Bernie.

"And I read it in high school at Ukarumpa," said Philip. "It opened my eyes to what was going on in the country I was in, more than anything else I had ever read. I later got in touch with your mom, Pam and Bob, when I was at Messiah College in Pennsylvania. I feel honored to meet you, Toropo," he said as he shook hands with her, and gave a gallant bow, as he said, "May I present my wife, Hannah, to you, Toropo?"

A look of astonishment crossed Toropo's face, and she shared her surprise with Tawa, as she accepted the hand of

Philip's wife, and gave her a big smile in turn. Why am I being so honored? she asked herself.

Pastor Rapea and his wife invited their visitors into his house where the talk continued until Rapea said something that made other conversations come to a complete stop. Every eye focused on the pastor.

"She says she might as well commit suicide because she must have committed an unpardonable sin. Her father and her brothers cannot forgive her. I know a pastor whose own daughter said the same thing, and she did commit suicide. What do I tell this sixteen-year-old girl here in Kagua High School? How do I keep her from killing herself?"

"Tell her we do not condone sex outside of marriage" said Norm Imbrock, "but it is not the unpardonable sin. It can be forgiven just like any other sin. It might be harder for the PNG man to forgive, if it is his own daughter, or sister, but he does have to forgive if he wants to be forgiven; the Lord's Prayer tells us that!"

"And Jesus said it elsewhere as well," put in Bob Kelley. "But as closely as we can understand God's Word, suicide might be the unpardonable sin because the person who commits it does not likely have time to repent of it and ask forgiveness."

"Right," continued Norm, "so you tell this girl, Pastor Rapea, not to commit suicide. God can and will forgive her if she asks Him, and people will have to, sooner or later, if they want to get to heaven themselves. You see how important it is for *men* to be pure? These girls need fathers whom they can look up to and respect; not fathers running after a second or third wife, and neglecting the spiritual education and training of their sons and daughters. I never knew a polygamist yet, who was a good father. What about you, Bob and Pam?" Pam and Bob both thought of little kids who played with their own children, who were sadly neglected by their polygamist fathers, even more than the kids might have been in their parents' time and the old-fashioned harem.

Pam spoke up and said, "My mom wrote about Kedle's harem in Piamble when she was a girl, but at least he stayed in one place, and was an on-site father even if he didn't interact with his kids much. Some of the polygamists of our day and time, have girls in various villages and towns, and the children only get one tenth of a father, or less, on site, and even when he is on-site, his attention is not in fathering, but on another wife he is wooing and buying, or politics or making money or many other things. Some of the things are legitimate enough, but I cannot imagine a childhood without my own father in it."

"Right," agreed Bob. "Actually as missionary kids we saw more of our father than a lot of kids in America see of theirs. We played soccer or basketball with Dad and other guys on the station every evening. We usually ate three meals a day with Dad and Mom both. I remember my little brother, Deanie, riding to town with Dad when I was in school and couldn't go. Not that I wanted to anyway, I always got carsick in those days on these bumpy roads. But some of my earliest memories are of my little brother helping Dad and Grandpa change a tire, unscrew the lug nuts, and entertaining the crowds who gathered to watch. Dean was a clown in those days. As a teen I often felt I had missed out on an American childhood, but when I was a father in the USA myself, I saw how hard it is to work at an outside job and be a fulltime father too. I came to the place where I saw I could envy pastors and missionaries who could homeschool their children and have almost twenty-four hours a day with them. I heard one radio preacher say, 'Every time I heard my father say "I love my work." I would think, then why did you have me?' This preacher said it takes two parents to nurture a child emotionally. A mother does not have enough reserves to nurture her children without the help of her spouse."

"Could we look at John 4 together briefly," asked Philip. "This is where Jesus was talking to a woman from Samaria at the well. Look in verse 18. He says to her, 'You've had five husbands in the past, and you're not married to the man you're living with now! You've spoken the truth!' (Complete Jewish Bible) We can gather that this woman was an outcast from other women, and that is why she went after her water in mid-day when the other women would not be at the well. She would rather endure the hot sun than their scorn and shunning. How shocked she must have been when Jesus spoke to her! And how amazed she would have been that He was willing to take water from her, a fallen woman! But she must have felt Christ's forgiveness for she immediately became a missionary to her own people.

"Verse 27 in the Complete Jewish Bible says, 'Just then, his *talmadim* arrived. They were amazed that he was talking with a woman; but none of them said, "What do you want?" or "Why are you talking with her? 28. So the woman left her water-jar, went back to the town and said to the people there, "Come, see a man who told me everything I've ever done. Could it be that this is the Messiah?"

"Verse 39 goes on 'Many people from that town in Shomron put their trust in him because of the woman's testimony. "He told me all the things I did." 40. So when these people from Shomron came to him, they asked him to stay with them. He stayed two days, 41 and many more came to trust because of what he said. 42 They said to the woman, We no longer trust because of what you said, because we have heard for ourselves. We know indeed that this man really is the Savior of the world.'"

"Would you say," asked Pastor Rapea, "that she believed in God and became a missionary to her own people because Jesus knew everything she had ever done, yet He talked with her, and accepted water to drink from her, and evidently forgave her?"

"Yes," agreed Bob, Norm and Philip together, because they could see that Rapea had directed the question to all three of them. He wanted to be sure he understood the white man's opinion on this mind-boggling issue to a Christian black man.

"Adultery is wrong, Rapea," continued Philip, "but it is not worse than murder, is it? Murder takes away the victim's right to make his peace with God. Is it worse than suicide? No, because one can repent of adultery, but not usually of suicide. It is very evident here that our Lord forgave this woman even though she may have had five divorces and was right then living in sin. Christ often said, 'Go and sin no more,' to those whom He healed and/or spoke with, and I believe this woman went and straightened her life up right then and there, and all was forgiven her. It may have taken the other Samaritans years to accept her, but on the other hand, it may not have, too, because she was the one who had led them to the Savior of the world. Isn't it wonderful how a testimony such as hers can change everything? However, I am sure there were still people who threw her past up to her. But the Master had told her, 'You have spoken the truth,' and so she continued to tell the truth from then on out, whether she was shunned or not. I feel sure of it!'"

"And I think you are right," agreed Pam, while Timothy Asi, Rebecca Mokanu and Rapea and others tried to take it all in. Other men and women were standing around listening, too, and seemed rather staggered by it all. Did Christ really forgive, even a *woman*'s sexual sins?

Norm sensed some were not believing they had heard right, and were not trusting their ability in English so he proceeded in Pidgin English, "Mi bin ritim wanpela buk i singautim ol gutpela man i tok, 'Mipela nitim yupela gutpela man bilong halivim mipela mama, susa-meri na pikinini-meri i kamapim gutpela yangpela meri.'"

He looked around at everybody crushing against him and wanting so much to hear what he was saying. "I am going to go to my land rover and get this book out of my suitcase, and read you some."

Rapea turned to the crowds at the open door and open windows and explained in Kewa what Norm had said. Bani did the same to the ImboUngu speakers, and chatter arose on all sides as they waited for Norm's return.

He came back in, showing the book, **Strong Fathers, Strong Daughters** by Dr. Meg Meeker, and proceeded to read in English, as little groups turned to translators in Pidgin, ImboUngu and Kewa.

"'Men, good men: We need you. We – mothers, daughters, and sisters – need your help to raise healthy young women. We need every ounce of masculine courage and wit you own, because fathers, more than anyone else, set the course for a daughter's life.

"'Your daughter needs the best of who you are: your strength, your courage, your intelligence, and your fearlessness. She needs your empathy, assertiveness, and self-confidence. She needs *you*.

"'Our daughters need the support that only fathers can provide – and if you are willing to guide your daughter, to stand between her and a toxic culture, to take her to a healthier place, your rewards will be unmatched. You will experience the love and adoration that can come only from a daughter. You will feel a pride, satisfaction, and joy that you can know nowhere else.'

"You understand, yupela manmeri, this author is writing to American men, and talking about the toxic culture of America. That means poisonous culture. PNG is not the only country that has a culture with poison or sin in it. Sometimes Papua New Guineans think America is a little like heaven, but let me assure you there is more sin in America than there is in PNG, but there are also more people fighting against all the evils of child abuse, women abuse, alcoholism, stealing, murder and so much more. Whereas you have one or two churches to a village, or sometimes none, most American villages of the same size have five or six. I remember some foreign students counting when they visited our country and saying this town is only big enough for one MacDonalds, but it has twelve churches! Each town also has several police officers on twenty-four hour duty, trying to arrest every person who wrongs another by theft or violence. Keep in mind this author is writing to American men, but every man in the world needs to read this. I am still on the first page of Chapter One of *Strong Fathers, Strong Daughters*.

"'After more than twenty years of listening to daughters – and doling out antibiotics, anti-depressants, and stimulants to girls who have gone without a father's love – I know just how important fathers are. I have listened hour after hour to young girls describe how they vomit in junior high bathrooms to keep their weight down.... I've watched girls drop off varsity tennis teams, flunk out of school, and carve initials or tattoo cult figures onto their bodies – all to see if their dads will notice.

"'And I have watched daughters talk to fathers. When you come in the room, they change. Everything about them changes: their eyes, their mouths, their gestures, their body language. Daughters are never lukewarm in the presence of their fathers. They might take their mothers for granted, but not you. They light up – or they cry. They watch you intensely. They hang on your words. They hope for your attention, and they wait for it in frustration – or in despair. They need a gesture of approval, a nod of encouragement, or even simple eye contact to let them know you care and are willing to help.

"'When she's in your company, your daughter tries harder to excel. When you teach her, she learns more rapidly. When you guide her, she gains confidence. If you fully understood just how profoundly you can influence your daughter's life, you would be terrified, over-whelmed, or both. Boyfriends, brothers, even husbands can't shape her character the way you do. You will influence her entire life because she gives you an authority she gives no other man.

"'Many fathers (particularly of teen girls) assume they have little influence over their daughters – certainly less influence than their daughters' peers or pop culture – and think their daughters need to figure out life on their own. But your daughter faces a world markedly different from the one you did growing up: it's less friendly, morally unmoored, and even outright dangerous. After age six, "little girl" clothes are hard to find. Many outfits are cut to make her look like a seductive thirteen- or fourteen-year-old girl trying to attract older boys. She will enter puberty earlier than girls did a generation or two ago (and boys will be watching as she grows breasts even as young as age nine). She will see sexual innuendo or scenes of overt sexual behavior in magazines or on television before she is ten years old, whether you approve or not. She will learn about HIV and AIDS in elementary school and will also probably learn why and how it is transmitted.'" (Dr. Meg Meeker.)

Bob interrupted, "Could I insert a word here, Norm? We had a world-wide children's choir come to our church in Lansing, Michigan. Probably a third of the children were from Africa, but others were from the Philipines, Laos and other countries, and they were all orphaned by HIV/AIDS. The children sang beautifully. They played African drums and performed amazingly well, touring all over America. But at half-time or in the middle of the performance they sat down while a film was shown of literally six million children orphaned to AIDS in Africa, and one man said, 'They just know their parents are sick. They do not know why they have this sickness. They cannot understand why their parents die, and some of their grandparents even, and why they have to be orphans.' Do you think children here in PNG know?"

"No. I don't think so," said Rapea. "What do you say, Bani?"

"I think you are right. We parents do not talk about this sort of thing with our children."

"What do you think about what author Dr. Meeker says about fathers and teen-aged daughters looking up to them?" asked Norm.

Rapea looked at Timothy Asi and then at Bani. It seemed no one wanted to answer.

Finally Bani said, "She may be right. It is something I have not pondered or thought that much about. Looking back, I realize that my sister, Toropo, surely felt that way about our father. She went to him and spent time with him, watching, hoping for some way out of her unbearable situation after she was burned and beaten by fellow wives and her husband." He turned his eyes to his sister.

"Is that right, Toropo?"

"Yes, my Brother. I read *Ara* Pidgin newspapers, and he listened to those. He spent more time with me than he ever had before, because I could read him something about the world. And I waited and hoped and prayed, but I never had the nerve to tell him what was on my heart even though I finally had his ear for the first time in my life."

"Tawa, do you listen to our father?" asked her older brother.

"Yes, Bani, I do. He has full authority in my mind, more than my teachers, more than my pastor, more than anyone in my world, because I know he can pull me out of school the moment he chooses and sell me to the man he wants to accept bridepay from. Can an American father pull his daughter out of high school and make her marry, Mr. Imbrock?"

"Oh, no! American young people are not allowed to marry until they are eighteen years old, unless the parents will give their consent and sign for them. No parent wants his daughter or son to drop out of high school to marry."

"*Aminienga glapa!* I did not know!" Chatter and exclamations erupted all around.

"Do you see, Mr. Imbrock, laws like that make us think America must be heaven below. At least it makes us *girls* think it!"

A babble of conversation in several different languages continued until Bob spoke again, and everyone strained to listen.

"The author's mention of a daughter even seeking eye contact with her father made me think of a story a missionary father in America once told." Bob looked around at everyone leaning in to hear. "His name is Marc Sankey, and his little son contracted some sickness and could not walk straight, or use his arms and legs correctly. He was not yet eighteen months, so he was not talking enough to tell his parents what was wrong or what was hurting. They took him to the doctor, and he was put through a battery of tests. It took blood work, and the nurses could not find his tiny veins to get blood out of him. The father held his son lovingly and kept soothing him through several tries. When they came at him with those needles a third or fourth time, little Cameron looked up at his dad. His dad looked down at him and made eye contact, and Cameron allowed them another try, and they succeeded at last. Marc said, 'All Cameron did was look at me, make eye contact, and ask if he had had words, "Do you see what they are going to do to me again, Dad? Is it all right?" and when he saw that his dad knew and was acquiescing, he could acquiesce too. Marc said it is that way with us, as children of the Heavenly Father. We just need to look up and make eye contact once in a while, and it will give us the strength to go on through hard places and through life.

"So I can believe, because I know my own children, that a child often needs to make eye contact with their father. I know I do it even yet with my own father. And I am a grown man and a father. Having a daughter of my own, I know it is not less with daughters than with sons. And I know I am already thinking about my daughter's future, and I hope she will listen to me when she is a teenager and it comes to matters of her heart. I am trying to treat her mother in such a way now, that Brianna and Cody both will respect their mother and always listen to both of us, when they are in their teens and beginning to make the choices which will affect the rest of their lives."

"Maybe I need to make a confession," said the evangelist. "I helped my wife raise her sister in our home, but when she became a teenager she did not listen to me. I washed my hands of her. She did wrong, so she did not need to look to me as a father, I said. Even now I feel estranged, but my wife keeps saying we have to forgive her."

"Your wife is right," said Norm. "You do have to forgive. We have to forgive if we want to be forgiven. Prea bilong Jisas i tok olsem: Lusim sin bilong mipela, mipela tu i lusim sin ol i mekim long mipela. Your adopted daughter wronged you, when she disobeyed. She needs to ask forgiveness, but even if she doesn't, you have to forgive her if you want to be forgiven, Timothy."

People looked at the white man with astonishment. Bringing it home to one in their own circle really made it register in their hearts and minds. Timothy Asi was looking at Norm, at Philip and at Bob. He was seeking eye contact, and each man looked him in the eye and nodded their agreement.

"Linda Kelley told Rebecca that, when she was here in 2008, but I thought perhaps it was just a woman talking."

"No, Timothy, it was a woman quoting Jesus Christ, our Lord and Master, our Savior, the Son of God, who became man, and spoke as a man among men and women."

"This is a woman writing this book," put in Philip, pointing to the book in Norm's hands, "but it is a woman who knows what she is talking about, a highly educated woman, who has doctored men and women and children for enough years that she knows whereof she speaks. Maybe men right here in Kagua, right here in the Kewa-speaking area need to learn to interact more with our daughters. We need to read the Bible more and seek out how God, our heavenly Father, speaks to women, and we need to be like our heavenly Father. This girl of whom Pastor Rapea was speaking needs to go to her father just as the prodigal son did and say, 'Father, I have sinned and I am no longer worthy to be called your daughter,' and if her father does not have the grace to say, 'You were dead in sin, and lost to me, but now that you have asked for forgiveness I restore you to your full rights as my child,' then she must still say, 'I will do what I can to make amends, and to serve you,' but I cannot kill myself because that would compound sin upon sin, and I could not repent when I am dead.' As far as we know from the **Bible**, choices in this life carry great weight before God and His mercy in the next life with Jesus for eternity."

The bell rang and Pastor Rapea stood to his feet. "It is time for service, you are all welcome to come into the church."

"I am sorry," said Norm, "but my little wife and I are weary and must get the rest of the way with our guests out to Wabi. But let me suggest that you get this book and read it. It has a message for Papua New Guinea which everyone needs to read. The very next paragraphs are about her son choosing to do a health assignment for school on HIV/AIDS, and PNG needs that message even more urgently than the USA, according to statistics."

Ellepe Nomi

Ellepe was my baby, Jeanie's cousin. You can read about her in MK's pp. 92-117. She visited me here in Michigan in 1995. She married Wiwa Korowi and went to Belgium & other countries with him as ambassadors for PNG. They have three sons Melvin, Leslie & Owen. Wiwa married more wives and later was knighted by the Queen & became Governor General of P.N.G.

y Unda, Lady Diana Morgan, Ellepe & Angela

Ellenie said, "I could say a psalm for her + sing her a song. And I

r saved

rica ne k.!

Ellenie on the trampoline

Lynnette is married to Melvin & the mother of Ellenie.

Ellepe's adopted daughter

Ellenie was 5 in April. Nathan is 4.

Owen

Owen won a basket ball scholarship to the University of Oklahoma but a rugby injury stopped him from coming.

Melvin

Leslie & Ellepe

Ellenie & Nathan, her cousin.

Nathan's father married a second wife, so his mother left her husband but couldn't take her son, of course. No one was taking care of Nathan so Lynnette took him. He gained 3 kilograms in

: of the flowers she brought me.

Chapter Eight

Pombo wasn't feeling well. Tawa-Ma had stayed home with him for two days, but this morning she had gone to the garden, determined to put in a good day's work.

Pombo had visited the aid post and received quinine, but he wasn't getting better. He felt something more than malaria was wrong with him this time.

As he sat by the dying embers of the morning's fire he suddenly passed out and fell forward. When he became conscious his first thought was "I'm burning. I must have died and gone to hell." He struggled to move, but felt too weak to even raise himself.

"God!" he cried out. "God, help me! Help me and I'll serve You!"

Within seconds strength came to him, and he pushed himself up out of the ashes and coals. For a few minutes he sat by the fireplace brushing himself off, then he stood shakily, rose, and walked outside to a water tank.

"I'm alive," he murmured aloud. "I'm still at Tona. I am not in hell. Thank You, God! Thank You for a second chance!"

He drank long and thirstily from the delicious rainwater in the tank, placed the cup beside the faucet and turned toward the church, the Papua New Guinea Bible Church and parsonage.

"Thank You for another chance, God. I realize it is not a second chance, maybe it is the hundredth chance You have given me. You have spoken to me so many times, God, and I've big-headed You. I am done big-heading, God. Forgive me. I promise to do everything You tell me to do from now on, every day You let me live. Every day I live and breathe I give to You, God. Show me what to do.

"Oh, God, let Pastor Mark be home."

As he neared the church he heard someone praying, and he went straight in and straight to the altar. He started to try to kneel, but he fell prostrate across the altar.

119

"Oh, God, save me!" he cried out in a loud voice. "Save me from hell. Save me from my sins! Forgive me all my sins, God! Forgive me, Jesus Christ! They tell me You died on the cross for me, Jesus! They tell me You shed Your blood for me, a sinner. I've heard them, God. I've heard everything Bani and Toropo and my wives and Pastor Mark have told me about You, but I big-headed them every time, God. I was so proud! I was so full of pride! But not any more, God! My pride all burned up in the ashes of that dying fire back there. Now I know it is only by Your mercy that I am still alive, still breathing.

"Save me, God, save me!"

Pombo was totally unaware of the people who gathered round him, helping him pray, and praying for him and with him. It was as if he were all alone with his God, and crying out for mercy and confessing his sins. The sins he focused on over and over again were his pride and disobedience. At one point he even told God he was done with his "big-headedness" just like he had taken off his big-wig years before, only he was done with pride and disobedience once for all! *Kamukumu*! He would never don them again, he promised, like he had the big-wig for subsequent singsings after its original removal.

"And I'm done with singsings too, God, forever! *Kamukumu tiro*, forever! No more singsings and mokas for me, God! I am done with trying to make a *Biknem* (big name) for myself, God. 'For Thine is the kingdom, and the power, and the glory.'" How did he know that last line? He wasn't sure. Where had it come from? It had just come out of his own lips!

"I'm not taking any more glory for myself, God, and I know You have all the Power, Lord. I tried to boss things myself, my whole life, God, and suddenly I realize I cannot even make myself keep breathing. I throw myself on Your mercy, Lord. I ask forgiveness. I ask forgiveness for stupid, stinking, rotten pride. All those times I ran out with gifts of pork in my hands, yodeling for all the world to see and give me '*biknem*,' give me glory. *Na pendepende teli-iyemu*, God, I'm nothing but a show-off! I thought I was so smart, now I know I was so foolish. Can you forgive me, God? Oh, forgive me!

"My pigs are all Yours, God! My tribe is Yours. My family is Yours. My sons are Yours, God, my daughters too. My wives are Yours, God. I won't buy any more wives!" He stopped in shock at what he was saying. He stopped and thought and realized he meant it. Suddenly he had no more desire to buy another wife. His life-long obsession with buying more wives and earning himself a big name was gone! Totally gone!

"Thank You, Jesus!" he screamed. He scrambled to his feet and began jumping up and down. Pastor Mark stood up with him. He grabbed the pastor's hands, and they jumped up and down together singsing-style almost, and all the while Pombo was shouting, 'Thank You, God! Thank You, Jesus! Thine is the kingdom, and the power and the glory! Thank You, Jesus!" He felt so free! He felt so light! He felt as if a great weight had just been removed from his shoulders, and he realized that it was the weight of sin removed from his heart.

Pombo stopped jumping. He raised both hands to heaven, shouting, "Thine is the kingdom, the power and the glory. Any kingdom I have ever had, I give to you, Father! *Kamukumu tiro.* Any power I have ever had, I give it to You, God. *Kamukumu tiro, kani.* Any glory, any biknem, *kamukumu tiro, Ara Gote. Nunge mendepogol, Ara Gote*! Thine is the kingdom and the power and the glory. It has always been Thine, Father! I am just a worm You could have squashed long ago if You had so desired! Oh, thank You, God! Thank You for life and breath! Thank You for forgiving my sins. Thank You for taking away all my desire for sin, for my own glory, for my own power, for my own kingdom! It's all Yours, God! Thine is the kingdom, the power, and the glory forever and ever!"

A small crowd had gathered by this time. Men had left their card games and their courts. Children had come to watch. Christians had gathered to pray and rejoice with Bossboy Pombo. Two of his wives and other women had come from their gardens to join in the praying and rejoicing.

Pombo suddenly realized he heard his first wife, Bani-Ma, praying and crying. He went to her. He bent over her kneeling form. He laid his hand on her back, and said, "Forgive me, wife." She raised up and looked him in the eye. He took her hand and pulled her up.

"Forgive me, wife. God has forgiven me." He pointed with his lips to his burned shoulder. She gasped when she realized it was burned.

"I thought the Creator and Judge had sent me to hell, wife, but He gave me another chance. He is giving me new life and breath. He has taken the load of sin from my heart, and I feel so light and so free and so strong again. I feel like I could run to the river! I feel like I could jump over logs! He is forgiving my sins. Will you forgive me?"

"Yes, my husband, I forgive you."

He went to Tawa-Ma. "Will you forgive me?" he asked as he took her hand.

"What does this mean?" she asked.

He stopped short. He looked her in the eye. "I'm not sure all it means. I'm a new creature in Christ. Old things have passed away. Look! All things have become new. I'm not sure all it means. I just know I feel like a different man. I have to get to know my new self before I can tell anyone else all it means. I'm just asking your forgiveness for any way I have wronged you."

He turned away from her to the pastor. "I ask you, Pastor, for forgiveness for big-heading services, for going my own sinful way and not listening to your preaching. God, have mercy. I have been so proud! Forgive me, Pastor."

Pastor came to him again and shook his hand, and laid his other hand on Pombo's good shoulder. "You're forgiven. God forgives you, and I forgive you."

They stood there face to face, smiling at each other; the glory of God's forgiveness shone on their beaming faces.

Someone started humming the tune to "God is so good." Soon they were all singing

God is so good, God is so good, God is so good, He's so good to me.

He took my sin, He took my sin, He took my sin, He's so good to me.

Pombo had sung with his arms raised to heaven. When they were done, he said, "I am free, folks. I'm free from sin. I'm free from guilt! I feel like I am out from under a terrible load! I feel as light as a tiny feather. I feel like a little wind could blow me into the sky, maybe clear up to heaven, and I'm ready to go now! If God should take away my breath I am ready to go to heaven! I no longer would go to hell! Oh, what a merciful God! Thank You, God! Thank You, Father!"

Overcome with emotion, Pombo sat down on the front seat, put his face in his hands, and cried. Pastor Mark asked if anyone else wanted to pray. "God is here! God is present! God wants to save."

Ten people made their way to the altar and the Christians gathered around them to pray with them. Kariyapa and his twin sons came and knelt beside Pombo. The twins were named Kera and Glopa. Even the little boys bowed their heads and prayed, crying along with their grandfather, and feeling the move of God in their own little hearts.

Much later that evening Pombo asked Kariyapa, "Why do these words keep going over and over in my mind? Where do they come from? *'Mele waiyema Nunge mendepogol, kombunu kinie, tondogol kinie, imbi-ogla-moglopili ugul akumu, takitaki.'?*"

"Oh, *Ara*, that's the last part of the Lord's Prayer that Christ taught His disciples to pray.

"Let's look at the whole prayer in ***Pulu-Yemonga Ungu Mare***. (***Some of the Source-Man's (God's) Talk***, in Kakoli or Kaugel.)

Matt. 6:9. Olioga Mulu-Koleana Moleno Lapamo, 'Nu ibi ola molopa, ye kake teli peagamo moleno' nigu yebomane pilku molagi!

10. Nu ye-nomi-kigimu molko yeboma nokoni-walemo opili! Nuge ugumu mulu-kolea pilku liku telemcle-mele aku-tiku ya ma-koleana pilku liku teagi!

11. Kine nomolo-kere-lagima olio kine tiyo!

12. Yebo-lupemane olio teko kejegi-ulume tie kolopo ulu-te naa temulu-mele olione Nu tepo kejemulu-ulumega aku-tikula tie kolko olio ulu-te naa teyo!

13. Olio 'Kodi-topili' naa nigu ulu-pulu-kerimene 'olio naa lipili' niyo. Kolea Nuge kinie, tondolo Nunge kinie, ibi-ola-molopili ulu akumu kinie Nuge medepolo, aileli aileli. Amen."

"Thank you, thank you, *nanga Magol*," said Pombo when Kariyapa had finished reading. "I'd like you to read it for me every day until I can say it myself like one of the tales from the Ancients which I learned when I was a child."

"*Kapogla, Ara*, I will be glad to do that, because the ***Bible*** tells us to hide God's Word in our hearts that we might not sin against Him.

"Let me read it for you in Pidgin too. You speak Pidgin so well. This will help you too.

Matt. 6:9 Papa bilong mipela, Yu i stap long heven. Nem bilong Yu mas i stap holi.

10. Kingdom bilong Yu i mas i kam. Laik bilong Yu ol i bihainim long heven, olsem tasol mipela mas bihainim long graun tu.

11. Na Yu givim mipela kaikai inap long dispela de.

12. Na Yu lusim ol sin bilong mipela, olsem mipela tu i lusim pinis sin bilong ol man i bin rongim mipela.

13. Na Yu no bringim mipela long samting bilong traim mipela. Tasol tekewe mipela long samting nogut. (Kingdom na strong na glori, em i bilong Yu tasol, oltaim oltaim.) Tru.

"That's good! That's wonderful! That's so true!" responded Pombo. "May the Lord help me to commit it to memory both in ImboUngu and Pidgin.

"I love it in English too," said Kariyapa. "See if you can say any of the words after me."

Kariyapa repeated it word by word, or phrase by phrase at times, and Pombo, Glopa and Kera did their best to repeat it after him. Glopa sat on Kariyapa's lap while Pombo held Kera, and the four of them went over the English Lord's Prayer together.

"Would to God I had learned it as a little boy as you two are doing, my grandsons," said Pombo. "I pray to God that you two never live the lives of sin that your old grandpa has lived. Please God, it's all going to change now! I'm done with sin now and forever! Oh, if only I could read the **Bible** so I wouldn't have to ask others to teach me everything!"

"You have lots of children, *Ara*, and thanks to you and the mission school at Kauapena, we can all read. And we all have **Bibles**. We can read to you. We can help you."

"I think we had better begin from the beginning so we don't leave anything out. I better buy my own Pidgin **Bible** and keep it with me, so I can be sure I have heard every word in it. I wouldn't want to miss one of God's Words to me."

"Next time we go to Hagen we can go to the Christian Bookshop and get you your own copy, *Ara*. That will be wonderful.

* * * * * * *

To Kariyapa and Pombo's great delight, Pastor Mark spoke about the Lord's Prayer in church the next Sunday morning.

"Pombo's continual repetition of the last line of the Lord's Prayer in his conversion this week has made me ponder it as I never have before. With it continually going through my mind I have decided to study it more thoroughly and preach on it this morning.

"Let's take a look at it together.

"It begins with the words 'Our Father.' This is the way Jesus tells us to address His Father, as 'our Father.' Doesn't that thrill you to hear that *linionga Ara*? Think of Jesus as our Brother, and every other child of God as our brother and sister. That makes us closer even than *wantoks*. Remember that, my people, everywhere you go. Christians are your brothers and sisters, the children of one Father. The blood of Jesus ties us together closer than language ties even. 'Our Father, Who art in heaven.

"'Hallowed be Thy Name.' All of us have been around *kiaps* and other people who curse freely and take the Name of our God in vain. May it not be so with us. May we always hallow the Name of our Father and His Son, Jesus Christ.

"'Thy kingdom come.' This is the second request in relation to God that we are to pray for. First we are to ask that His Name be hallowed, secondly that His kingdom come. What does that mean to you? When you think of God's kingdom, what do you think of? At the end of this prayer we say, 'For Thine is the kingdom and the power and the glory.' All kingdoms belong to God because He created them, but the prince of the power of the air is trying to take them away from God, and has done so, at least temporarily, all over the world except where men love God and give themselves back to Him of their own free choice, of their own free will. Where people worship ancestors and spirits of the mountains, spirits of the lakes, and all these *tambaran* they are honoring Satan instead of God, and taking away His kingdom from Him.

"Also I think the kingdom of God is the Christian family, the Christian brotherhood. I believe somewhere it says in the Bible, 'His kingdom is within you.' So that is God reigning in our hearts and being our Sovereign there, and God being the King over us and our brothers and sisters in Christ.

"Another part it doubtless means is the heavenly kingdom, or the eternal kingdom of God, which will not be in its complete fullness until Christ returns, and the devil and his angels are cast into the lake of fire. So we want to be praying for the return of Christ, and the coming of His kingdom, just as the New Testament ends by saying, 'Even so, come, Lord Jesus.' And if we are praying for Christ's return *moabeta yumi wok de na nait bilong bringim ol haiden i kam insait long lain bilong God. Yumi taitim bun na wok hat bilong kamapim lain bilong God!*

"Thirdly, is the phrase 'Thy will be done.' How often do you ask for God's will to be done in your daily lives? Do you not more often say, 'Let me do this or that today, God; let me go here or there and keep me safe?' How many times do we ask God to have His way in our lives? Let us remember daily to pray, 'Thy will be done on earth, even as it is in heaven.' This is the second mention of heaven in this short prayer. We are calling on our Father, Who is in heaven, and now we are asking that His will be done on earth, even as it is in heaven. In heaven there is harmony; there is obedience and happiness. I imagine as I read God's Word, the angels are happily going about God's business, doing all He asks, following His every command, and enjoying heaven to the fullest. We know that He sends them to guard us; we know that He sends them in answer to our prayers. We can read that in the book of Daniel and elsewhere. We know that they are invisible to our eyes while they are here on earth, except when God gives us spiritual vision on occasion as he did for the young man for whom Elijah prayed, 'Lord, open the young man's eyes.' When God opened the young man's eyes he saw the armies of God all around, on beyond the armies of Israel. Those were God's angels acting as soldiers for the battle in answer to the prayers of God's people.

"Let us learn to pray for God's will to be done in our lives and in each life we come in contact with, day by day. This ends the first section of the Lord's Prayer—three requests concerning God: His Name, His kingdom, and His will.

"Now let us look at the next requests: First for us is, 'Give us this day our daily bread.' How many here know what it is to be hungry, and have nothing to eat?" All of the adults in Pastor Mark's congregation raised their hands, and some of the children.

126

"Thank God, there are children here who cannot say they have ever known the hunger we knew in our own childhoods. And it was worse in our parents' childhoods. My father and Bossboy Pombo and others tell us tales of the olden days when they wore big bark belts which they sewed onto themselves, and when there was no food, they stuffed more and more leaves between their stomach and the bark. Those times of great hunger occurred far too often in the olden days when frosts killed our gardens, and there were no stores to go to, to buy fish and rice. Now we are affluent, by the standards of the olden days. Now we can work to get money, and with money we can buy food, whether there are sweet potatoes in our gardens or not. My generation has grown a whole head taller than my father's generation. If we continue to work hard, maybe our children can be the size and character that God meant for them to be. But there can still be times of hunger due to sickness of our wives, or one reason or another. Let us thank God for daily food, and pray that each one in our family, each one in our tribe, each one of our *wantoks*, and each child in God's family is given their daily bread. If your heart grows big enough in God to pray for the whole world to be given their daily bread, wonderful! So be it! I try to pray for children everywhere that they will have enough to eat. And as I pray that they may have their physical bread, I pray also that they may have their spiritual bread. Jesus is called the Bread of Life, you know. May all men everywhere eat of that heavenly Bread and repent and turn to God.

"The second request for ourselves and all humankind is 'Forgive us our debts, as we forgive our debtors' or 'Forgive us our trespasses as we forgive those who trespass against us.'

Another way we might say it is forgive us our sins as we forgive those who sin against us. However, many of us are Christians and we are doing our best to live a life without sin. Why then does Jesus tell us to forgive our debtors if we want our debts forgiven? Let me tell you how I see it.

"You know how self-centered a little child is? You know how they cry and sometimes throw a temper tantrum if they cannot get their own way? Well, some of us are still pretty self-centered. Maybe all of humankind is. The Apostle Paul said in I Corinthians 13, 'when I became a man I put away childish things,' but some of us men are only men in our outward growth; we have not become a man in our inner spirits yet. We have not put away childish things and self-centeredness entirely, and when someone does something that isn't just the way we want it, we get angry with them, and we want our own way. The next time that happens to you, whether it is your child who offends you, your wife who offends you, your brother, your father or mother, your tribesman or a stranger, try immediately to say in your heart, 'Forgive me my debts, Father, as I forgive my debtors.' Lots of times it is not sin on the part of others that offends us, in fact most of the time it isn't.

"First of all we have to forgive other people for their sin if we want to be forgiven. Secondly we have to forgive them for the times they put themselves ahead of us. Thirdly we have to forgive them for things or ways in which they do not even know they have offended us. One of my teachers used to say that everyone is always worrying about what other people think of them, and if they only knew their minds, they would know how little they think of others, and how much their minds are taken up with themselves. It is human nature to be self-centered. Hopefully when we become parents we think as much about our children as we do ourselves, and that is one part of maturity. I am afraid a polygamist is often thinking more of getting another wife than he is in providing for his children, but now in the Christian way, we men are marrying one wife and committing to her 'till death does us part' so we have time to think of the welfare of our children, of their education, and of their physical needs and happiness, as well as of their spiritual needs. As a pastor my job is to think of the spiritual needs of all of you. I need to make your spiritual welfare my concern, and be thinking of you more than I do of myself. May God help me to mature more and more in Him, and be a true shepherd of my sheep, and not a hireling. May God help each one of us to forgive our debtors as we want God to forgive us. He made us for His own, and we have big-headed Him over and over, all our lives long, just like spoiled children. Let us ask His forgiveness and then forgive others for every way we feel they have wronged us. We did not create other people; why should they worry about pleasing us. God created us, and yet we have gone our own way instead of obeying Him. Can you see, my people, how much more we have wronged God than any person has wronged us? Let us remember that and pray humbly, 'Father, forgive us our trespasses as we forgive those who trespass against us.'

"Thirdly, we are to pray, 'Lead us not into temptation.' My teachers at Tambul Baibel Skul told me this could also mean 'Lead us not into sore trials' or things that would pierce our hearts. The older we get the more sadness we see in this world. The closer we are to God the more it grieves our hearts to see our grown children making wrong choices, or people everywhere reaping the rewards of their sins. The longer we live the more death we see, and death is so final in this life, and in the next because our spiritual condition determines where we spend eternity. Oh, that God would lead us not into piercings of our hearts, livers, souls and minds.

"Fourthly, we are to pray, 'Deliver us from evil.' Satan is the prince of this world, and he is all around. In fact some translations and some languages pray it, 'Deliver us from the evil one.' We are no match for him and his wiles, my people. He was once an angel of light, living in heaven, living with the blessed Triune God, and then he disobeyed and fell like lightning from heaven. But he is far more experienced in this world than you or I. We need deliverance from him, we need protection from him, and any form of evil that he would get anyone else to use to influence us. Let us never forget to pray daily, 'Deliver us from evil.' And notice again it is us, not me. We are to pray for others, as well as ourselves, that they might be delivered from evil. As a father, may God forgive me for the times I have not prayed for God to deliver my children from evil. As a pastor, may God forgive me for the times I have not prayed that my congregation would be delivered from evil. As Christians, let us pray for one another. And then there is a verse in God's Word that says God desires all men everywhere to repent. So let us pray for all men as well. Let us pray that God deliver us ALL from evil. Let us pray that God would send forth the third person of the Trinity to convict men of sin all over this world and cause them to repent. Christ is teaching us here in this prayer that this is our responsibility to pray that we all might be delivered from evil.

"So now we see we have prayed three things for God and four for ourselves and mankind, and now we pray a fourth thing for God—that He might be glorified as He ought. We acknowledge that the kingdom and the power and the glory are all God's forever and ever. How many men do you know who want the power and the glory for themselves? Those feelings are widespread here among our tribe, among our *wantoks*, wouldn't you say? Perhaps it is universal. Perhaps it is why tribes fight with other tribes, wanting the land, or in other words, the kingdom, as well as the power and the glory. Doubtless it is why nations fight against other nations for that matter. It is why we had our pig killings in the past; instead of killing a pig and eating it so our bodies could have the nutrition we need to stay healthy, and our children could have the nutrition they need to grow, we saved all our pigs for a big pig killing, so we could give away pork, and our names could be great, in other words, so we could get the glory. God made the pigs. If God has given us pigs, let us thank Him for giving us our daily food, and eat them as we need.

"Bossboy Pombo prayed again and again, as God was saving him, 'for Thine is the kingdom and the power and the glory.' You who have walked in this Christian way longer than Pombo, examine your hearts. Do you really want God to have the glory and the power? Or do you want it for yourself? I am examining my own heart, along with Pombo here. May God get the glory for Pombo's conversion; may I not want it for myself. May God have all the glory for everyone who turned to God this week, as they heard Pombo pleading his way to the Father! May this be God's kingdom right here at Tona, and may no man claim it for his own, least of all me, who am meant only to shepherd God's sheep, and to go out and seek lost lambs.

"Let me read you some verses from Psalms 66 before we pray together: The Psalmist says in verses 17-20, 'I cried out to him with my mouth, his praise was on my tongue. Had I cherished evil thoughts *Adonai* would not have listened. But in fact, God did listen; He paid attention to my prayer. Blessed be God, who did not reject my prayer, or turn His grace away from me.' CJB.* The **Pidgin Bible** has verse 18 translated: '*Tasol sapos mi tinging pasin nogut i samting nating, orait Bikpela i no inap harim beten bilong mi.*' Let us not 'regard iniquity in our hearts,' as the KJV says it, or the Lord will not hear our prayers.

"That word *Adonai*, that you heard me use, is the name for God that Jewish people put in place of Yahweh which means Jehovah. They feel that name is so sacred that we should not speak it, just *think* it! In English we do use the name Jehovah, and God, but let us say them reverently and carefully, my brothers and sisters. Let us never use them in vain or in cursing and swearing.

"Oh, my people, pray for me, as I pray for you. And pray with me in unison, 'For Thine is the kingdom, and the power, and the glory, Amen.'" His congregation repeated that line with their pastor and bowed their heads, and fell on their knees and continued to pray fervently that they might not fail God in all this new light they had received that morning through the simple Lord's Prayer in Matthew Six and the heartfelt words of Pastor Mark.

*Scripture quotations are taken from the *Jewish New Testament*, copyright 1979 by David H. Stern. Published by Jewish New Testament Publications, Inc., 6120 Day Long Lane, Clarksville, Maryland 21029. www.messianicjewish.net/jntp Used by permission.

Puri Pastor and family. The pastor's wife is Lovedy Kupaloma pictured on page 89 with the Kelley boys and her sister, Aisapame.

Marilyn Lavy in High School

Marilyn in College

Marilyn Lavy Sturtevant with Jason

Marilyn Lavy Sturtevant with Stephanie

Steve & Marilyn Sturtevant, Jason & Stephanie with Paul Wagun in PNG

Marilyn

Marilyn Lavy Sturtevant just before she passed away

Jason & Joanna Sturtevant & their children, Jessica and Joshua, in Ukraine

Chapter Nine

Linda Kelley sat down on the bench beside the tiny cemetery at Pabrabuk, Western Highlands Province, thankful that someone, Someone had placed a bench there. There had been no place to sit beside the two graves and four markers when she had been there in 2008, and her friends and she had planted four new rose cuttings, one at each corner of Marilyn Lavy Sturtevant's grave. The pink rosebush Marilyn's husband, Steve, had planted long before, was in full bloom at bottom center of the grave. She could see that three of the red rose cuttings had rooted. Two had red buds on them and one had both buds and full blown red roses.

"Thank You, God, that they grew," she murmured in prayer. "I don't have the green thumb that Marilyn had. In 2008 I walked all around Marilyn's yard and touched the exotic plants she had planted that were still growing. I must find time to do that again, Abba. Now I know Richard Peki lives there, so I will ask him and his wife to walk with me, so I can talk about Marilyn with them. Help me to remember to tell them the things You want said, Abba. And to Toropo now, as she joins me to learn about Marilyn—probably the dearest, godliest woman I have ever known on earth. I have the poem and tribute I wrote to her in my Bible here, Lord, but I don't know how to say some of this with the language barrier. Help me, Abba."

Linda sat there in the hot tropical sun looking across the station and down the length of the soccer field at the crowds of people gathered here for camp meeting. How could she ever find Toropo among them? What if Toropo had never even received her message? She sat there whispering a prayer that God would help Toropo find her if He wanted them to get together.

And He did! He brought Toropo straight into Linda's arms. Linda stood and they hugged each other tightly.

"Toropo, my Konopu! How good to see you again! How good to feel your arms around me, to feel your flesh and bones again!

You're alive! You're real! You're here in person, not just in my dreams as you have been for the last twenty-five years! Thank God for bringing us together again here on earth and not making us wait until heaven!" Linda said as the tears ran down her cheeks.

Toropo was crying too. "Konopu, my konopu!" she was whispering over and over. After several minutes of crying and hugging she pulled away and pointed to her mother with her chin and drew her into the circle of arms saying, "This is my Ama," and pointing again with nose, chin and pursed lips she said, "This is my Ara, the man you know as Pombo, Bossboy Pombo, but he is not the man you wrote about many years ago, Konopu. He just got saved a few months ago, and now he's a new creature in Christ."

Linda shook hands with this glowing man saying, "Thank God! You are now God's son, and my brother in Christ Jesus!"

"This is my sister, Tawa," said Toropo as she drew her sister closer by the arm, into the circle of four, making it a circle of five.

"I am so glad to meet you," said Tawa. "We read the book you wrote about my sister in our literature class at Ialibu High School. You gave me words in English for my feelings, and I just can't tell you how much that means to me! You helped the inner me to grow!"

"Why thank you, Tawa! That is so kind of you to give me such a compliment! But I must pass it on to my Heavenly Father. He gets the glory because it was He Who spoke to my earthly father, Robert Harvey, and called him to New Guinea, (back before it was called Papua New Guinea) and when I was just a child. In that way I learned ImboUngu and Wiru as a teen at home with my parents, and because He, **Abba**, which means Father in Hebrew, guided us to Piamble, I got to know your sister, Toropo, and *Abba* gave me the privilege of writing about her!"

Tawa pulled Annie into the growing circle and said, "This is my friend, Annie Yakura."

"Oh, I know you, Annie," Linda exclaimed as she hugged her. She turned to Tawa as she said, "Annie shared her bedroom with me one night in 2008. She gave me her bed, and she slept on the floor!"

Annie ducked her head and blushed as Linda said, "Thanks again, Annie."

"And this is your namesake, your Nopi, Linda Stanley," said Tawa.

"Oh, yes," said Linda as she hugged her in turn. "I met you in Mendi in 2000. How is your mother, Nogo, and your father, Stanley Unda?

"Daddy is well and strong though his hair is as white as yours and Pombo's now. But Mama's knees are bad. She can't walk well enough to come here to camp meeting."

"Oh, if only they could do knee replacements in PNG like they do in America! My friend, Liriyame at Maiya, in the Wiru, has so much pain that she cannot walk at all. She says it is because of all the children she has borne. God bless her! She and her husband, Timba, are such great prayer warriors and two of their great grandsons are already little preacher boys and pray-ers too at ages 12 and 13! Have you heard of Japhaniah and Mesgun?"

Both Annie and Linda Stanley nodded.

"I hope I see your Dad again, Nopi. He and I were kids with our parents at Mele once upon a time, though I was a little older than he. I was already a teenager when my mom started your dad and six of his siblings in first grade English all in the same year! Your dad and George were the oldest ones."

"Yes, I have heard my dad talk about your mom. He and lots of other people from the Wiru say she was a strong lady and their Mother-in-Israel, their Mother in the Christian faith."

"Yes, I thank God for my parents," said Linda again. "And now I would like to tell you about my friend who is buried here. That's why I asked Toropo to meet me here." Linda put her arm around Toropo again and asked her to sit down on the bench with her. Her father and mother seated themselves on the grass in front of them, along with the Trio, and soon others did the same.

"Tawa, I have this poem I wrote about my dear friend, Marilyn Lavy Sturtevant. Do you think you could translate it or at least parts of it for your father and Toropo's mother and anyone else who wants to hear? My ImboUngu is not up to it. *ImboUngu nimboi tero waddle nanga akumbettle topettle mapettle teremo.*"

Pombo and several others laughed so hard at this surprising sentence in their language from Linda's lips that it drew a larger crowd around them. When Linda could be heard above their laughter and chuckles she began her story of Marilyn.

"I was in my junior year at Adirondack Bible College, having done two years by correspondence from God's Bible School while I was at Mele, when my mom was teaching your fathers, Annie and Nopi," she said, glancing at each in turn.

"But at this time I was in the USA in the state of New York, at A. B. C. or Adirondack Bible College, and the whole school or most of them anyway took a trip to Washington D. C., to see our nation's capitol. We stayed overnights with Rev. Sherwood Weeks and his family and congregation in Harrisburg, Pennsylvania, and commuted from there to Washington and Gettysburg each day.

"A lot of people there had a lot to say, but I found this one young girl, not saying a word, taking care of two little children. Someone told me her name was Marilyn Lavy, and she was a nanny for those two little Jewish children. I was missing my orphan babies from New Guinea very much, so I was drawn to them, but even more I was drawn to Marilyn. I followed her around and asked her questions and tried to get to know her. She hardly responded. If she answered at all it was only in the fewest words possible. I asked her about her family, and she said, 'This is my family,' pointing to the two little tots. When I pressed her for more she started asking the little Jewish girl to talk to me. 'Tell her about Purim,' she said to her. 'Tell her the words you said at the table at the feast of Purim.'

"For that visit I had to give up. I could not get to know her even though we spoke the same language.

"The next conference year saw a change of presidents at Adirondack Bible College. Rev. Harold Cranston was replaced by Rev. Sherwood Weeks. We young people were scared of Rev. Weeks. He was such an ascetic, and we thought we could never measure up. He was a powerful preacher, and he even preached against wearing colors. I was extremely poor and wore only what I had been given. I did not have the money to change my wardrobe to one of black and white (which I mistakenly thought he wanted), so I just tried to stay out of his way at camp meeting after his appointment to A.B.C.

"I was shocked when he confronted me one day of camp and asked me if I would be returning to Adirondack Bible College for another school year.

"I said, 'Yes, but I would go anywhere else to get Greek II and Hebrew I if I had the money.'

"'I'll teach you Greek II,' he said.

"'You know Greek?' I asked, surprised.

"'Yes. I had five years of Greek at Bible College and Seminary.'

"'Wow! Five Years!'

"'And we will have Hebrew I also.'

"'You know Hebrew, too?'

"'No, but I will buy books, and we will study it together!'

"I looked up at him in awe, amazed, said 'Thank you!' ducked my head, and scuttled out of his presence.

"I canvassed the small student body begging everyone, anyone to take Greek II and Hebrew I that year. I didn't want to be his only pupil in any class because I was still afraid of him, and did not realize what an honor and privilege it would be to have his entire attention focused on me!

"The year before we had started Greek I with Rev. Glenn Pelfrey (whom I will say more about later because he came here to Pabrabuk!) and the largest class there had ever been in any subject at Adirondack Bible College. But students kept dropping out until we were down to three by the end of the school year.

"I begged Beatrice VanCise and Lorana Moshier to continue Greek II with me, but they declined. 'We just don't like languages as well as you,' they said to me, and of course they hadn't had the privilege of living in New Guinea and learning languages from such wonderful people as I had.

"Two young men started Hebrew I with me. Steve Sturtevant and Paul Jukes were very brave to try Hebrew when they had not learned Greek first, and understandably, they found it just too hard. The Hebrew alphabet is exceedingly difficult. I remember I went out on the Prayer Rock to tackle that alphabet. I sat there on that hard seat focusing all my mental powers for over two hours on it before I learned it. By the end of that afternoon I could read Hebrew, however slowly and laboriously. But Steve and Paul were busy men, too busy to give a whole afternoon to just one subject, and they dropped out.

"'I know someone I think I can get to join us,' said Rev. Weeks when he saw how devastated I was by their withdrawal.

"'Who?' I asked, skeptically.

"'Marilyn Lavy.'

"'In Hebrew or Greek?'

"'Both.'

"'Has she taken either one yet?'

"'No, but I will get her started now. I imagine she will be able to join us second semester when she comes here to teach. She has to complete her contract teaching Junior High Biology and other science with the Harrisburg School District before she can come to us. But she's a real student and very capable!'

"Marilyn Lavy, I pondered. I remembered how hard I had tried to get to know her, but I hadn't succeeded. I remembered how something within me had called to her. Later the Psalmest gave me words for it in Psalm 42:7, 'Deep calleth unto deep,' and I don't mean that to sound proud, but just that something in the depths of me called to the depths of her, and vice versa.

"Marilyn came. She studied Greek and Hebrew alone first, asking Professor Weeks questions by phone, and then she came to Adirondack Bible College.

"We took classes together, but we did not become close friends at first. It was my fault more than hers this time. I had always had this thing about revering my teachers so much and putting them on such a high pedestal that I could not speak to them out of class. Outside of Greek and Hebrew (where she was a student) she was a teacher. Even though she was not my teacher, I could not speak to her on a casual basis. I still could not be comfortable with her out of class, though every fiber of my mind and soul thrilled to the vibrations of hers and Rev. Week's in class. As we studied the New Testament in Greek God met with us, and that little spot in the back of the dining hall where three people met with their God became hallowed ground to me. I caught a glimpse of God's great glory there and have studied deeply into the word 'glory' in Greek and Hebrew and English since, still trying to understand it!

"And then one day in late spring the tree whose branches touched my upper story window began to leaf out. This girl who had come from five years in the tropics, almost sitting on the equator; sixty months of purest ever-greenest green in PNG, was having a hard time making it through the long snowy upper New York winters!

"So I flitted down two flights of stairs and lighted briefly in the kitchen to announce joyfully, 'My tree has buds on it!'"

"Three teachers laughed. Then one asked, 'How is it your tree?'

"Marilyn's question surprised me and I stopped to consider.

"'...because it touches my window. It touches Lois' window, too. She can claim it if she wants.'

"They all laughed. 'So you like trees?' continued Marilyn.

"'I *LOVE* trees.'

"How about taking a walk in the woods with me?'

"'I'd love to. When?'

"'Tomorrow afternoon.'

"And we did. And we were friends forever from that day on."

Linda reached out and clasped Toropo's hand briefly, then Tawa's, Annie's, Linda's, and Toropo-Ma's (better known to most as Bani-Ma.)

"A wonderful poet by the name of Robert Frost wrote a great poem beginning '*Tree at my window, window tree*,' and I have borrowed that line or title from him.

"We can back up a few paragraphs and let the poem take over:

Love Tree — Philodendron

Tree at my window, window tree
'Twas you who once brought a friend to me.
I loved you so, I called you mine.
She came to ask, "How yours? How thine?"

We walked into the woods that day,
To see your sisters. What'd she say?
She spoke not of the 'outer weather'
As we went strolling on together.

"You know, Pombo," Linda said, "when Imbo Imboma meet on the road they say, 'Nu tendo puni?' but Americans say, 'How are you?' and then they start talking about the weather. Well, Marilyn and I never talked about the weather. Right from the first we began baring our souls to each other.

139

She spoke of inner thoughts, the heart
She sought mine out. Though worlds apart
We grew to one. We learned to meet
At the Father's throne, the Mercy Seat.

In school again at the feet of the master
We studied Greek. I never passed her;
I never reached her. She forged ahead;
I followed on tiptoe wherever she led.

"Dendron" means tree. It seems so right!
Philodendron — love tree!" Shining light
Lit our faces. Teacher shook his head.
"Oh, you two!" was all he said.

"Rev. Weeks was the Greek Teacher, the Master, Toropo,"
Linda said, looking her in the eye, "and he just shook his head at
us. He was such a godly man and so interested in each one of us
spiritually. He used to search our eyes to see how our souls were
doing. I couldn't meet his eyes because of adhering to PNG
culture for five years where modest young ladies at that time
were supposed to keep their heads down, their eyes lowered. But
finally, I learned to look this Man-of-God in the eye to show him
I wasn't trying to hide any sin.

I took my turn and did the leading,
New Guinea my world; His call, my heeding.
We spoke not of the 'outer weather'
As we sailed the seas and skies together.

Alone, together, in a foreign land,
Alone, and parted, in His Hand.
Though tribes and languages apart,
We met in letter, in thought, in heart.

She came to visit my little cane hut.
We mourned our Teacher. Heaven unshut!
We hid away by the Kawe River
And sought new life, from Christ, the Giver.

"She was in the Kewa language area at Katiloma, and I was in ImboUngu at Kauapena. But when Rev. Weeks was killed in a truck accident in the Adirondack Mountains when his brakes gave way on November 1st, 1967, she came to my tiny house at Kauapena, and we mourned our loss and celebrated his life together. He had been her mentor for many years; he had only been mine for one. She loved him far more than I, but I too had taken his measure in the Lord, and knew what a Man-of-God he was! As I became a more mature teacher myself in later years I realized how magnanimous it was of him to be willing to teach me alone in two language classes that one semester, and to go on doing the same for just two of us the second semester!

"How I thank God for Rev. Weeks and his protégé, Marilyn. I bless their memories!

"I had a cleft in the rocks along the Kawe River (when I lived at Kawe-pena, or Kauapena) where there was an overhang of vines. People could go up and down the river without seeing me. Marilyn and I could hide away in there together and read our Greek New Testaments and pray without anyone being aware but God.

I visited her in her hut, "Shalom"
Grass roof, cane floors, a humble home.
We hardly noticed the outer shell,
We communed in mind, where spirits dwell.

"She had the Hebrew letters — שלם cut out of paper and pasted on her door. There at Katiloma I married George Kelley and she was maid of honor in my wedding.

"Two years later she went back to America and married Steve Sturtevant. George, Bobby and I followed. My second son, Deanie, and her first child, Jason were both born in 1974, so we 'played dolls' together!

In America then, together again
Communion in word, in look; no pen.
We played house and we played 'dolls'
Our husbands near. No fear. No walls.

Then back again to our calling dear
Where the huge Rekari spreads its cheer.

Our children, our books, more language study,
Outstations, bush trails all wet and muddy.

"When we came back to PNG, George and I were at Katiloma in the Southern Highlands Province again, but she and Steve came here to Pabrabuk in the Western Highlands Province. We both had baby girls by then. I had been here fifteen years earlier when I was fifteen years old, writing language lessons for the missionaries in the Meyamo dialect of ImboUngu or YamboUngu, so I now helped her learn this local language, and she became my mentor for my studies from Azusa Pacific University at Ukarumpa. She loved to visit Katiloma, and one time she and her two children, I and my three children and five children of Neil and Edith Taylor went down to the Sugu River where the great Rekari or rain tree spreads itself in all its glory. Remember, we both loved trees, and it was a tree that had brought us to friendship. It took two adults and nine children to be able to encircle that huge tree with our arms outspread.

And the gorgeous burning tropical sun
Black hearts made white in the Blood of One;
Black women crushed in pain and fear
We shared our love, we shed our tear.

"We shared together the sad plight of women here in PNG, and she really cared as I do, though she never wrote a book about it as I did. Her book, **Orchids on a Waste Hillside** is about PNG men, conversions, and tribal fighting.

"We loved discussing C. S. Lewis' books together and doing Greek Word Studies as I said. Let me digress a minute here to share the word glory, which I have studied for a couple years thoroughly, every where I can find it, in this last decade. I taught my tiny little four, five and six-year-old students at DayStar in Michigan to say 'Kavod Elohim hasatar davar; lekavod malachim haCHar davar.' Isn't that beautiful. In only eight Hebrew words there are four rhymes! At least if you pronounce it the way Rev. Weeks and the **Strong's Concordance** says to do. My Israeli friend pronounces it a little differently; perhaps in modern Hebrew. Anyway it is Proverbs 25:2, and I translate it this way: It is the glory of God to hide a word, but the glory of kings to seek a word. Kids love hide and seek, you know, and so I tried to show them how to have fun with God in seeking for words and the meaning of them in His Word. Davar is translated word in most places, only rarely thing, as in this instance in the **KJV**. Those little kids delighted in learning Greek and Hebrew words with me. They could also recite John 1:1 in Greek: In the beginning was the Word, and the Word was with God and the Word was God. That's logos in Greek, you know: Εν αρξη ην ο λογος και ο λογος ην προς τον θεον και θεος ην ο λογος.

"This great joy I have in word studies I first learned with Marilyn and Rev. Weeks, and always when I do it yet, I feel a fellowship with them, a fellowship of the saints!

"At that time, then, I went back to America in October of 1984 and my dear friend died here at Pabrabuk in 1985. My husband gave me the sad news at the home of my father and mother-in-Israel, Robert and Dorothy Symons of Aliquippa, Pennsylvania.

My sister, my friend, my Poroman!
C. S. Lewis, Greek words, the Palm of His Hand!
My husband came with the words of a song...
"Honey, listen. Take it easy. It's Marilyn. She's gone."

"She's gone to Glory. She's 'Over There'!
She's sitting at the feet of the Master fair.
She's learning the Whence, the Why, the When.
She's understanding what we canna' ken."
Tree at my window, window tree,
You that once brought a friend to me....

God of the gallant trees, help me keep growing
Learning, living, giving, knowing.
May I follow Marilyn as she followed You,
And see Your Plan, Your Pleasure do.

"'God of the gallant trees' is a phrase from one of Amy Carmichael's poems, and she was my heroine when I was a teenager at Piamble. Pat Andrews, who was a missionary here at Pabrabuk then, mentored me and introduced me to her writing.

"My whole heart cried out, "Marilyn, wait for me!" for I could see her sitting at the feet of the Master Teacher, Christ, learning lessons I haven't imagined yet. I wonder if our earthly teacher, Rev. Weeks, might be there too, and perhaps Rev. Pelfrey too in that circle of eager students. I have a feeling that any of us who want to learn will get to study all we want about the deep things of God. Sometimes I can hardly wait to get started. Now it has been twenty-four years since Marilyn died."

Linda started to read the article she had written "In Memory of Marilyn" when Richard Peki and Pierre came down the gorge, and all eyes followed their descent and ascent. They made their way to Linda and Toropo's group and listened to the remainder of the article. Linda introduced both of them to each of Toropo's family.

"This is Richard Peki, the academic dean here at Pacific Bible College, and this is Pierre Simon (See-moan), the evangelist from Haiti. Pierre is Peter in French."

Richard and Pierre shook hands with each of Toropo's family.

Richard was talking to Linda Stanley when Pierre said to Tawa, "And you are Tawa?" and shook her hand.

Our Tawa felt a physical shock go through her whole body as she raised her eyes to his. She felt like her heart was knocked off its feet. "What a powerful personality he has," she thought.

Pombo too was drawn to this young man, and he followed him when he left to go to the tabernacle. Tawa's eyes followed her father and Pierre as they walked down the sidewalk together and were soon swallowed up by a crowd of other followers. Pierre was tall enough that his head showed above the crowd.

"Whose is the other grave?" asked Linda Stanley.

"Dale Mahan's," answered Linda. "He was a young missionary who lived here at Pabrabuk with his wife, Cheryl, and his daughters, Julie and Dana.

"Dale was born to Eugene and Laveta Mahan in rural Kansas on November 16, 1954, when I was eight years old. As a young boy, Dale worked on the farm raising cattle and crops with his father and brothers, but it soon became evident that God had given him a very creative mind and the ability to understand and fix mechanical things. Even as a boy, he built and repaired farm equipment and household items, and won a prize in a farm newspaper once for a hay caddy he designed and built.

"One of his pastors used to take household appliances apart and try to fix them. He usually ended up carrying the pieces in a paper sack to Dale, and Dale put them back together for him.

"Dale attended high school at a Bible School in Independence, Kansas, working on cars or projects in the shop every chance he got. Winston Wehrman, our missionary at Kauapena, went to speak at a chapel service there, and Dale heard him, and also heard God speaking to his heart and calling him to be a missionary. During his high school years he met Cheryl Shreffler from Barnsdall, and they were married a year after Dale graduated.

"Dale and Jerry Schenk had been best friends all their childhood and youth. They were only six weeks apart in age and only three miles apart in geographical location. They grew up going to church and school together, and after high school Dale held down three jobs, one of which Jerry also held. They were both working for a man in their church named Bill McCormick and challenging each other to see which one could weld the best weld on the most unlikely surface.

"Jerry married a girl named Becky the same year Dale married Cheryl, and they just went right on working together, and doing many things together. What one didn't think of, the other one did, people say!

"God gave Dale and Cheryl a baby girl whom they named Julie Lavon, on the 11th of September 1977. Then He gave them Dana Marie on the 29th of June 1979. Dale and Cheryl moved to Independence Bible School as dorm parents in 1980.

"Dale bought an old drilling rig, repaired and rebuilt it and drilled several water and gas wells in the area.

"In 1982 John and Sharon Davolt came to speak at Independence Bible College. They had been long-time friends of the Mahans and Schenks before they came to Papua New Guinea and did missionary work at Mt. Hagen and Kauapena. Rev. Jacob Miller was with the Davolts in that service in Parsons, Kansas, and he spent time afterwards talking with both the Mahans and the Schenks about coming to Papua New Guinea as missionaries.

"Jerry and Becky did come to PNG in February of 1983 and Dale and Cheryl came later, that same year right here to Pabrabuk! Dale was in charge of the jointery shop, the mechanic shop, and making trips to Mt. Hagen and Lae for supplies for Pabrabuk Station and all the missionaries and school students who lived here at that time.

"Dale was able to buy an old outdated telephone system here in PNG, and he revamped it to work for Pabrabuk. Each home on campus had a phone in it, as well as the mission store, the workshop, and the business office. The service was only local, but it saved many steps and many many minutes and hours of everybody's time.

"Marilyn Lavy Sturtevant's son, Jason, loved Dale Mahan and his three-wheeler. Any time Dale stepped outside and started his three-wheeler, Jason was right there and rode along with him. They went everywhere together, and Jason worked with Dale any time he could get out of school.

"One Sunday in 1985 Steve Sturtevant was gone, perhaps holding a service elsewhere, and the Mahans and three Sturtevants started out walking to an outstation together. Marilyn and Cheryl became tired and hot and sat down to rest. As they sat in the shade trying to catch their breath they decided to shorten their trip and go to a different outstation closer by, but when they started out again Marilyn was unable to go on. They turned back towards Pabrabuk, and Jason ran ahead and got the three-wheeler while Dale, Cheryl and local people supported Marilyn and helped her try to walk. When her son reached them with the three-wheeler at the edge of Pabrabuk Mission Station, Jason drove her home while Dale sat with her and supported her on the vehicle.

"Marilyn lost her sight for a while after that, and Steve bought tickets for them to return to the USA. One day Cheryl ran to Marilyn's house from the school and found Marilyn sitting with her *Bible* on her lap. Marilyn greeted her with the words, 'I can see.'

"Steve cancelled the tickets to America, but one Saturday evening Marilyn wasn't feeling well, and that evening he walked her down that little hill from her house, just like we saw Richard and Pierre walking a moment ago. Steve said she paused to look at flowers along the way and spoke of their beauty. She loved flowers. You can see that by the look of her yard and the title of her book. Steve walked her to that little house there behind that big eucalyptus tree with the fireplace in its trunk. Wane and Kinza Ninjipa live there now. Pelfreys lived there then, and Dorothy Pelfrey was a nurse. Steve thought she could care for Marilyn better than he. Unbeknown to Steve and Marilyn, the night before that, Pastor and Evangelist Kandulopi Yakumbu had seen angels coming to get a white woman at Pabrabuk. He was

Kandulopi

not told which one. But that very night, Kevin Reali, who was a registered nurse at the Pabrabuk Clinic at the time, saw angels coming for Marilyn, his first teacher at his childhood home of Katiloma. And the angels did take her that night."

"*Yarayowe!*" sighed Linda Stanley.

"*Na kondo teremo*," said Toropo and Tawa together.

"Dale Mahan and Jason Sturtevant built the casket together, and they held the funeral that Sunday. I cannot imagine Jason's heartbreak as he helped Dale nail those boards together. He was only ten years old.

"Mahans went on furlough in December of 1986 and returned in January of 1988. Though they were living here at Pabrabuk, they were asked to help out as part-time missionaries to Baiyer River where my parents had started a station, and the Haynes family, a Filipino couple, and the Glicks later served. Every other weekend Dale and Cheryl drove to the Baiyer River and spent the weekend ministering to people there. The Mahans had shipped a container of equipment and supplies for Dale to use upon his return which included a drilling rig. Dale had found this old rig for sale in the States while he was on furlough and purchased it for PNG.

147

"On the first day of April in 1988 Dale Mahan and Jerry Schenck drove the Fuso truck from Lae to Pabrabuk heavily loaded with the drilling rig and much more from the container. While driving through mountains between Lae and here, police stopped them and told them a roadblock was set up ahead. The police chief got in the front seat of the truck, with Dale driving, and other officers got on the back of the truck and hid under the tarp. Jerry was told to go ride in the police wagon, and they would meet up at the other side of the roadblock. As Dale drove up to the area there was a tree felled across the road. He stopped the truck, and a man came to his window and held a gun to his head while demanding his money. Before Dale could respond, a gunshot was heard, and the police chief demanded that Dale drive through the roadblock. As Dale obeyed, he realized that the officers on the back of the truck had shot the would-be robber. They drove a ways and then waited there for the police to bring Jerry. Those officers had stopped where the incident had occurred and found that the gun that had been held to Dale's head was loaded. They were very blessed to have God's protection in the form of a police escort. They arrived home shaken but thankfully safe.

"Dale took an old truck and built the drilling rig on the back of it. He drilled a water well here on Pabrabuk station as well as a few others for the mission elsewhere. Another big project Dale was working on was a hydroelectric plant for electricity for Pabrabuk. He drove an old yellow bulldozer clearing a road at the end of Pabrabuk Station to the water way down below. He worked very late many evenings trying to get the road cut out of the side of the mountain so he could get supplies down to build the hydro plant. He then rebuilt an old defunct hydro that he had purchased. Up until then Pabarabuk had had electricity only three hours a day when they ran a large generator in the evenings. Dale enabled the station to be supplied with electricity twenty-four hours a day on a daily basis.

"On the thirtieth of June, 1988, Dale and Dean Rose loaded the small mission bulldozer on the Fuso and drove it to Kundiawa in the Tsimbu Province to clear land for a church. They made the long drive and worked the rest of that day clearing the land. They spent the night there with the pastor and his family and then began work the next day finishing the clearing

Dale & Cheryl Mahan with daughters, Julie & Dana

Dana Mahan grown up and married to Larry Jones; they have Kartyr and Karlye.

Julie Mahan married Wesley Rummell and they have Brianna and Kierra.

and making a driveway from the highway into the church property. In the early afternoon of the first day of July, Dean watched from the truck as Dale was making the finishing touches on the driveway. The dozer tipped and fell into a ravine, to Dean's great horror. Dean and the pastor ran to get to Dale, but the dozer had drug him down into the ravine. The dozer was still running backwards, and the elephant grass on either side was very tall and thick and difficult to walk through. Just as Dean got to the dozer to try to shut it off, the motor died. Dale was lying lifelessly, just behind the bucket. The back of the dozer was at the edge of another deep ravine.

"Dean and his helpers retrieved Dale's body from under the dozer and carried him to the road where they flagged down a passing truck. He was taken to Kundiawa Hospital where he was pronounced dead. John Davolt, our mission pilot, flew to Kundiawa to pick up Dale and Dean. And so there was a second missionary funeral here at Pabrabuk less than three years after the first and nine years after Tracy Rose's memorial service here, and his funeral at Tongo River.

"Now the Pelfreys, who nursed Marilyn her last night on earth are both with Jesus, too," Linda continued. "They are the ones who planted this row of gorgeous palm trees, — the only such coconut palms in the highlands, to my knowledge."

"Do they bear coconuts?"

"Yes, they do. The Pelfreys later followed God to Ukraine, where Mrs. Pelfrey died, and is buried at Kenyazachee.

"Rev. Glenn Pelfrey was my first Greek teacher, you recall. He was teaching in a Bible School in Belize when he died, and that's where he is buried."

"You loved them too, didn't you, Konopu?"

"Yes, I did. They were dear to my heart. Rev. Pelfrey introduced me to Greek, and it is still the love of my mind. One whole day in Ukraine I shelled beans with both of the Pelfreys and got to know them better than ever before. They had grown those beans in their garden at Osikovo, and they gave them to hungry widows and poor people there. They were so kind! They also went as missionaries to Jamaica and Zambia."

"And who is Susie Lorimer whom this marker names?" asked Tawa.

"She was an older missionary lady who first came to PNG when her children were grown. I think she had ten children. See that yari tree down by the church with the scarlet bougainvillea growing up the trunk and through its branches?"

"Yes, I have looked at that tree more than any other since I arrived here," said Toropo.

"Susie Lorimer planted those two together, and they grew together, the tree supporting the bougainvillea all this time. It reminds me of a poem I wrote at Katiloma years ago. I'll have to share it with you some time, ladies. It's my picture of marriage in Christ."

"Oh, please do share it," said Tawa.

"And this other stone is a marker for G. T. Bustin," said Annie. "He started Evangelical Bible Mission and was the first white man to come to Pabrabuk and Tambul in the Western Highlands, and Kauapena and Mele in the Southern Highlands."

"Right, or at least the first non-government white man. And one of his first converts, if not his very first in 1948, was the young teenager, Kandulopi. Have you heard of him?"

Kandulopi, G. T. Bustin, unknown

Many of the listeners nodded their heads, but others said they hadn't.

"He started his pastoral work here at Pabrabuk after he was converted, and he was taking pastors' classes at Kauapena when we arrived there in January of 1960. My dad had the privilege of teaching him in those classes for a few weeks, and he was a great blessing to my father then, and to our whole family when he visited Piamble in later years.

"After he pastored here, his son, Gideon Gamaliel says he went to Tambul, and then Kauapena, Mele and Piamble, before coming back here to start his little church in his home village of PapeKolia. He also was used of God to reach out to Minj, Banz, and Kudjip. He and his wife, Takame, already had a son named John when we came to Kauapena, and God later gave them Ruth, Gideon, Orpha, Leon and Wendy. John Kandulopi lives in Australia now; Ruth started a Christian school here in PNG; Gideon is doing his graduate studes in the USA; Orpha is married to a businessman; Leon was at home with his father when he died last year; and Wendy is married to Pastor Luke Pena, also at her father's home. Luke pastors the little PapeKolia Church. Kandulopi asked to be set up or set forward on Friday evening about 8 P.M., October 23, 2009, and said, 'Gote okomo.' God is coming. I heard there was an earth tremor here at Pabrabuk, just like there was at Tambul when the Patriarch Sarowa Kimbu died.

"Becky Schenk said that Kandulopi visited Summerfield, Florida, and though he spoke Pidgin, he did not know English. After a while his ears were opened, and he understood what was being preached. Isn't that exciting? Wane Ninjipa said he talked with angels in his sleep before G. T. Bustin first came to his village. Wane also speaks of his ministry at Kauapena in the sixties, and the great sweeping revivals God sent upon his village in the 80s and 90s. Wane called him a 'man of prayer' and says he never complained to anyone about anything. His wife had preceded him in death on the 13th of January 2007."

"Did you know both Rev. Bustin and Kandulopi personally yourself?"

"Oh, yes. I'll never forget hearing Rev. G. T. Bustin preaching when I was just a child. He talked about New Guinea in such a wonderful way that I couldn't wait to get here, right along with my parents! And my last memory of Kandulopi is when I was here in 2008. I heard his arthritis was bad, so I took him some medicine one day to his home at PapeKolia, and we sat on his front porch and chatted. He was getting close to eighty years old, but his mind was so clear, and we reminisced. I asked him to pray before I left, and I shall never forget the clarity of his mind, as he prayed for my children and me, and oh, so many others. It is a memory I shall cherish forever, or as long as God lets me keep it!"

"Thank you for telling us about these people," said Toropo. "Now my parents and I will look forward to seeing them when we get to heaven. "

"Can you imagine what it will be like in Heaven, getting to know the people who have gone on before us? I don't think there will be any language barriers in heaven."

Just then two beautiful women approached the group. Tawa was thinking they were the most beautiful women she had ever seen when Linda jumped up saying, "Agape, who do you have with you? Oh! Florida, is it you?"

"Yes, it is I," said the Popendetta woman shyly, as Linda wrapped her arms around her.

Then she presented her to Tawa's Trio and Toropo saying, "My friends, this is Florida Pugupia, a poet from Popendetta!"

"Is this all there is to life? Male tyranny, polygamy and bribes?" quoted Tawa.

"Ah, yes," said Linda.

Florida turned her beautiful eyes on Tawa and said, "You have read my poem?"

"Yes, we studied it in literature class at Ialibu high school. Have you written others?"

"Yes, I have, but let me introduce you to my friend, Agape, from Eritrea in Africa. She will tell you of something as bad or worse than male tyranny, polygamy and bribes or any male domination."

"What is that?" asked the Trio in unison, as they turned to the beautiful African lady.

"Domination by the government," said Agape. "In our country our government has taken away our right to worship God and has closed our churches."

"Oh, my, *yaruyowe!*" exclaimed Linda Stanley, as the others made similar sympathetic sounds and exclamations.

"Right now some of my people are imprisoned in cattle cars, and have been for years."

"What are cattle cars?"

"Iron railroad cars belonging to a train but shunted to the side. Even cows cannot stay in them too long, for they suffer the heat by day, and the cold by night, and die, but somehow our Christians have survived years of this suffering!"

The girls made velar clicking sounds in their throats, and continued to express their sympathy as they gazed at this most beautiful dark-skinned lady who looked like she should be a queen in a palace, and instead was speaking of suffering at the hands of government.

"What race are you, Agape?" asked Florida. She could see the question in the eyes of the girls and voiced it for them.

"Our ancestors say we come from three different races, African, Israeli or Jew, and Arab."

"Oh, my," exclaimed Tawa, "there is beauty in the mixture of races, then?"

"Beauty for ashes," said Agape.

"Is that poetry? What do you mean?" asked Tawa.

"It is from the Bible. 'To appoint unto them that mourn in Zion, to give unto them beauty for ashes, the oil of joy for mourning, the garment of praise for the spirit of heaviness, that they might be called trees of righteousness, the planting of the Lord, that he might be glorified. Isaiah 61:3.'

"It may mean different things to different people. It is an interesting verse to study. But there's the bell for service. I can't wait for the next service! I am so enjoying the freedom to worship as we desire here in Papua New Guinea!"

"And there is the mention of trees again in that verse in Isaiah," said Linda, as they all rose to their feet. "May God of the gallant trees, and trees of righteousness, and trees at our window, and rekari trees help us be trees of His planting as He did the people who are buried here and the others we have just talked about, that He might be glorified! Amen!"

"Who is preaching this time?" asked Annie, as they began walking toward the tabernacle.

"My nephew, Steven Harvey," said Linda Harvey Kelley

Just then a truck pulled up, driven by Mike Davis.

"Oh, Anna," exclaimed Linda, as she ran around the other side to embrace this God-given daughter, also. To her surprise, out clambered Brody, Wyatt, Pam, Vicki and Brianna. Hugs all around ensued and introductions, before everyone rushed down the soccer field for service.

154

Miss Jo Eleanor Jones leads Tambul Christian Academy; she does a great job! They're top winners at conven...

Students on the PNG-shaped m
in the schoolyard.

Tambul
Christian
Academy

Lining up for inspection &
marchin...

TEACHERS MINUS Jo Eleanor Jones
Betty Kome, Melissa Talpa,
Charlie & Janet Koi & Helen
Charlene & Sandra Serowa Mapikon

The Students

155

July 4th, 1960 Robert é Lily Harvey took two more babies into their home at Paamba in the foothills of Mt. Giluwe. One was "Kanambo" from Lkia and they re-named him Steven K. Harvey.

At 4 months Stevie says "H I"

Linda & Stevie

3rd birthday

4th birth day

Stevie on his second birthday

"Don't posi-lutely me, Linda!"

teve

Harvey

Kelley

Henry

Stevie & Champ

akatoa, Stevie & John Mandare

& Family

Lily   Susie   Pamela

Kevin

Stevie & Valerie & Evan-geline Smith

Lily Harvey 3.10.94

10.11.92 Susie Harvey

Another birthday

Chapter Ten

"I want to talk about forgiveness today," said Steve Harvey as he came to the pulpit in the huge tabernacle. "I have learned that '*payback*' is one of the main tenets of your culture. I want to begin by reminding you of Romans 12:19: 'Dearly Beloved, Avenge not yourselves, but rather give place unto wrath; for it is written, Vengeance is mine, I will repay, saith the Lord.'

"Also in Hebrews 10:30 David H. Stearn has translated it in the *Complete Jewish Bible*, 'Vengeance is my responsibility; I will repay.'

"Africa's biggest poisonous snake is called the black mamba. It is native to at least sixteen African countries. It is called the black mamba because its mouth is inky black. Its actual color is dark olive, olive green, gray-brown or metal gray. Average adult black mambas are eight feet long, but they can grow as big as fourteen feet. It is known for being very aggressive when disturbed or confronted, and it strikes with deadly precision.

"This black mamba which is said to be the most deadly snake in the world, along with the King Cobra, has one magnificent characteristic. The black mamba takes only one partner for life. There are many animals and birds that do that. A few are Gibbon apes, wolves, coyotes, barn owls, beavers, bald eagles, golden eagles, condors, swans, brolga cranes, French angel fish, sandhill cranes, red-tailed hawks, ospreys, prairie voles (which is a rodent), black vultures and others. All these creatures set us a good example in doing what God commanded in Genesis 2:24: 'Therefore shall a man leave his father and mother, and shall cleave unto his wife, and they shall be one flesh.' Notice that is wife in the singular. It does not say a man shall cleave to his wives. I hear that polygyny is another problem here in PNG. If you want to become a great nation you need to follow all of God's laws. I can read you verse after verse in the *Bible* proving that God blesses the nations who follow His laws. Notice also that this verse begins with the word therefore. You know when a verse starts with therefore, you have to look back to see what it is there for? Verse 23 says, 'And Adam said, This is now bone of my bones, and flesh of my flesh; she shall be called Woman, because she was taken out of Man' and in the Hebrew that is, she shall be called Isha, because she was taken out of Ish. If English followed the Hebrew feminine marker, woman would be called manna! But English made its own rules, of course!

"Let me read you those verses in the Complete Jewish Bible. Let's back up to the fifteenth verse of chapter two of Genesis: *Adonai* God, took the person [Hebrew: *adam*] and put him in the garden of Eden to cultivate and care for it. 16. *Adonai*, God, gave the person this order: 'You may freely eat from every tree in the garden 17. Except the tree of the knowledge of good and evil. You are not to eat from it, because on the day that you eat from it, it will become certain that you will die.'"

"18. *Adonai*, God, said, 'It isn't good that the person (*adam*) should be alone. I will make for him a companion suitable for helping him.' 19. So from the ground *Adonai*, God, formed every wild animal and every bird that flies in the air, and he brought them to the person to see what he would call them. Whatever the person would call each living creature, that was to be its name. 20. So the person gave names to all the livestock, to the birds in the air and to every wild animal. But for Adam there was not found a companion suitable for helping him.

"21. Then God caused a deep sleep to fall upon the person; and while he was sleeping, he took one of his ribs and closed up the place from which he took it with flesh. 22. The rib which *Adonai*, God, had taken from the person, he made a woman-person [Hebrew: *adamah*] and he brought her to the man-person [Hebrew: *adam*]. 23. The man-person said, 'At last! This is bone from my bones and flesh from my flesh. She is to be called Woman [Hebrew: ishah] because she was taken out of Man [Hebrew: ish].' This is why a man is to leave his father and mother and stick with his wife, and they are to be one flesh. That is the end of this reading in the CJB.

"Wikipedia says the ***Bible*** condones polygymy, but I think God makes it very clear that the 'times of this ignorance he winked at but now commandeth all men everywhere to repent.' Acts 17:30, or as the ***CJB*** puts that verse 'In the past, God overlooked such ignorance; but now he is commanding all people everywhere to turn to him from their sins.'

"Wikipedia would be more correct to say that the **Bible** *reports* polygamy, not *condones* it. Over and over again, all through the **Bible**, God had His writers report sin. He never tried to hide sin from us. Adam Clarke was a Hebrew scholar who lived over two hundred years ago. Actually he was born in 1760 or 1762, and after he was converted he spent forty years writing six volumes of commentary on the Bible. I imagine you have his commentaries here in the John Wesley library at Pacific Bible College. He was John Wesley's greatest theologian and he was my grandparents' favorite commentator. They even bought his commentaries for their kids for their graduation gift when they graduated from Bible School.

"Adam Clarke writes about Genesis 4:19 which says Lamech took to himself two wives: 'He was the first who dared to reverse the order of God by introducing polygamy; and from him it has been retained, practiced, and defended to the present day.'

"But remember, my friends, he was a great, great, grandson of Cain who had killed his brother and been banished from worship, or excommunicated from the family worship, Adam Clarke believes, and he was perhaps far from those who were worshipping God as had been commanded, and in his carnal, depraved nature he thought of doing this thing and did it. Islamic countries and Africa and Papua New Guinea continue it to this day. There is even a sect called Mormonism in America where the men try to practice it, and our United States law has outlawed it. Recently there was a community in Texas who may have been practicing it, and a girl escaped from this enclosure and called the police. The U. S. army went in and took it over. Later they apologized and gave the children back to the families, but most recently another woman came forward and said it was true. And that they take their teen-aged boys and leave them on the streets of Los Angeles in California, because older men in the communisty do not want these young men taking the youn-ger women. How wrong is that, men? It is not fair to young men, any more than what older men in any of these cultures I have just listed for you are allowed to do.

159

"However, I was saying that my message is to be on forgiveness, and I have taken it largely from a man in my church named Rev. Paul Wolfe. He does not talk about the black mamba or polygamy, but let me get back to my illustration of the black mamba. The black mamba takes one partner for life, and if its partner is killed, the second snake, male or female, will often wait for the killer to return, and it is prepared to lose its life getting vengeance for its partner. The black mamba believes in *payback*. The black mamba does not give credence to God Who says, and let me repeat it, 'Dearly Beloved, Avenge not yourselves, but rather give place unto wrath; for it is written, Vengeance is my responsibility, I will repay, saith the Lord.'

"Let me urge you, men and women of PNG, let us not try to avenge ourselves. Let us leave vengeance to God, and let me tell you why. The reason we need to forgive everybody who wrongs us lies in the verses of Matthew 18. I am going to call my friend Roger Kewa Timba up here to read verses 23 to 35 in Pidgin for you. And after he reads that, he and the other Patriarchs are going to sing for you.

Roger stepped up to the pulpit and began to read: "Olsem na kingdom bilong heven em i olsem wanpela king, em i laik stretim dinau wantaim ol wokboi bilong en. / Em i statim wok bilong stretim dinau, na ol i bringim wanpela man long em, em i gat dinau olsem 10 milion dola. / Tasol em i no gat mani inap long bekim dispela. Olsem na king i tok long ol i mas baim dispela man wantaim meri pikinini na olgeta samting bilong en, na kisim dispela mani bilong bekim dinau. / Olsem na dispela wokboi em i lindaun long graun klostu long king na i tokim em, i spik, "Yu sori long mi na wetim mi! Bambai mi bekim dinau long yu." / Na bikpela man bilong dispela wokboi em i sori long em na i lusim em, na i lusim dinau bilong en tu.

"'28 Na dispela wokboi i go ausait na i lukim wanpela wanwok bilong en, em i gat dinau long em olsem 100 dola. Na em i holim pas dispela wanwok na i pasim strong nek bilong en, na i tok, 'Yu bekim dinau bilong yu olgeta!'

"'29 Olsem na wanwok bilong en em i lindaun na beten long em, i spik, "Yu sori long mi na wetim mi! Bambai mi bekim dinau long yu." / Tasol em i no laik. Nogat. Em i go putim em long kalabus, bilong em i ken i stap inap long i bekim dinau.

"'31 Na ol wanwok bilong em ol i lukim dispela pasin na ol i bel nogut tru. Na ol i go kamapim dispela olgeta tok long bikpela bilong ol. / Olsem na bikpela man em i singautim dispela wokboi na i tokim em olsem: "Yu wokboi nogut! Pastaim yu krai long mi, na mi lusim nating dispela olgeta dinau bilong yu. / Mi bin sori long yu. Na watpo yu no sori tu long wanwok bilong yu?' / Na bikpela bilong en em i belhat na i putim em long han bilong ol man bilong givim pen long em, bilong em i ken i stap inap long em i bekim olgeta dinau long em. / Sapos long bel bilong yupela, yupela olgeta i no lusim sin bilong brata bilong yupela, orait Papa bilong mi i stap long heven em tu bai i mekim olsem tasol long yupela.'"

As Roger ended the reading, his wife Anna, and his sisters, Barbara, Beulah, and Leah came and stood with him and sang the Lord's Prayer in English. Tawa and Toropo thrilled to every nuance of melody and harmony as the five Patriarchs sang together. The Presence of the Lord was felt in all hearts, Tawa realized, as she looked at the congregation, not just her own. Especially as they sang, "And forgive us our debts, as we forgive our debtors," Tawa felt her whole heart vibrate with the chords of the instruments, with the voices of the singers, and with the power of God's Holy Spirit. God is bearing witness to His Word, thought Tawa. Oh, God, help me forgive those who have wronged me, just as I want you to forgive me for all my sins. Likewise all the thousands must have been thinking, for a holy hush fell on that huge congregation. Not even a baby cried. No sound was heard except for the incredible harmony of the Patriarchs as they sang in the Spirit.

Steve Harvey came back to the pulpit as the Patriarchs took their seats and began his message.

"There are some of you here this morning who, in your past, suffered unbelievable hurts. There is a parent who took advantage of you, a close relative who did you harm; there is a situation, maybe, for a pastor where there was a church problem; you didn't come out on the right end of the problem; and it damaged you. It hurt you unbelievably. There are church members here this morning who have been hurt by church situations; there are people who have been wronged by other individuals; there are families that have been torn apart by some silly quarrel that was never mended, never resolved; and that was allowed to continue festering and infecting the entire family until not only have family reunions gone the way of the past, but now there is no longer love and communication between family members.

"You say, 'Pastor, how do you know this?' It is because we are human, and hurts and wrongs done to us, and unpleasant situations, and misunderstandings, and unresolved conflicts are all a part of human experience. Not a one of us will go through life without experiencing something that will hurt us or cause us pain or rip at our hearts or torment our soul and our spirit. There will be unpleasant circumstances, unjust circumstances, wrongs done to each one of us, so I know in this congregation today, I'm speaking to people who have experienced those kinds of circumstances in life.

"Some of you have moved on. God's grace was real in your life, and though the pain was deep, and though there may be a scar that every once in a while you can run your finger over and remember the battle, or remember the conflict, or remember the problem, you've allowed God's grace to flow through you and you have moved on. But I would believe in a congregation this size there are others here this morning who are remembering just like the black mamba. And for you the pain and the hurt were too great, and you have never moved on. You have never allowed the wound to heal. You have never come to the point of releasing that past hurt or bitterness to God, and so for you life stopped, at least your spiritual life, and maybe even your emotional health, at that moment of great injustice, that unkind word, that cutting remark, that moment of abuse or terror. You cannot think of anything besides getting revenge.

"Jesus told this parable that Roger just read to you because it deals precisely with this situation about a king who was going through his accounting records one day, and called in all of his regional directors, if I understand the setting correctly, and he was asking them to give an account for what they had done in their particular providence, or regional areas, whatever was in their control. All was going well until he called a certain servant in, one of his rulers, and he began to demand of him what he had done with the tax money he had collected, and he found out this man owed him an incredible sum. The story, as people who write about this particular period say, is that the debt that this man owed was equivalent to ten years of tax collections for the region.

"The king demanded of him where his money was; after all, he had a palace to run; he had things to support, and the man admitted he didn't have the money to pay him. So the king ordered his wife and all of his possessions and the man to be sold into debtor's prison. That servant fell down at his king's feet and began to beg and plead, and he began to say, 'Will you have mercy on me. Give me time and I will pay you all.' This king was merciful, and seeing the distraught and humble condition of this servant, the **Bible** tells us that his heart was moved with compassion, and he said, 'I forgive you all. Go your way.'

"Can you imagine the relief that servant experienced? He sprang up, undoubtedly, with hearty and warm tokens of gratitude towards this man who had been so kind to him. He ran from the palace, and on his way out he sees one coming towards him, one of the men who he has control over. And this guy, in common terms, just owed him a few dollars. He grabbed him by the throat and said, 'Pay me what you owe me.' And this man who had just been forgiven millions and millions of dollars or kina in today's terms, threw this man into prison for a matter of just a few measly dollars or kina.

"Well, the palace was swarming with people who had witnessed this, and those servants ran back to the king and told him exactly what had just happened. In Jesus' parable, it says the king became angry, and he called that servant back to him and said, 'What do you think you are doing? Didn't I forgive you all of this debt? I wiped it out. I gave you a clean slate. I allowed you to start over. It cost me millions and millions of dollars, but I forgave it of you freely. How dare you treat your fellow servant that way over just a few dollars?' In reality, it wouldn't have mattered if that servant had owed him millions as well. After he had just been forgiven, why shouldn't he have forgiven the other man regardless of what he had owed him? But Jesus was making a point. Then the king gave a command, 'Throw him into the prison; deliver him to the tormentors; he will not come out until he has paid everything.' And then I imagine Jesus' hearers were just about as quiet as you are this morning. Jesus drove home His point with forcefulness.

"That's how my Heavenly Father treats every one of you who do not freely, from your hearts, forgive your brother his trespasses. That's pungent truth for the day that you and I live in because we have all seen families split apart over bitterness and unforgiveness. We have seen churches and ministries wrecked by bitterness and unforgiveness. There are businesses that have been wrecked over bitterness and unforgiveness. And there are personal lives where people have allowed their emotional clocks to stop at the point where someone wronged them, and have never moved beyond, much to their own hurt.

Pombo sat in the congregation that morning, thinking of many things. Something Steve Harvey had just said reminded him of some words of Toropo's years ago, after he had sold her to that old man, Kedle. Why was he thinking of this now? Such a great sadness overwhelmed Pombo as he thought of the wrong he had done Toropo.

Next he thought of his multiple wives. Steve had said many animals choose a mate for life, and this is God's plan, just like every white man he knew had done. One man leaving his mother and father, to be joined to one wife, to be one—one in flesh, one in spirit, one in mind, he thought. That is why a man is to leave his father and mother and stick with his wife, and the two of them are to be one flesh. The words kept running over and over in his mind. God what can I do? How can I right things now? I promise not to sell Tawa to an old polygamist, God, or my other two younger daughters, but how can I ask Toropo and Mombo to forgive me?

And what do I do with all the wives I have bought? Oh, God, my heart is breaking with grief in all the wrong I have done them, but what do I do now? Suddenly he realized he was not paying attention. Maybe this young man, Steve Harvey will give me some answers if I will pay attention. He sat up straighter and opened his mind to God and listened with all his mind and strength.

"Can I suggest four great truths this morning about what it does to us when we refuse to forgive freely from our hearts? First of all I believe it demonstrates incomparable ingratitude when you and I cannot forgive others for the wrongs they have done to us. Why do I say ingratitude? Because every single one of us here this morning, regardless of the state of grace you are in, whether you are saved or whether you are unsaved, have been the recipients of grace in your own life. If you are here and are not a believer this morning, you owe gratitude to God and to your fellow believers simply for the fact that God allows His sun to shine on you, and He allows His air to fill your lungs, and He allows you to go on day after day shaking your fist in His face, extending to you the mercy of a new morning, giving you more and more time to get right with Him."

Immediately Pombo's whole heart said, "Amen! I am thankful for air in my lungs, for You allowing me to be alive to come here and hear this, God. I am sorry I was shaking my fist at you all those years!"

"At a very basic level, every one of us should have gratitude towards God and a free spirit towards our fellow men, simply in light of the mercies of God that every one of us experience on a daily basis," continued Steve. "But for those of us this morning who are sitting in this auditorium as believers, who have experienced the incredible mercy of a Heavenly Father, who though we had infinitely sinned against Him, because a sin against an infinite being is an infinite sin, when we had sinned against Him to the extent that we had, He loved us enough to send His Son for us, and though we did not love Him, and though we were unlovely and unworthy, though we merited not but to die, in His grace, and in His mercy, and in His love, He chose to send His Son, that we, through faith in what Jesus has accomplished for us, could experience forgiveness for everything we had done against Him freely given.

"You and I are the recipients of a powerful forgiveness. And when we choose not to forgive others who have done us not an infinite wrong but a finite wrong, those who have just harmed us physically, or maybe those who have harmed us financially or emotionally, not anything in comparison to our great hurt towards our Heavenly Father, if He can so forgive us, then it reveals the height of ingratitude to not also forgive others for what they have done to us.

"Doesn't the knowledge of what God has done for us, propel us to wanting to forgive those who have done us wrong? I believe that Christianity calls us to such a grateful spirit towards God for what He has forgiven us for and saved us from that we can do no less than forgive our fellow men freely. To hold a grudge, to hold on to bitterness, to refuse to forgive, reveals incredible ingratitude to the God who forgave us.

"Secondly, to refuse to forgive no matter the wrong is to place ourselves in the role of debt collectors. And that, my friends, is a role that belongs only to God. 'Vengeance is mine, I will repay,' saith the Lord. But when we hold on to a hurt, to a bitterness, to a grudge, to an unforgiving spirit, when we refuse to release to God the things that have brought us pain, and have caused us hurt and harm, when we want to hold on to them, when we want to nurse them in our memory, when we want to relive the situation, when we want to find an opportunity to strike back at the person who hurt us so deeply, then we are assuming a role that was meant for God and God alone.

"You say, 'Pastor Steve, you don't know the depth of what they did to me.' I don't. 'You don't know how deeply it hurt.' I may not understand that, but I want you to know that there is a God Who does, and He is the One Who is asking you to release those hurts and release those grudges and unforgiveness to Him. He is the one saying to you, "I understand how deeply you were hurt. I am touched by the feelings of your infirmities. But I am still asking you to freely forgive from your heart regardless of what they did. Forgive them.'

"God doesn't call you or me to do His job. He doesn't ask us to hunt down everyone who does us wrong and hurt them or pay them back. One of the basic principles in the Sermon on the Mount is that we are able to bless when we are reviled. We are able to do good when we are persecuted or to return good for evil. That's very basic to being a Christian.

"Sometimes you say as I just said, 'You don't know what a terrible thing they did to me, but other times, if you will be totally honest with yourself, you will find it is just a little thing you are not forgiving. Wives, do you get mad when your husband leaves his socks on the floor instead of putting them in the laundry? I heard a woman say that bothered her so many times, every day over the years that she had to take it to God and ask His forgiveness for this petty anger against her husband. You know how God taught her to forgive her husband after that? He whispered to her to pray for her husband every time she had to pick up his socks. And she did that for a few months, and do you know, women, that man later started putting his socks in the laundry without any reminders from her! She had learned her lesson to pray more for her spouse, so God didn't need to give her those reminders any more.

"What is bugging you? At least half this congregation are not wearing socks, so that wasn't a very good illustration to use I guess. Maybe this one from my grandmother's journal would be better. Back in 1962 when she was at Mele she was doctoring Tanguwe for some illness, and he was very weak. He reported to her that his wife had not brought him water that evening to take his medicine with, and she refused to get him water. My grandmother was thinking of spanking this young wife; can you imagine? But when she found her the next day and asked her why she did not bring him water at his request Wingime answered that Tanguwe had set a rat trap and put it among the food she was preparing, to tease her. So I guess she was angry at getting her hand caught in a rat trap when she was trying to prepare supper in the semi-lit pitpit hut. I myself was shocked to think that a man would try that way to tease his wife. I think that's worse than leaving dirty socks on the floor, but anyway, whatever you have to forgive your spouse for, whether it is little or big, do forgive. Remember, Christ is forgiving you from sin and saving you from hell. You can forgive your husband for leaving his dirty socks for you to pick up, or even for setting a rat trap to give you a scare! I hope you husbands love your wives too much to deliberately hurt them physically or emotionally. And wives, I hope you love your husbands enough to respect them and support them in their work for God!

"Do you want to know something? Forgiveness does not mean ignoring what has happened. Forgiveness does not mean glossing over the event like it never took place. It doesn't mean refusing to deal with issues. It doesn't mean that you just let things go by and never deal with it, if there was a real problem there. No, forgiveness is choosing not to hold someone accountable to you for what they have done to harm you. It's a choice of the will. It's not just based on pure emotions. You want to know something; those can take a long time to get over. It is the choice of the will to release the offender to God. It is the choice of the will to say, 'I will not hold you accountable to myself. I will not spend the rest of my life trying to exact punishment on you. I will not spend time on trying to find ways to get revenge or cause you pain and harm for what you have done to me. I am choosing to release your punishment to God. I am choosing to allow Him to deal with the situation as He wants to deal with it.' The memory, the event, the circumstances may never be wiped out of your mind. Your brain cells have permanently recorded it. You may not ever be able to block the pictures or the horror out of your mind, but I want you to know something. You can choose to release them to God, and choose to do it as often as is necessary to maintain the victory.

"Forgiveness is not a one-time event, I don't believe. There are some offenses that are so horrific, some abuses that are so terrible, some pains in our past that go so deep that from time to time when it comes up, and when the devil may try to bring it to your mind again and try to stir up those feelings of bitterness and grudge holding, that you may have to time and again go back to the feet of the Savior and pour out your heart to Him, and tell Him you are making a fresh commitment right this moment to forgive. 'I'm choosing right now again to release it to you.' That may take years.

"I know a lady who experienced a deep hurt in her life. It took her the better part of ten years before the memory had so faded that it wasn't a problem. I can remember her calling out in prayer over and over again for God to give her new grace, and new strength, and a new ability to choose forgiveness, for a while on a daily basis. God didn't call us to be debt collectors. He called us to leave the choices of vengeance and punishment to Him. He called for us to release the offender and to be models of the grace and forgiveness that we have received.

"Do you want to know something else? Be careful with your motive on this one, but God can do a much better job of holding the offender to account than you can. God can deal with the situation much more fairly than you would deal with it. His justice is more pure than ours is. His eyes see a little more clearly than ours do. His Spirit searches not just what happened externally but what the motive of the heart was, and therefore, He knows how to judge perfect judgment. Release it to God.

"Number three: When we choose unforgiveness, bitterness, and grudge holding, we are not harming the other person. We are causing ourselves to be tormented. Jesus said, 'Deliver this man to the tormentors.' I have seen people live with a grudge for decades, an unforgiving spirit, and the person they have held all this malice towards, didn't suffer one iota. But their health suffered the ill effects, their mind was in constant turmoil, they were at the altar all the time struggling, wondering why they couldn't get victory, and wondering why they weren't able to move on. It was their children who were infected with that same bitter and unforgiving spirit, and it passed on for a couple of generations, leaving their children the legacy and their grandchildren a debt to try to deal with because they wouldn't choose forgiveness, and all the while the offending party just went on, and it didn't affect the offending person or party a bit.

"Proverbs says that a critical spirit, an unforgiving spirit, eventually shows up in the physical body as well. It shows up in sleepless nights, panic attacks, nightmares, in spiritual instability and sometimes literally in the bones, according to the Proverbs. When you choose not to forgive, you choose to hold on to bitterness and unforgiveness. You are harming no one but yourself.

"Steve and Annie Chapman sing a song that I've listened to over and over again, about a wrong that was done. Steve sings it as a solo. And he decides that he will throw the offender into a prison cell. And it says that he did, and he locked him up and kept him under guard and key. But then he tells about one day when the spirit began to deal with him, and he decided that he would forgive and set the offender free, and so he visits the cell block, and he turns the key in the lock and opens the door to allow this prisoner that he has held there for years to go free, only to have himself locked out. When we choose unforgiveness we deliver ourselves to the tormentors, and we pay the price, not the offending party.

"Number Four: Perhaps most serious of all: Jesus said if you are going to call yourself a Christian, or number yourself as one of the believers, and yet harbor unforgiveness in your heart, don't bother. The truth is unmistakable. When we refuse to forgive at this level, we are not forgiven at this level. That's not me preaching that. That's verse 35: 'So likewise (or in this same way) shall my Heavenly Father do unto you, if ye from your hearts forgive not everyone his brother their trespasses.' If you want mercy, you have to be merciful. If you want forgiveness, you have to grant forgiveness. If you want God's pardon, you have to be one that freely pardons all and any who trespass against you. That's serious truth, friends. Because what it tells me is that when we deliberately choose unforgiveness, when we refuse to resolve unresolved issues, when we allow a grudge to go on and develop and to harm, when we sit in our pews Sunday after Sunday knowing that there is an unforgiving spirit, knowing that we are not willing to release someone who has done us wrong, I believe that God is teaching that we are not experiencing forgiveness from God in our own lives. That's serious truth, friends. That's serious truth.

"I said that as a pastor I would repeat these series year after year. I haven't done it yet. But I believe the truth is so essential because this is as close to where we live as anything is. This is where the rubber meets the road. Great theology is important but we have to live it out, and in this area of unforgiveness, bitterness and grudge holding, there are so many people in our church pews trapped right there.

"You know, I'm not going to pretend for a minute, that forgiveness is necessarily easy, but I am going to tell you this. There is incredible grace for the singer who sings with the Patriarchs, 'Oh to be like Thee' and 'The Lord's Prayer,' for the believer who says, 'I want a heart like Christ'; who says, "I want the mind of Christ to be in me." For the believer who says, 'I want all of my life to be a shining testimony to everyone around me for the grace that I have received, the love that has been shed abroad in my heart.' I want you to know something, if you want to purpose that in your heart that you want to be that kind of believer, there is all the grace in heaven to enable you to release offenses and offenders.

"Parents, God's forgiveness includes forgiving our children when they sin. It includes forgiving our daughters. It even includes forgiving them for losing their virginity before marriage. I hope you Papua New Guinea men are not like the Muslim men who kill their daughters and call it 'honor killing.' There is no such thing as an honor killing in God's eyes, my friends. The Muslim man murders his daughter supposedly to protect his honor. No way, men! That is a terribly distorted view of honor! Becoming a murderer is what destroys this man's honor, not his daughter. We cannot usurp the place of God in even our daughters' lives, men. God forbid that they should be defiled before marriage, but if they do, that sin is between them and their God, between them and their future husband, between them and their own conscience. Even in this you must let God avenge the wrong. You cannot, you dare not, take their eternal soul into your hands and snuff out their lives or shun them into suicide. Oh, my brothers, hear me, this morning, if you do, you will go to God with blood on your hands. And who did He say can stand before Him—only those who have clean hands and a pure heart.

"God never says anywhere in His Word that a man's sin is any different than a woman's sin. For adultery, in the Old Testament, God said both the man and woman had to be brought before the church leaders and stoned to death. In the New Testament dispensation Christ said to the woman taken in adultery, 'Neither do I condemn thee, go and sin no more!' He wants us to forgive likewise. What we do, men AND women, is what defiles our hearts and destroys our honor. Our teenagers do not value their virginity enough some times, and they throw it away without thinking first. But whether they are boys or girls, they are destroying their own honor; they are sinning against God, and they need to seek God's forgiveness. God has a thousand ways to wreak His vengeance. He will repay the sinner. Let us hold our children close in family altars. Let us pray over them and with them. Let us beg them to choose purity and commit themselves to it with all of their sober minds. Let us beg them to promise themselves, us, and God to walk in the paths of righteousness, and not the broad road to hell.

"Satan is an adversary going about seeking whom he may devour, and he is determined to get our young people, and to ruin and wreck their lives while they are young. If he trips them up, don't take your anger out on them, my friends! Take them before the altar of God, in His house, prostrate yourselves before God, and beg His forgiveness with them, that they do not carry this guilt into eternity, that they may find forgiveness before they die."

Steve paused and turned toward his family, on the right side of the platform.

"Raequelle, come up here on the platform," he said.

Steve and Kelly Harvey with their children, Keenan, Cade and Raequelle

Raequelle made her way through the thronging children to the steps of the platform and climbed them. She walked straight to her father, and he laid his right arm around her shoulder.

"This is my firstborn. When Raequelle was born and I held her, my first child, in my arms, all sorts of love names for her came into my mind. I called her Sunshine! I called her Sweet Pea, and I even called her a nonsense name, Buqudoop. As far as I know, that last one doesn't mean anything.

"Do you know, my PNG brothers and sisters in Christ, that's what the Heavenly Father does for us? He gives us a love name. Isa 62:2 says, 'Thou shalt be called by a new name which the Lord Himself shall name.' And Revelations 2:17 says, '...and I will give him a white stone, and in the stone a new name written which no man knoweth saving he that receiveth it.' God has a love name just for you which He is going to give you on a gemstone some day, and it is going to be a secret between you and Him. Isn't it exciting to serve a God like this, Beloved? Isn't it exciting to worship such a personal God?

"Some of you knew my grandfather, Robert Harvey. He was a man who gave nicknames or love-names to his wife and children. He called my dad, Brian, who was his youngest son, Drut. He called my Aunt Linda who is sitting here today, Slap-hap-a-bad-babe, and when she got older he shortened it to Slaphapabettyb, or once in a while, just Bettyb. My Uncle Jerry whom God promoted to Glory in July of last year, Grandpa called Coocoo-bug-DD, or just DD. He called my grandmother Flairts. Often, Aunt Linda tells me, when he got home from work as a young man, he would come in and tickle Grandma and call her Flairts and kiss her, and then he would go to each of his children, hopping sideways toward them, so full of energy, excitement and love, and tickle them and kiss them and call them his love name for them.

"My grandfather and grandmother came to Piamble in 1960. Grandpa had a broken leg and had to be carried cast and all, on the shoulders of three men at a time, all the way from Kauapena to Piamble. In 1971 they were living here at Pabrabuk and trying to buy the coffee plantation from Jim Thorp, and this mission station. They did not have the needed funds, so they went on to Baiyer River and bought a plot of ground there, and began a ministry there.

"Grandpa received criticism from people in America for bringing his daughter here to a third world country. Nobody said he shouldn't bring his sons, but that's the way we feel about our daughters in America. We want to protect them from anything hard, anything dangerous. We consider them our great treasures. Grandpa Harvey felt God was calling him and his whole family to come to an unknown tribe and an unknown land, so he did that for God. He committed his children to God, and he brought them here in obedience to God. And God rewarded them. I am sure some of those years may not have been easy for them and for Aunt Linda, but I know she says today, and I heard it read at her father's funeral, that one of the greatest things her Daddy ever did for her was to bring her to New Guinea, where she learned three languages, and learned that she loved to teach and loved to write. She wrote her first two novellas in the ImboUngu language while she was still a teenager. God has wonderful ways of rewarding us for doing right, just like He has ways unknown to us to wreak vengeance on those who do wrong and those who will not forgive.

"Dr. Dobson had a speaker once who said that a man's daughters go wrong if they see their father going wrong. My grandfather was an honorable man, a pure man, who lived a pure life, and his daughter never got into any trouble as a teenager when she lived here. You men cannot expect to live lecherous, unbridled lives with many wives, and then expect your daughters to control their emotions. The sins of the fathers will be visited on the children, and that is how you will lose your honor; by your own sinful example.

"Men, if you want your sons and daughters to be godly and live pure lives, you must set the example. Dr. Dobson and one of his speakers recommend taking your daughters out on a special date, and having a talk with them about the great gifts God has given them, and how they can use those gifts for Him. If you honor your daughter in this way, it will make an impact on her, and she will be more likely to remember and to pay attention.

"Realize, though, my brethren, that no one can guarantee that a daughter or son raised right, by right-living parents, will make all the right choices in life. You are giving them more chance to do right, but you must realize, each child you bring into the world is a free moral agent. You have eighteen years to train them to choose God's path, and to influence them in that direction. During those years you need to help them see that the **Bible** is true; the wages of sin are death, and everything which God prohibited is harmful, and He only made these rules for our happiness and our good. If you are not convinced of that yourself, you will not be able to convince your children.

"I hear of birthday bashes for sons with unlimited alcohol, even for the minors, and by that I mean children under eighteen years of age. Oh my people, this is so sad. Let us train up our children aright. Giving our children alcohol makes them lose more of those inbuilt principles unawares, because they may not even know what they are doing when they are inebriated. I heard a Native American woman say in a testimony, 'When you are drunk you don't know, and it's just a warm body to turn to,' and that's how we hear the Muslims got Dutch New Guinea men to go in to prostitutes infected with AIDS. Stay away from all alcohol and illegal drugs, men and women, and teach your children to do likewise. My Dad and my Uncle George and Aunt Linda have spent years in social work in America. Sometimes we think drugs and alcohol are the curse of our country. Never, never give them to minors. It is against the law in the USA!

"Before I return to our main topic and bring this to a close I promised to give you an example, better than the one with which I began this sermon. I will choose the bald eagle, because this is the symbol and logo for my country, the United States of America. Perhaps the bald eagle was chosen at that continental congress in 1782 to represent America because of its beauty, power, grace and spirit. However here is another good reason. The bald eagle is a bird that chooses a mate for life. One famous artist has portrayed how every year, the eagle clasps claws with its mate and starts a wild cartwheel of a dance and free fall to the earth. Imagine the risk! Imagine the thrill! Go out and take a risk for God with your mate. Clasp the same spouse by the hand, year after year, and go out and attempt great things for God! Men, don't put all your energies into raising another brideprice and buying another bride. Malachi 2:15 says, 'Take heed to your spirit, and let none deal treacherously with the wife of his youth.'

"Back to forgiveness, let us endeavor to forgive those who have wronged us. Our parents, our children, our brothers, our sisters, our spouses, our friends or our enemies, we must forgive them all! Let us ask God to help us forgive, and keep on asking every time we remember the wrong.

"That situation of which I have preached this morning has churned in your mind and heart. That person's face that just keeps coming before you, that old memory that any time you hear a message on this sort just rises to the surface it's right there, something in your life that you've never moved beyond, even if it was a wrong done to your tribe in the past, and your father and grandfather passed it on to you, and said 'We must be avenged.' Oh, no, my friends, we must let it go. We must give it to God.

"Maybe God has tenderly dealt with you this morning about a grudge, or an unforgiving spirit, something that you have never released, and His spirit is saying to you, 'I want you to release that to Me. I want you to choose willfully this morning to let it go, and let me begin the process of healing in your life. I'm not going to give an altar call, because there is no room with all this crowd, but in the silence of these next few moments I want you to examine your hearts, and if there is an issue you need to release to God and you really mean to do it by His grace, I want you to simply lift up a hand and open a palm to God, symbolically give it to Him. If you really mean to forgive, lift your hand, palm up. Does anyone have anything they need to release to God this morning? Hands are going up across the congregation. You are choosing to release it to the Lord. You are choosing to release the accountability of what was done to you to Him. You are freely saying to Him, "I yield to you the right to worry about the situation. I'm giving this person, this memory, this event to you, whether it occurred in my lifetime, my father's or my grandfather's. I give it all to you, God. Let us pray."

As Steve knelt to pray he heard the sound of a mighty volume of voices rising to God in prayer. It swelled and swelled till he felt wafted to the heavens on the tide of that prayer. "Thank You, God! Thank You, God!" he sobbed.

Pabrabuk Camp Meeting
Photo by Randy & Sharrona Dimmett

Maiye

Alu é Pulumanu with their daughter, Dianne's, 3 sons.
Dianne died in March, 2000, seeing angels who came for her.
Dean, Daryl & Darin

Roger & Tedla

John Kewa & Tedla's family

Timba's Family

Polly Wini & Julianne Magdalene Alu & children.

Timba & Litinmuy & last son, Daryl (H.S. teacher)

Polly & Julianne are teachers.

Jacob
(Walea)
@
Katiloma
1967

Jacob and son, Isaiah

Shallome
Georgette

Christine, Norah Sh

March 17, 1989

"Osi" Mark Tua

Jacob @ the botanical gardens, POM 1979

For the last eleven y. Jacob has been helping to Christine's three nephew gelos (24), Joel (10th gr), s teacher (18). Their father pino + forced to leave f 1989. Angelos + Joel are gifted in music. They pl trombone + sax + every instrument they see. An is doing computer engine @ Queensland Uni. the o a music scholarship @ U.F

Jacob in Wyoming

May 11, 2000

Jacob Mambi
with N.B.C.

Jacob, deer-hunting with the Kelleys in PA. National Broadcasting Commission
Radio   Southern   Highlands

Linda Pauline N

& Grandpa "Nic" wil
the wild horse he caug
and gentled, named
"Snip."

"My fingers feel like bananas."
(when cold)

Chapter Eleven

"I promised my friend, Toropo, and her sister, Tawa, and a few others that I would share with them a poem I had written about thirty years ago at Katiloma, because I loved bougainvillea like Mrs. Susie Lorimer who planted it with this yari tree right outside the church here. This is a poem in free verse. It has no rhyme and no meter:

Two Became One

Long ago in antediluvian Eden
God planted a great Oak tree
At the point of the V
Twixt the River Tigris and the River Euphrates.
The Oak tree sent his roots
Deep down in the soil
To gather sweet moisture and food.
He sent his branches
Up, up above
To nod and wave at his Creator.
And God pitied the Oak's loneliness
And transplanted a Bougainvillea sweet
At the base of the Oak,
At the great Oak's feet.
She sent her roots down among his.
They intertwined.
They found moisture sweet.
She put forth tentative tendrils
Along his tall strong body.
He held onto each one.
Encouraged, she wrapped herself
Around the very heart of him.
She drew strength from him.

He drew tenderness from her
Which seemed to enlarge him, and make him even stronger.
Nourished, cherished, strengthened, secure,
Her tendrils covered him,
And reached to his very top
Where she too, waved to her Creator
And sent out purple, blooming bracts
To cover her every leaf
In ultimate self-actualization.
The Oak breathed in her scent
And grew stronger to support her,
Sent roots deeper to sustain her,
Grew taller to elevate her,
Grew broader, reached farther to enhance her
Until with the very tip of his branches
And her tendrils,
Hand in hand,
Or bract in leaf,
They beckoned to their God.
And God bent low His ear.
Beneath Him He heard the birds and animals,
Relaxing in the shade of the glorious couple
Saying, "There never was such a pair!"
Above Him He heard the angels
Exclaiming at this picture of pristine perfection
A Perfection in and of Duality
We've never seen an Oak so noble, so proud,
Nor a Bougainvillea so beautiful,
So bountiful, so beneficent!
And now we understand
Why God planned for two to become one.
The pair heard not the animals nor the angels
For they were communing with their Creator.
"Thank You, God, for life and breath,
For your love, our Creator,
And for giving us each other."
And then the Voice of God boomed forth

In terrible, awful splendor,
"What I have joined together
Let no man put asunder!"

"I saw such beauty about seven years ago when I was in the Dominican Republic. Bougainvillea hung from the great trees in a park there, and I gazed in awe, and thought about the picture of marriage I had drawn with words many many years earlier.

"I believe God's plan is one man and one woman with a heart that He has united into one, to such an extent that they could not be torn apart without it being such a rent, such a wound, that they would die of it, but for God. Long ago I caught a glimpse of such a marriage when I read the words of Dietrich Bonhoeffer who gave his life for God under Hitler in Germany. I was here in PNG when I read those words, and I do not have them to hand, now, and cannot quote them, but I believe they are what inspired this poem.

"An oak can stand alone and often does. And I love a glorious oak. A bougainvillea can stand alone. The scarlet bougainvillea the Lytles planted at Katiloma did, and was beautiful. But it never grew as tall as that I planted by our two-story house nearby. And neither of them was ever as tall or as well-rounded as those I saw in the Dominican Republic, draped over the trees on every side, or as this one you see outside this sanctuary.

"The heart of the oak continues to grow and strengthen into more bountiful wood as it supports the bougainvillea, and they are a sight worth seeing. As the husband nourishes and cherishes the wife, he adds character and spiritual stature. As the wife nourishes and cherishes the husband and puts him ahead of herself she grows more beautiful and becomes more secure, better rounded, and better able to serve her God.

"Christ chose this picture to represent the church. Not my picture of the tree and flower but the picture of marriage. You have all heard that and read it many times in different passages such as Romans 7:4 …that ye should be married to…him who is raised from the dead. Second Corinthians 11:2, I have espoused you to one husband. And the most well known, Ephesians 5:25, Husbands love your wives; even as Christ also loved the church, and gave himself for it.

"Let's take a look at marriage gone wrong. Let's take a look at Papua New Guinea right now. Man buys a wife here, and if women are for sale, men can buy as many as they can afford. The older men have longer to aquire wealth, so they can keep buying young girls. Boys have no wealth accumulated, so the picture looks very bleak for young men. Their hormones are raging, and they go out and rape and plunder. News has stated that Port Moresby is the most unsafe capitol in the world because of the rape of injured girls in accidents, and gangs going out to find who they will, and gang-raping girls stolen from vehicles at roadblocks.

"HIV/AIDS is skyrocketing until it has been predicted that the country will cause its own genocide with this infection. Still the old stigma of a deflowered female makes women the scum of the earth, in spite of the fact that they had no protection from these rampaging males. When my husband heard of a man giving his niece up at a roadblock, for a gang to rape, he said, 'That's the difference in a PNG man and an American man. An American man would fight to the death before he would give up a girl to such a fate.' And can men in PNG ever feel differently as long as they can buy and sell their daughters and their wives? And can the country of Papua New Guinea, or Africa, for that matter, ever become great without changing their attitude toward women, without cherishing their daughters, without learning to build self-esteem in the mothers of their sons?

"Neela Sukthanker did a study of girls in the education system in Papua New Guinea here, and published the results in an article titled 'Math Education in PNG: A Challenge.' She said the education of a girl does not necessarily increase her brideprice, whereas if the boys are educated they can contribute to their own brideprice more effectively. So you see, by this, dear friends, that brideprice is still blocking the education of your daughters for some of our tribes and provinces here in our land.

"A Huli woman I read about in the *Cultural Survival Quarterly* said, 'In the past many Huli women asserted, women were the valuables for whom one gave bridewealth; now, cash is the valued item for which one gives women.' This woman had been raped while her husband had gone to work in a gold mine. She told her brothers, and they didn't do anything, saying her husband had paid brideprice and it was his responsibility 'to

182

take the culprit to court and demand compensation.' This woman became so angry she considered committing suicide, but decided instead to engage in extra marital sex. I cannot follow her thinking about how that was getting even. But earlier, people needed to stop the rapist by putting him in jail. No compensation can pay for the pain and humiliation of rape. And if something is given, it needs to be given to the victim, and not her husband!

"You women all know that no man will come near a haemorrhaging woman. I told in my first book how a woman was not even allowed by PNG men to be taken to the hospital in a truck because she was 'unclean.' It was a woman just like this who touched Jesus in Luke 8, when Jesus asked, 'Who touched me?' He knew, of course, because He knew all things, but He wanted all the crowds to know, too. And He wanted you and me to be comforted by the story two thousand years later. He wanted women everywhere to know that He healed a bleeding woman when she touched Him. Even His disciples were amazed at His question in that crowd of people, because when He said, 'Who touched me?' they answered Him, 'Rabbi! The crowds are hemming you in and jostling you!' *CJB* 8:45 46: But Yeshua said, 'Someone did touch me because I felt power go out of me.' 47: Seeing she could not escape notice, the woman, quaking with fear, threw herself down before him and confessed in front of everyone why she had touched him and how she had been instantly healed. 48 He said to her, 'My daughter, your trust has saved you; go in peace.' *CJB*

"Some of you women have felt even you could be contaminated by another woman's blood.

"I remember when I was pregnant for my firstborn I helped a friend who was delivering her baby. I recall the women scolding me when I caught the baby whose mother was kneeling to give birth, because I did not want it to be hurt by falling on the floor. They said, 'Now your husband will sicken and die, because you have contaminated yourself with another woman's blood.' My husband, George Kelley, did not die. He has carried a woman in childbirth for a long ways; he carried her in his arms, and got her blood on him. She was giving birth to twins, and he carried her to the mission truck because he could not drive the truck back into the bush where she was dying. He saved her life.

He carried more than one such woman. He is still alive and well, and a hard worker, and a good provider for me, and our children and grandchildren. Such acts of courage in many different situations and different cultures have doubtless only made him stronger, like the Oak I just told you about in my little '*tok bokis.*' You people are so good at making up riddles, metaphors, analogies yourselves, that I know you can understand mine.

"Reach out to the women around you, my dear sisters in Christ. Don't let a woman suffer in childbirth alone, without someone even to wipe away her perspiration with a cold, wet cloth, or warm one, whichever she wants. And don't let her baby fall and suffer head injuries like I have seen on newborns in my Mom's clinic. Don't be afraid of the contamination of another woman's blood as you were taught traditionally. You do need to use protection such as latex gloves to keep you from the contamination of HIV/AIDS now, but we still need to reach out to such people too. Jesus did.

"Warn your daughters that girls who get pregnant before they are sixteen years old are four times as likely to die from pregnancy-related causes as girls over twenty. Explain this to your menfolk so they won't sell their daughters so young. Treasure the lives of your daughters just as you do your sons, my dears. Why should you love them less because they are female when you yourself are female? Don't be a traitor to your own gender! And please don't say, I had to suffer so they must suffer too. That is jealousy, dears! Not wanting your daughters to have things better than you had it shows the traits of the carnal heart. You want God to cleanse you and make you whole and free and truthful and loving to the core of your being!

"Girls are no more to blame for a premarital pregnancy than boys are," Linda went on to the group of girls and women who had asked her to have a women's meeting with them in the church. "In fact your PNG traditional belief is that man makes the child totally. Women provide only the sac to grow it in. But we know enough now to realize that men provide the Y chromosome and women the X chromosome, and a child cannot grow in the womb unless both are provided. Both the boy and the girl need to accept responsibility for that child. If possible they should marry. If that is not possible the boy or father should pay child support, and the mother should be a mother to the child.

"If her parents are willing to help her care for the child until she finishes her education or until she turns eighteen, that is well and good. However, unless she finds someone who wants to adopt that child, she needs to own up to the world that she sinned, that she is taking responsibility for her act, and she will only marry a man who will accept her and her child."

Someone gasped.

"Yes, it could mean she remains single. That may be the price she has to pay for her wrong choice. But educated women can make it as mothers in this modern world. It is not what is best. God means for every child to have both a mother and a father in the home.

"God can give you the strength and moral character to remain pure until marriage, young people. Wait for marriage to have children!

"'This HIV/ AIDS epidemic will wipe out the population of the small country of Papua New Guinea by the year 2020,' Paul Harvey News said in 2008, 'if it continues to increase at the present rate.'

"Muslims perform FGM which stands for Female Genital Mutilation, on little girls to keep them pure until marriage. Six thousand little girls are cut every day in 28 countries of Africa. Many die. You can read all about it in Waris Dirie's book **Desert Flower** and in Ayaan Hirsi Ali's book, **Infidel**. But God can give you enkrateia εγκρατεια inner strength, to keep yourselves pure, both girls and boys. FGM isn't necessary for purity any more than brideprice is necessary 'to keep the marriage tight' as some PNGns say. Christians keep their word. They commit themselves to marriage between one man and one woman 'until death does them part' and they keep that commitment. They believe in the Truth. They hold to Truth with their whole inner being as well as on the outside. They believe in Christ, Who said, 'I am the Way, the Truth and the Life.' Jesus is the Truth. Real Christians should also be Truth or Truthettes just as they are followers of Christ—Christians.

"God puts in every girl's heart the mother instinct. It's the parents' job to raise those girls to be pure. Perhaps our greatest job as parents is to 'touch the palate of the child with righteousness and truth,' to create such a hunger for God in them that they won't depart from this true way when they grow up and go out from their parents' home, Proverbs 22:6.

"Papua New Guinea with its boarding schools takes children away from their parents sooner than that happens in the USA. This is another cause of the spread of HIV/AIDS. It breaks down the authority of the home, the learning of parents' values, and it puts children too much on their own, before their parents' values have become their own, and before they have the self-control and maturation they need to withstand the temptations.

"When I was nineteen years old and in Bible School at Adirondack Bible College in New York State, a sixteen-year-old girl said to me, 'I want a baby of my own so badly I am willing to be a bad girl to get one.' I couldn't believe my ears. I thought she could not mean it. I thought she was just saying that to shock me. I graduated and returned to PNG to do Bible translation and did not hear from her until five years later when I was on furlough again in the USA. In those five years this girl had gone out and done what she said she wanted to do. I was married to George Kelley and had one son. She had a son to an African American man who was legally married to an African American woman. Over the next several years she had five children to this man, between beatings from his legal wife!

"Today all three of her sons are in jail or in prison for life. One son has overdosed on drugs and been in a coma for the last year. He is like a vegetable. He has killed his brain, so to speak, on drugs. Oh, the heartbreak of sin! Young women, you need to commit yourselves to God and determine never to depart from His Way of Truth and Righteousness. Derek means Way in Hebrew. Jesus said, 'I am the Derek, the Way, the Truth and the Life! No man comes to the Father except by Me.' Any 'way' that claims to get to the Father without going through Jesus Christ is not THE WAY and not Truth and not Life.

"Jesus loves you so much, young people. He forgives. I wish I had time to read you pages 165-173 of *God So Loved the World*, by Elizabeth Goudge. She is one of my favorite authors.

"Turn in your Bibles to John 8:3. Elizabeth Goudge pictures Jesus telling this parable of the Good Shepherd and the lost sheep. Imagine Him leaving 99 sheep in the fold and going out in the dark and the weather to search for that one lost sheep.

(Luke 15) And when He finds it, He lays it over His shoulders! Remember, it's a sheep! Not a lamb! He carries it back to the fold, and by the way, ladies, it was doubtless a ewe, a female sheep. (Isn't it interesting that in the animal world, the females are more wanted than males, usually, since they produce young. Here in PNG and in Africa the men think women are almost sub-human, instead of thinking females are special! America probably gives women more freedom to be themselves and respect for their individuality than any other country. Could that be the reason God let them be a superpower for a while?) But the Good Shepherd is so happy when he gets her back to the fold that He calls in His friends and neighbors, or the angels in heaven and says in verse six, 'Rejoice with me! Let's celebrate! I have found my sheep which was lost.'

"Then Elizabeth Goudge pictures Jesus being interrupted by the scribes and Pharisees, the religious leaders bringing in that woman 'taken in adultery' in John 8.

"You see, they only brought the woman, even though she was 'caught...in the very act' (v. 4), so there had been a man there too. They were breaking their own rules, because in two different books of the Pentateuch God commanded that both the man and the woman be brought before the priests.

"The Muslims nowadays take it even farther. In November last year they stoned a thirteen-year-old Somalian girl named Aisha Ibrahim Duhulow, who had been gang-raped by three men. Somalia isn't far from Ethiopia and Eritrea, where our dear Agape comes from. But this thirteen-year-old girl told her dad. He told the imam or religious leader and fifty men stoned her to death. Three days later American people voted in Barack Hussein Obama as the 44th president of the United States of America even though he spoke of his Muslim faith, and said he had burned our flag, and he would change the flag and change our national anthem. The majority of my countrymen do not seem to care about the countries already torn apart by Islam. We give Muslims free reign to worship their own way in America, just like we do other religions. We vote in a man who says he is going to solve economic problems and spread the wealth around. He says openly, braggingly that he is all about change. America has already seen some of the sad changes he has made.

187

"Two Taliban assassins shot and killed Malalai Kakar as she left for work in Afghanistan's largest southern city on the 28th of September, last year. She was a policewoman herself, and she led Kandahar city's department of crimes against women. She was forty-one years old, and her son who was on the motor cycle with her when she was killed was gravely wounded also. Though President Hamid Karzai condemned the targeting of Malalai Kakar, she was already dead, and the Taliban had shown women they better not stand up for other women, no matter how bad the crimes against them. That is not justice, ladies!

"In Iran a woman cut up her husband for raping their daughter, and she was hung by the neck until she was dead, in a public hanging just twenty-three days after we elected Obama for our president.

Let me read you a letter written in America by a man named David Barton, founder and director of WallBuilders, if I understand correctly, and sent to me by Elizabeth Rivard on the day the Muslims met on Capitol Hill for the first Muslim prayer meeting ever, there where presidents had been inaugurated.

Calling Muslims to the Capitol?

As nations such as Canada, Great Britain, the Netherlands (and many others in Europe) have become more secular, they have demonstrated a willingness to embrace virtually anything — anything *except* their traditional Christian foundations. In fact, they now regularly repudiate those foundations, promoting abortion, legalizing homosexual marriage, and changing their traditional  legal codes. And accepting the falsehood that all beliefs are equal and that truth is relative, they have even been willing to incorporate Islamic Sharia law into their legal codes in order to protect the special practices of some Muslims living among them. This has energized many Muslims in those countries and they are displaying a new boldness that is vocal, visible, and demonstrably assertive.

Each year, nearly 5,000 Muslim "honor killings" occur across the world (a practice whereby parents kill children who alleg-

 edly bring "dishonor" on Islam by dating non-Muslims, wearing western garb, converting to another religion, etc.). Dozens of those murders are committed in Europe, but in many of these formerly Christian nations, those who commit the "honor killings" (i.e., the murder of their own children) often go unpunished since the death of their child was "required" by Islamic law (now included in the legal law of the land). Additionally, many public personalities across Europe who criticized Islam have been murdered, causing Parliaments in the Netherlands and other European countries to forbid criticism of Islam in an effort to prevent further murders. These nations, having given up precious ground, are now having difficulty retaking it.

Historically, on this continent Christian America adopted an open free-market approach to all religions from the beginning. American Christians then (and now) were not fearful of other religions. They were confident that Christianity would prevail on its own merits and they therefore followed the Biblical precedent set forth in both the Old and New Testaments of simply presenting God's word in a straightforward manner, expecting that the Holy Spirit will confirm His word in the hearts of hearers. Christians believe that on a level playing field, Christianity will always prevail through the voluntary choice of the people.

As a result, Christian America welcomed all religions, with Muslims arriving here by 1619, Jews establishing their first synagogue in 1654, and Buddhists, Hindus, and others also being present from the early days. Significantly, only America extended (and continues to extend) a free-market religious tolerance to others while still preserving the core societal values of our Christian heritage. But the culture has begun to shift. The level playing field is being eroded. As in Europe, Christianity is being knocked down and Islam elevated.

For example, a federal court of appeals ruled that public schools in nine western states can <u>require</u> a three week

indoctrination to the Islamic faith in which all junior high students must pretend they are Muslims and offer prayers to Allah (students are further encouraged to take Islamic names, call each other by those names, wear Islamic garb, participate in Jihad games, and read the Koran during those three weeks). Yet that very court also ruled that it was unconstitutional for those same students to voluntarily mention "under God" in the Pledge of Allegiance. Likewise, a federal court on the east coast ruled that public schools may display Islamic holiday symbols but not Christian ones. And the University of Michigan recently spent $25,000 of taxpayer money to install foot-washing facilities to accommodate the religious practices of Muslim students but made no similar expenditure on behalf of students from any other religion.

As a result of such actions, many Muslims are exercising a new boldness in America. In fact, Muslim "honor killings" have now arrived in the United States (most recently in Texas); and just a few weeks ago, direct action was taken to prevent the honor-killing of a 17-year old Muslim girl in Ohio who converted to Christianity and, in fear of her life, fled from her parents to Florida.

American Muslims have also enjoyed the direct support of President Obama. In April, he traveled to Egypt where he told the Muslim world that America no longer considers itself a Christian nation. He later traveled to Turkey and announced that America was one of the largest Muslim nations in the world (despite the fact that 78% of Americans claim to be Christians but only 1% claim to be Muslims). Then in May, President Obama refused to invite Christian and Jewish leaders to the White House to participate in the National Day of Prayer (as former presidents have done), but in September, he did invite Muslim leaders to the White House for a special Muslim Ramadan celebration to commemorate Allah delivering the Koran to his prophet Mohammed.

Heartened by this new encouragement, Muslim leaders have called 50,000 observant Muslims to come to the Capitol this Friday, September 25, for a day of Jummah (Friday congregational prayer). The sponsors promise that from 4AM to 7PM, "the Athan [the call given five times each day for Muslims to participate in mandatory prayer] will be chanted on Capitol Hill, echoing off of the Lincoln Memorial, the Washington Monument and other

great edifices that surround Capitol Hill." The goal of this event is that "the peace, beauty and solidarity of Islam will shine through America's capitol." In fact, their website for this unprecedented event proudly and unabashedly declares, "Our Time Has Come!"

As Bible-believing people, let's also make this Friday a day of prayer – and please encourage others to participate with you. We know that our contest is with spiritual forces (Ephesians 6:12), and we firmly believe that He Who is within us is greater than any other god or force (1 John 4:4), so I encourage you to fill America with prayer to the True God this coming Friday.

God Bless!

David Barton of WallBuilders
WallBuilders Info: info@wallbuilders.com 1-800-873-2845.

"Oh, my dear girls and ladies, it is so important for us, and for our men too, to get our eyes on Jesus! Let's take our eyes off money. Let's stop giving precedence to polygamy, male supremacy, being 'lords of the earth' and let's give precedence to Jesus!

"As Miss Goudge goes on to picture the Bible story, even though these men reminded Jesus, 'Moses said she should be stoned, but what do You say?' hoping to trick Him, to trap Him. Even though they had flaunted the words, '…what do YOU say?' He didn't answer a word at first. He just stooped down and wrote on the ground.

"They got upset. He was acting like He didn't even hear them! (verse 6) So they repeat, 'What do You say?' and they keep on asking Him again and again until He raises up and says, 'Let the one of you without sin be the first to throw the stone at her!' Miss Goudge thinks maybe Jesus was so hurt by the evil in their eyes and the knowledge that they lusted to kill her as much as they desired to trip Him up and cause His downfall that He stooped to hide His face from them. Or she wonders if He was remembering Jeremiah 17:13 which says, 'O Lord, the hope of Israel, all that forsake Thee shall be ashamed, and they that depart from Me shall be written in the earth, because they have forsaken the Lord, the fountain of living waters!'

"If He did write their names in the earth, He must have begun with the oldest, for that is the order in which they filed out, v. 9. And did He perhaps write after their names some of their sins? I have heard my mother say he wrote down the names of women with whom they had committed adultery. At least no one pretended. No one said, 'I haven't sinned.'

"Miss Goudge says the first one to leave was a very old, very brave man, a Pharisee who by his act of leaving was crying aloud, 'Lord, have mercy on me, a sinner.' After they had all silently admitted their sin and gone out praying for forgiveness, realizing this Man was God and knew all, Jesus turned to the woman they had wanted to kill and said, '*Ambo*, where are those accusers of yours? Has no one condemned you?'

"Startled by the mercy in the Master's eyes, she thinks of the mob of angry men who had just been jeering at her, dragging her along by her clothes or any way they could without touching her, promising to kill her. She thinks of how they all melted away.

"She lifts her eyes to look into those kind eyes, and says, 'No man, Lord.'

"And He says, 'I don't condemn you either. Now go, and don't sin any more,' and she makes her way softly out, knowing she has so much to be thankful for. She has seen other women stoned. She did not doubt those men would do it to her.

"So what does God say to the Somalian Muslims who stone a 13-year-old girl, when three men had gang-raped her?

"How many girls here in Papua New Guinea have been raped? How many have died from AIDS? Be careful, girls. Don't take unnecessary risks. Remember to stay in groups as much as possible if you don't have a man around to protect you. I want so badly for you all to get as much education as you can get, but I am so worried about you riding buses alone, and traveling home from high school or college alone. They told me at Adirondack Bible College, if I would dress modestly I could trust to God for protection from rapists. There is no doubt that modest dress is *a help* in this respect. Years ago, Paul Harvey, news commentator, said that most women in the USA who are abducted are wearing shorts and halter. Dress is a privilege we can avail ourselves of, girls. Back three hundred years ago Arab and Caucasian men, and even African men were capturing Africans and putting them on slave ships for other countries. These slavers used to make the slaves dance naked on the decks of their ships. Usually it was the only time the poor people got to come on deck and get out of the filthy holds in which they were kept like animals and in which they died! But imagine the degradation of being made to dance in the nude. Oh, we are so blessed to be able to cover our bodies and dress modestly. Back just fifty years ago in your own history most highlands women wore only a purupuru held onto their bodies by a single bark string. My mother always said that was man's decree, so that when men wanted to beat their women, and the women tried to run away, all they had to do was hook a finger in that string and break it, and the woman would crumple in shame at his feet, not moving, only trying to hide her nakedness with her hands, and the man could beat her to a pulp or just as long as he wanted, without any interference.

"You know we holiness people say it is better for women to wear skirts and dresses because the **Bible** says women should not wear that which pertaineth to a man. Some people argue that women's pants are different, so they are not men's apparel, but if you look at the logo of public toilets (which are called restrooms in the USA) the logo for women is always a woman wearing a skirt or dress. This has been considered proper dress for a woman in Europe and America for centuries. Besides girls, you know how angry it makes most men in PNG for women to wear pants, so why add that irritant to men, and stir up their anger against you?

"Let me tell you about a time I reminded God of what they had told me at Adirondack Bible College. George and I were engaged to be married in 1969. We were both living at Katiloma in the Southern Highlands Province at the time. I was planning to go to Port Moresby Teachers College to do the 'E' Course and get my accreditation to teach English in the schools here in PNG. My parents were getting their masters' degrees at Aldersgate School of Religion in Florida, and would not be back in New Guinea (as it was still called then) until the latter half of 1970. The Expatriate Course (called the E Course for short) for teaching certification was to start in February of 1970, so George and I were going to marry after the course was over when my father could be at Katiloma to give me away. However, as George was listening to the radio up in the bush house in the Southern Highlands Province in November of 1969 he heard on the news that an expatriate woman staying at the YWCA in Port Moresby had been raped and murdered by a New Guinea man there.

"'You can't go to Port Moresby alone, Honey,' he said to me. I had been planning to stay at the Y as well. 'We will have to get married and go down to Port Moresby together, so I can protect you.' So we set up our wedding date to February 3rd, and asked my older brother, Jerry, with whose family I was living at the time, to give me away to George, and he did. People came from Kauapena, Mele, and Kagua to attend our wedding and reception. Our Katiloma people had a pig feast for the occasion.

"In Port Moresby we rented a small apartment or flat as the Australians say, in the basement of a well-to-do lady by the name of Mrs. Barker on what was known as Snob's Hill, overlooking Ela Beach. The kitchen and bathroom were so small you could stand in the center and touch the walls on either side, and the bedroom-living-room-combination had only windows on two sides, without proper ventilation. There was no air conditioning, and the heat was so intense (and we never had visitors) so when we were home, we shut the heavy drapes, and turned our fan on, and undressed to our underwear. There we had our extended honeymoon because the 'E' Course lasted six months. George got a job for Watkin's Construction Company because our mission allowance did not even pay the rent of that tiny apartment. He made enough as a contractor to take flying lessons one night a week, so he got his pilot's license, and later flew us back to Kagua on his first cross-country flight.

"One night about midnight we were wakened to the sounds of Mrs. Barker's screams, 'George, George!' George jumped up, jerked on his jeans, and ran out to find her lying on her driveway, and a man running off in such a hurry he had left one of his flip-flops behind. He had thrown Mrs. Barker up against the retaining wall of stones when she had come out of her garage. George helped her up and into her house whereupon she called the police, who did not come that night. The next morning Mrs. Barker was vomiting blood so she went to the hospital where she was admitted. That afternoon, the policeman finally arrived. He got the facts from George and then he said, 'Is there a younger woman living here? That man wasn't waiting for that old lady.'

"'Yes,' answered George, 'my wife and I are newly married.'

"'Let's look at your window screens. I bet he has been a peeping tom.' The policeman showed George a hole in each lower corner of every screen. 'He inserts a wire here and pulls the drapes aside and watches you.'

"He took George to the highest window. 'See here is the mark of a five gallon drum. I bet we will find it behind the garage.' George followed the policeman behind the garage, and sure enough, a drum was hidden there. 'He brings it out each evening, and stands on it, watching you.'

"When he had gone, George entered our flat with a big pipe which he stood beside the door. 'Honey, whenever you go out, always wait for me to go first, and I will go armed.' And he explained to me what the policeman had told him.

"But I arrived home from school about 3:00 each afternoon and climbed the hill from the bus stop alone. I let myself into my apartment with my key and locked the door behind me. However, I had to go up behind Mrs. Barker's house to do our laundry in her half-walled hut in her back yard. One afternoon as I was putting my clothes through the wringer, I felt eyes on me. I turned around and searched the yard and saw no one. I turned back to put more clothes through the wringer, and felt more strongly than before that someone was watching me. This time when I searched the yard I found the man standing in a flowering bush. His eyes gazed boldly into mine. Fear leaped up in me. I found it hard to breathe.

"'God,' I prayed, 'I am in Your hands. They told me back at Adirondack Bible College if I would dress modestly You would take care of me. Here I am with a skirt on and long sleeves and nylon hose, even in this terrible heat. It's up to You, God.'

"God said, 'Break eye contact and turn around.'

"I obeyed reluctantly. I turned around saying, 'Oh, God, I am so vulnerable now. I won't be able to tell when he is coming my way, when he is going to grab me. Oh, God,' I moaned inwardly. But after a little while I stopped feeling eyes on me. I turned around and looked and he was no longer standing in the bush. I searched the yard; he wasn't in sight. I turned off the washer, left the clothes in the water, went down around the house, and let myself into my apartment and locked the door behind me. I collapsed on the bed, pouring out my thanks to God for deliverance. I wondered how he had kept the man from grabbing me. But I didn't need to know. I was safe, and that was all that mattered.

"Later we learned it was the Tsimbu cook at the house next door who had attacked Mrs. Barker and doubtless watched for me as well. And years later God showed me a verse in His Word that says, 'God put a river between me and my enemy,' and I responded, 'Oh, is that what You did, God, back there when I was in Mrs. Barker's backyard?' Or maybe He put a hedge around me like He did Job, in Job 1:10. Notice in that verse, Satan is accusing God of putting a protective hedge around Job, so he could not get to him. Maybe that is what God did for me that day. Anyway, we know when we obey God's commands in all things we can trust Him to take care of us. He will not allow us to be tempted or tested above that we are able to bear. After that day George helped me with the laundry in the evening, and I never went into the backyard alone again. My understanding is that we need to take every precaution we can for our own safety, and that includes reading God's Word daily and knowing exactly what He wants of us in the culture in which we exist. I believe He can speak to us individually through many ways, but primarily through His Word. Isn't God good?

"Furthermore, girls and women, when we live in a less-than-perfect world with non-Christians all around us, and even Christians who have a lack of thorough training in their background, or baggage they are carrying from their own experiences that they haven't yet let God heal, women are going to be mistreated. Let me read you a poem written by my friend, Missy Haynes, who came to PNG when she was eleven years old with her missionary parents.

The 'Me' Within
(For All Girls Young and Old)

Down deep inside where no one goes,
I am 'ME!' The one I know.
There I sing and trill with ease –
Swing and dance beneath the trees.

Within my heart I can perform
Music graceful, deep and warm.
Inside me there are no limits
Of capabilities or minutes.

This outer frame is just my shell –
And sometimes doesn't work too well.
(Everyone has limitations –
Just different types and variations.)

God has a plan that's just for me –
Walking with Him, He'll help me see.
His plan is for my whole life long
And so I will keep dreaming on.

Keep dreaming on and living well,
For without dreams I am just a shell.
Let 'Me' live on and sing the song
God has for 'Me!' my whole life long.

Down deep inside, where no one knows
Dreams and hopes bloom as a rose.

m. a. kinnet
8/22/06

197

"Let God plant a dream in your hearts, girls, and when I say girls, now, I mean all of you, even if you are as old as I am. Inside I still remember and often feel like the little girl I was fifty years ago. Last year when I came back to PNG I had a dream. I wanted to tell all the old women, my age and older, that even though they are crippled with arthritis and cannot do the work they once did, and so we feel old, useless and worthless, I wanted to tell them that God still loves them. God sees the heart inside. He knows how we still long to serve Him. He knows we are sorry we are so old and wrinkled and unappealing. And by the way, GIRLS, no matter how old you are, you are allowed to wear nice clothes and look appealing! God wants you to be clean and neat and as well-dressed and modest as you can continue to be, without spending money on attire that should be put into His work. I remember when I was thirty-eight years old, at Katiloma. I had been called *enagaesi* for so long, (you ImboUngu speakers, that means, *ambo amboi*) that I really felt I was an old woman. One week in my spare time I made a beautiful embroidered denim skirt and vest for myself, and then I felt ashamed to wear it. I thought I was too old to wear something new. I had absorbed the PNG attitude of the 80s that old women deserved only the old rags, or worn-out cast-offs of other women. That is wrong, GIRLS. You can still be called girls, no matter how old you are, by other girls, at least, and then you can know that inner girl who can still dream and hope, dance and sing, joy and rejoice in her great God.

"I discovered last year that I was too late to tell the older women that God still loved them, at least in church, because they fell asleep too quickly to hear me. Their bodies are so tired they just want to sleep. You younger women, cherish and care for your elder sisters. PNG homes have such little comfort. I am so sorry for women my age who do not have soft mattresses to sleep on, when their bones hurt so badly. I brought magnets last year and this year to give to my friends with arthritis. I could not have come back to PNG last year if I had not discovered the help magnets can give you, wrapped around your aching limbs at night, to take the pain away. I showed my magnet wraps to the pharmacist here in Mt. Hagen last year and asked her to order some from China. She was Chinese, and I pled with her to order these from China and sell them here in her pharmacy. She said, 'No, we have enough jewelry for sale here. We don't want to order more.' I tried to explain to her that even though these look like jewelry they are really magnets, and they take away pain for seventy-five or -six percent of the population. I could not convince her, but I will try again to get someone to buy these from China for all of you people with *skru-pen*. Tell any buyers you know they can get them from Golden Eagle J. Inc. Wholesale Import, and it is called magnetic jewelry. You can type that in on Google, and bring it up.

"Please remember Melissa Haynes Kinnett's poem, and be all you want to be for God in the 'ME' inside you. Please ask God for a dream, and feel it and live it, deep within, even when you cannot do it on the outside, thus offering God the service of your heart.

"I am going to ask the four female Patriarchs to come up here and sing another one of Missy's poems for you that her Mama put to music, her God-given Mama, not her birth mother. God gave Missy a wonderful person to mother her when she was as old as I was at Katiloma, having been called enagaesi for five years! Even when we are old we need the ministry of our sisters, much older than we, or even younger, to *need* us and to bless us with their love. I am sure God has blessed Missy's Mama as much through her ministry to Missy, as He has blessed Missy, herself, through this ministry of her Mama. While I am speaking of her, Missy told me that even though Mama is single now and never married during her sixty-six years on this earth, she had proposals from several men and even from one Arab man! She always asked the men if she could have her music, and the Arab man said, 'No, but you can be the first wife, and you will get to help me choose the other wives!' Of course she turned him down! You women need the same freedom to say no to the man you do not want to marry!

"Before they sing let me tell you the story a Mendi woman told me in May, 2000. She said her husband, who is an educated man, had taken many more wives after he married her. Soon he just started living off the salaries of his educated wives. She herself was a bankteller and made a good salary. When he took a second wife, back when she was much younger, she wanted to commit suicide, but she had a son whom she could not part with, and she decided to kill him, too, to keep him with her and to get even with her husband who was not showing their son enough love. Preachers in America tell you the best way a man can show his child love is to love the child's mother and keep the marriage happy. This woman's husband certainly wasn't doing that. So this little lady was going to overdose her son on camoquin and then overdose herself, but our loving heavenly Father said to her with so much love she heard and understood, 'My Daughter, if you do that, your little son will be with me for all eternity, but you will be separated from him and Me.' So this lovely and loving little lady who is here this morning, and who can tell you who she is, if she wants to, said to me, 'I have not committed suicide or killed my son. I am still here, and my husband keeps replacing each successive wife with a younger one, but it still hurts just as badly when he prefers their children over mine, who are his children also. And if I could not come here every week to this women's meeting and get these ladies to pray for me, lay their hands on me and pray for me, I could not make it through the week.'

"Your sisters need your ministry to them, my Dears. Some of you women are pastors' wives, or the wives of men who do not and will not take a second wife, thank God! You women need to reach out to your sisters who are hurting so badly. Some of your sisters are bearing burdens I could not bear. I do not know how you do it, but for God! And God can minister to these hurting sisters, through you, and me, Dearly Beloved! We can be God's Hand extended to these hurting ones. Let such ministry be a part of your inner dream, if you will.

"Leah, Anna, Beulah and Barbara, Patriarchs, will you come and sing "Forgotten Dream" for us?"

Three of Timba and Liriyame's beautiful granddaughters, and one 'granddaughter-in-law' came to the front and melted the hearts that were not already melted, with their beautiful harmony.

Forgotten Dream

There is a dream down deep inside
Where bright sunshine and laughter hide.
Sometimes I catch a glimpse of it –
Slip teasing from the rainbow mist.

I'd like to cross the chasm wide
And live upon that other side.
Whenever I start to cross o'er
Fear and guilt press even more.

'Know the truth and be set free'
(Free is what I long to be.)
Loving God by faith alone
More than rules set in stone.

Free to know God's joy and peace –
Tension, doubt – to Him release.
See in Him His face alone –
And hear Him say I am His own.

This dream looks like a meadow fair
With pink-hewn clouds and crystal air.
Perfumed flowers give nectar sweet
And in the trees the songbirds tweet.

Jesus Himself each day is here
With open arms and listening ear.

m.a.kinnett
8/14-15/05

As the women and girls were leaving the sanctuary, Tawa
slipped up to Linda and asked, "May I have a look at your Bible,
the one you call *CJB*? May I read it until the next service?"

"Certainly, you may," said Linda. "Better yet, keep it until
tomorrow at this time, and then bring it to me before the
evening service, okay?"

"Okay," said Tawa, accepting it gratefully.

Helen Rakua Kelley (Kotapu) Tua was the orphan daughter of Pastor Rakua and his wife, Nasupi, both of whom died of cancer, asking the mission to help care for their daughters. Her grandfather, Kotapu, would not allow his name to be used by her and her sisters because he did not want to pay their school fees, so we put our name on her school records, as well as seeing to their other financial needs, though their grandmother did most of their care. Helen attended Tambul Baibel Skul and pastored for two years before she married Pastor Tua, a Wiru widower, father-in-law of famous pianist Jack Kipoi of HSBC, currently studying again in Florida. Their daughters names are Vicki (not pictured) and Rowena. Helen teaches religious instruction, and reading and writing to women and children at Aponda Community School, as well as being an active pastor and pastor's wife.

Chapter Twelve

The Patriarchs were singing when Pombo's family entered the tabernacle. Out of habit the women went to sit on the women's side, and Pombo and his sons and grandsons went to sit with the men. Even in the confusion to find a seat, Tawa and Toropo did not miss a word of "The Gift of Music," by Melissa A. Kinnett.

Music is a gift of love
Because it lifts the soul above –
And is an avenue to flee
When life is like a stormy sea

Music gives the soul a voice
When the time comes to rejoice.
Whether sung or softly played –
Still the message is conveyed.

Music clears the path to God
Examining the way we've trod.
Drawing to a true repentance –
Grateful for the lifted sentence.

Music is a discipline –
Giving joy while reigning in.
Music gives to those who hear
With the heart and with the ear.

Music of the ear alone
Is cold and bare – without a home.
It takes a heart to let it feel –
To set it free and make it real.

Music will reverberate
When we enter Heaven's gate.
Bowing low before our King.
Forever of His love we'll sing.

When the Patriarchs took their seats on the platform the tall Haitian man unfolded his long thin body and stood to his feet. He walked gracefully to the pulpit. Linda was reminded of her godly mentor, Rev. Sherwood Weeks, who moved so gracefully on the platform she used to think it was almost a dance, a sweet, solumn, sanctified dance. Certainly it was nothing carnal, sensual, or detracting from grace. Rather it was the very picture of grace! Both spiritual and physical!

"'Music will reverberate,
when we enter heaven's gate.

"The book of First Thessalonians has a double theme, as my Studies in Holiness teacher, Dr. Paul Kaufman, taught me and one of them is about the second coming, or 'when we enter heaven's gate' though we can also do that by dying in Christ! Open your **Bibles** to First Thessalonians and keep them open, as we are going to be reading a lot of scripture in this service.

"The entrance of Thy Word gives light. God's Word, the **Bible**, is our main source of light. You can never read too much Scripture!

"This book of First Thessalonians has a double theme as I said. One is holiness of heart; the other is the second coming of our Lord. Let us see if we can make this sermon one with two themes, just like the book of First Thessalonians. The last two verses of chapter three will combine these two themes nicely for us and give us the double thrust or the double barrel for this sermon:

"'And the Lord make you to increase and abound in love one toward another, and toward all men even as we do toward you. (13) To the end he may stablish your hearts unblameable in holiness before God, even our Father, at the coming of our Lord Jesus Christ with all his saints.'

"These two verses bring out the return of our Lord and the second work of grace, giving it two of its many names here: holiness and abounding love or perfect love, as it is often called.

"We want to be ready for the Lord's return by making sure that we are living above sin and our hearts are pure. This is necessary if we are to be included in that word 'saints,' His saints; His holy ones would be another way to translate it from the Greek.

"Before we seek holiness, my friends, we need to establish the fact that we are saved. We have to have had that repentence that the Patriarchs sang about, that caused 'the lifting of the sentence.' Do you know you are saved? Dr. Kaufman told us to look at these four facets of salvation:

- Justification: a legal act that takes place in heaven as Romans 5:1 tells us.
- Regeneration: a new birth; born again, like a new baby
- Adoption: you have new relatives. Christians are now your *wantoks*!
- Initially sanctified: as holy as you know how to be. You are not completely sanctified, as I will continue to show you.

"To live above sin we have to first understand what sin is. John Wesley said, 'If I hold the standard too high I drive people to distraction. If I hold it too low, I drive them into hell.' We have to endeavor to keep between those two extremes.

"The first thing necessary is to understand sin. It is also necessary to realize that there are degrees of perfection. John Fletcher wrote an eight-page sermon with that title, 'Degrees of Perfection.' You Pacific Bible College students will want to look that up in your library. It may be hard reading, but if you don't already study it in one of your classes, form a small group to read it together and help each other study it and understand it.

"The second work of grace is to be both instantaneous and gradual. The two Wesley brothers decided between them that Charles would press the crisis experience, the instantaneous work, while John was to emphasize or press the process as opposed to the crisis, the gradual workings of the Spirit in our lives to continually help us to mature and grow in grace. I hope I am remembering that correctly from Dr. Kaufman's lectures. Anyway, they agreed for one of them to emphasize one, and the other, the other.

"Chapter four, verse three, gives us another name for this second work of grace: 'For this is the will of God, even your sanctification.' Sanctification means to be set apart from something, in this case, sin.

"What is sin? Sin is a willful transgression against a known law of God. If we know something is wrong and we do it, we have sinned. But the born again Christian does not willfully do anything wrong. He wants to obey God. God has forgiven his sins when He took him as His child, and this child of God wants to obey God in all things and do only what is right. As First John 3:9 says, 'Whosoever is born of God does not commit sin for his seed remaineth in him and he cannot sin, because he is born of God.'

"If you know you have been to Calvary and had your sins forgiven, when the devil brings up your past, remind him of his future!

"But there is another type of sin. Pride is sin. Jealousy is sin. These are involuntary reactions. They are carnal traits that we have in our hearts. We do not willfully choose to be proud, or to be jealous. Sanctification will root out the carnal nature; sometimes it is called the death of the old man. Let the old man die."

Pombo sat listening and pondering in his heart. More and more, he had realized in this camp meeting he had lived a life of self-centeredness, selfishness. He had not considered others. He had only used others. He had pandered to himself, pandered to his own pride, and here this man was saying, pride is a carnal trait, pride is an involuntary reaction. He thanked God for forgiveness for every sin he had committed in the past. He wanted to obey God now. He was not committing any willful sins, but he knew now he wanted rid of the pride in his heart that had ruled so much of his actions all his life long. God was surely turning his heavenly spotlight onto the root of sin in Pombo's heart!

Pombo's mind had been occupied with himself and things God was pointing out to him for some time when he suddenly heard some more words the man of God was saying.

"I grew up in the country of Haiti, a poverty stricken country where some of the leaders long ago decided to follow evil in many forms. It is called Haitian voodoo, and it is syncretism of many beliefs, but it includes Satanism. All around me people died in their sin and poverty, all through my childhood. The children do not have enough to eat, and they die like flies. The greatest percentage of adults do not have enough to eat and are sometimes even reduced to eating what they call 'clean dirt' or soil from the riverbed.

"I attended four years of training at Hobe Sound Bible College, and I often got together with the three or four students from Papua New Guinea there. Some years there were as many as six or seven. We ate meals together and discussed our homelands together. I learned that you people almost all own land. You all have places you can make gardens and grow vegetables. Some of the PNG students feel people are beginning to move to the cities more and more, but they always come back to their villages for special times, for holidays, for deaths, for celebrations. In Haiti for several hundred years now people have multiplied in the cities, and they have no villages to go to, no land that their grandparents owned. My country is one of few that gained their independence through a successful slave rebellion. None of those slaves owned land, and even though they took over the properties of the people they rebelled against, they probably did not understand how to care for them properly. Realize the value of your land, folks, and treasure it. Don't become rootless in the cities. If you have a job in the city on the coast, maintain your inherited spot of ground back in the highlands or in your village. Take a vacation there, build a house there, and then some day if you lose your city job and cannot afford to keep living in a city, you can go back to the village with some savvy about how to better your life there. God can use you to be a blessing in your village and help raise the standard of living there.

"I was blessed to have been taken in by missionaries and raised by them, and trained in righteousness, in the ways of God.

"I gave my heart to God as a small child. I remember going to the altar in a little brush-arbor church and feeling forgiveness for my sins. At an early age I knew I was a sinner. I had lied. I had been mean to other children. I had stolen. I did not need the preacher to tell me I was a sinner. I knew that well, but God forgave me and made me His child, way back there when I was seven years old.

"When I was sixteen years of age I became impressed by the man of God with whom I lived and his prayer life. He used to rise at four o'clock every morning and go over to the church to pray.

It was a nice church building by this time, and a large one. One evening I asked him to waken me before he left the house the next morning, and he did. I began a routine of seeking more of God for myself as well as praying for my people every morning. I grew in grace. There came a day when I realized I had the root of sin in my heart; I had the Old Man on board. I began seeking God at the altar in church every time somebody preached. And I continued to seek Him in His fullness each morning in my room while my spiritual father prayed in the church.

"Sometimes I would think I had reached through and attained the experience, and I would testify to it. Then I would see the evidence of carnality in my life again, and back I'd go to seeking sanctification again.

"Finally God sanctified me wholly! The next day that my classmates made fun of me, I just laughed along with them. I felt no anger rise up in my heart against them. When that happened, Brothers and Sisters, I was so happy, I jumped to my feet and began running outside. I ran and leaped over the low wall that enclosed the school yard. I felt almost like I had wings. I felt like I could run through a troop and leap over any wall the devil cared to try to build around me. I knew then that my God is invincible! Oh, the power of the indwelling Holy Spirit I felt within me!

After quoting the words to the children's chorus by Ruth Harms Calkin, the glowing happy preacher broke into song, and sang them in a lovely bass voice, repeating the last two lines twice. The people thrilled to every note.

My God is so Big
Ruth Harms Calkin
©2002 Nuggets of Truth Publishing BMI

My God is so Big
So Strong and so Mighty
There's nothing my God can not do

Verse 2
My God is so Big
So Strong and so Mighty
My God can make everything new

Verse 3
The mountains are His
The rivers are His
The stars are His Handiwork too

Verse 4
My God is so Big
So Strong and so Mighty
There's nothing my God can not do
(For you)

He pointed a long shapely finger at the huge congregation, delighting them, and then added, "For you and for Haiti! There is nothing my great big, invincible, omnipresent, omnipotent, omniscient God cannot do! All He needs is enough people who will obey Him fully. He can take a weak man like me, from a poverty-stricken country, a motherless kid with a father who didn't want him, who had abandoned him and left him to die. He can take a child who stole, cheated, lied and was violent, and make that kid over anew! He can take a proud, angry, jealous teenager and remove every bit of carnality from that kid's heart, and turn him into a vessel of honor—not for the kid's honor, but for the King's honor, for God's glory! Imagine us weak human beings being vessels of glory for our great God! Can you imagine it? Can you fathom it? Can we wrap our weak minds around that truth? The God of Glory, the Creator of the universe, took on the form of man and 'tabernacled' among us, as the Scriptures tell us. He lived with us, and died with us, and for us. He was buried, but He rose again, and ascended into heaven where He sits at the right hand of the Father, but He's coming back, people! He is coming back soon! One of the PNG students at Hobe Sound showed me how you people measure something small by putting your thumbnail against the tip of your little finger, and he told me he had had a dream, and an angel had told him to get ready, to be prepared because Jesus is coming back this soon!" Pierre Simon measured his little finger tip with his thumbnail with both hands and held them up to the congregation! This soon, the Spirit told him! I remember when he told that in Studies in Holiness class. I remember how my heart lept within me! My spirit bore witness to the Spirit of God as that truth was delivered by one of your countrymen in Florida, USA.

"Holiness or Christian Perfection is on a sliding scale, Dr. Kaufman used to say. Abraham never reached the level of perfection Paul did, even though God said to him to walk before Him and be perfect. I may never attain to the level of perfection Dr. Kaufman has, but I can walk before God and be perfect before Him, and that is Christian perfection.

"Dr. Kaufman said, 'God demands moral perfection.' Matthew 5:48: 'Be ye therefore perfect, even as your Father which is in heaven is perfect. Let us go on to perfection as Ephesians tells us because God created us to be holy.'

"Dr. Kaufman talked about 'fasting with his eyes.' Do you know what fasting is? Have you ever fasted a meal to pray?" People raised a loud chorus of assent. "So you know what fasting is. Well, in the cities of America, as in the cities of Papua New Guinea, and the cities of Haiti we can see things we should not see. My teacher said we can look away. We can fast with our eyes. If people are not dressed modestly we do not have to let our eyes rest on their immodesty. We can look away. We can fast with our eyes.

"I said we need light. 'Light is God's opinion on any matter,' as my professor always says.

"Do you know God has an opinion on how you dress? He has an opinion on the music you listen to. He has an opinion about every facet of your life and your behavior and your walk with Him. When He says, 'Walk before me and be thou perfect,' He wants you to line up with His opinion in your walk, in your dress, in your recreation, in the music you listen to, in the books you read, even in the thoughts you think."

Pastor Pierre paused and looked around. He smiled at everyone. A big smile that spread across his whole face and showed all his teeth! "You know what, folks? I love preaching to you! You are so open! You are so accepting! My heart tells me you are so willing to obey all that God asks of you! You want to walk before God and be perfect in His sight. You have turned from idols to serve the living and true God as First Thessalonians, chapter one, verse nine says. 'And to wait for his Son from heaven, whom he raised from the dead, even Jesus, which delivered us from the wrath to come.' That's verse ten, the last verse of the first chapter of First Thessalonians.

"There is that underlying theme of the Second Coming of Christ again. Turn over to the last verses of chapter two. 'For what is our hope, or joy, or crown of rejoicing? Are not even ye in the presence of our Lord Jesus Christ at his coming? For ye are our glory and joy.' I think Paul was just as excited over the Thessalonians as I am over you. He must have enjoyed writing these words to them like I am enjoying reading his words to you and preaching to you!

"Then there is the last verse of chapter three which I have already read to you, but I am going to read again. Listen with all your ears and all your hearts! 'To the end he may stablish your hearts unblameable in holiness before God, even our Father, at the coming of our Lord Jesus Christ with all his saints.'

"Are you getting excited about the Lord's return, folks?" Pastor Pierre held his hands aloft, measuring his thumbnails against the tip of his little fingers, and all knew what he meant. The Lord's second coming may be this close! After walking back and forth across the platform, smiling at them all the while, showing them his littlest finger tips, he said, "We have read the last verses of each of the first three chapters. Now let's look at chapter four and read the most quoted passage about our Lord's return in the last six verses of that chapter.

"'But I would not have you to be ignorant, brethren, concerning them which are asleep, that ye sorrow not, even as others which have no hope. (14) For if we believe that Jesus died and rose again, even so them also which sleep in Jesus will God bring with him. (15) For this we say unto you by the word of the Lord, that we which are alive and remain unto the coming of the Lord shall not prevent' or precede 'them which are asleep. (16) For the Lord himself shall descend from heaven with a shout, with the voice of the archangel, and with the trump of God; and the dead in Christ shall rise first: (17) Then we which are alive and remain shall be caught up together with them in the clouds, to meet the Lord in the air; and so shall we ever be with the Lord. (18) Wherefore comfort one another with these words.'

"Isn't that beautiful, folks? Have any of you lost a loved one in the last week, the last month, this last year? Well, those verses tell us that those who are asleep in Jesus, who died believing in Him, will rise to meet Jesus first when He descends with a shout. Then we who are alive, and remain on this earth, and who believe in Him, will be caught up with them in the air together! And so shall we ever and always for all eternity be with our Lord! Isn't that exciting? Oh, my Brothers and Sisters, it makes me want to run and shout and leap over a wall! I can hardly contain my joy when I think on the Lord's return!

"First Thessalonians isn't the only book where these two themes run together. It's in many other places too. Before we look at the last chapter of this book, jump quickly over to First Peter, chapter one, verse two: there Peter talks about the 'sanctification of the Spirit,' and then in verse three he talks about the 'lively hope by the resurrection of Jesus Christ from the dead.'

"Hebrews 12:14 says, 'Follow peace with all men, and holiness, without which no man shall see the Lord.' You see, it is talking about holiness and seeing Christ all in one verse.

"Now we have one more chapter in this book, and one more Second Coming passage, as well as one more exhortation to be sanctified. There are twenty-eight verses in this chapter, and the last several verses are the closing of the letter or epistle. Verse 23 says, 'And the very God of peace sanctify you wholly; and I pray God your whole spirit and soul and body be preserved blameless unto the coming of our Lord Jesus Christ.' Isn't that beautiful, my people? Isn't that a beautiful piece of literature, combining those two themes like ribbons running through the whole letter, braided and intertwined, about our heart purity and the second coming of our Lord! It is worth living for, my friends. It is worth dying for. Whether we are dead or alive, when Jesus returns, we are going to rise to meet Him in the air. And so shall we ever be with our Lord. I want to rise, friends. I want to go meet my Lord in the air. I don't want any root of sin holding me down, any evidence of carnality or the old man messing things up for me. Let us pray for God to sanctify us wholly and purify our bodies, souls and spirits. Let us bow to God, and let us pray."

And the thousands bowed their heads and prayed, including Pombo, his wives, his children and grandchildren.

Tawa prayed for this second definite work of grace which Pierre had preached, and she committed her whole life to God and His service. The longer she prayed the more she became aware of a dream growing in her heart. She not only loved the message. She realized she loved the messenger. It seemed so impossible, humanly speaking. Probably every girl in this congregation of thousands felt their hearts drawn to this godly young man from Haiti! How could he notice her among the thousands of her people?

However with God, all things are possible! She had heard the speakers here at this camp meeting say those very words! God, are You giving me this dream? Is this just my own desires, or is this a God-given dream? Can I believe that You are implanting this dream in my mind as I commit my whole life to You and ask You to do a second definite work of grace in me? Oh, God, I am such a bundle of emotions. Why did You make me so emotional? Can I ask you to cause this man to love me, and then trust You to bring it to pass?

I remember a year ago, Father, I wondered if it was all right to ask You to keep my father from making me marry an old polygamist! Now, just one year later, I heard *Ara* say that he will never make me marry an old man or a polygamist! Thank You, Father! That is a miracle! Just one year ago I did not even know if I could ask for such a large thing. Now pastors have told me You say to ask largely! Can I ask this, Father? Can I ask you to let me marry a man from another country who probably does not know anything about brideprice, and would not have a tribe to help him raise it, if he did know and believe in the custom?

Tawa felt a deep peace steal into her heart. She felt patience. God answered my prayer of a year ago in just twelve months. I believe He will answer this question for me too, in His time.

She recalled the words she had heard the Patriarchs and Kelly Harvey and Pierre Simon sing in one service, *In His Time.*

In His time, In His time, He makes all things beautiful,
in His time.
Lord, please show me every day
As You're teaching me Your way
That You do just what You say, In Your time.
In Your time, In Your time, You make all things beautiful,
in Your time
Lord, My life to You I bring
May each song I have to sing
Be to You a lovely thing, in Your time

Diane Ball © 1978 by Maranatha Music and CCCM Music/ASCAP
All Rights Reserved. Used by permission

Tawa opened Linda Kelley's **Complete Jewish Bible** and her eyes fell on Luke 7:39. When the *Parush* who had invited him saw what was going on, he said to himself, "If this man were really a prophet, he would have known who is touching him and what sort of a woman she is, that she is a sinner.

40. Yeshua answered, "Shim'on, I have something to say to you.

"Say it, *Rabbi*," he replied.

41. "A certain creditor had two debtors; the one owed ten times as much as the other.

42. "When they were unable to pay him back, he canceled both their debts. Now which of them will love him more?"

43. Shim'on answered, "I suppose the one for whom he cancelled the larger debt."

"Your judgment is right," Yeshua said to him.

44. Then turning to the woman, he said to Shim'on. "Do you see this woman? I came into your house – you didn't give me water for my feet, but this woman has washed my feet with her tears and dried them with her hair!

45. "You didn't give me a kiss; but from the time I arrived, this woman has not stopped kissing my feet!

46. "You didn't put oil on my head, but this woman poured perfume on my feet!

47. "Because of this, I tell you that her sins – which are many! – have been forgiven, because she loved much. But someone who has been forgiven only a little loves only a little."

48. Then he said to her, "Your sins have been forgiven."

49. At this, those eating with him began saying among themselves, "Who is this fellow that presumes to forgive sins?"

50. But he said to the woman, "Your trust has saved you; go in peace."

And I will go in peace, thought Tawa. I will pray that God will bring His will to pass, and I will believe Him capable of doing it. Here she was a woman, and a prostitute, I believe, and she was allowed to weep her tears of repentance on to His feet. She was allowed to hold His feet, and dry them with her hair. She was allowed to kiss His feet again and again, to show how much she loved Him. Oh, God, You have done so much for me. You have saved me from marriage to an old polygamist. You can bring to pass my marriage to the man You choose for me. I will go in peace and rest in Your loving care. I hear You say, in Linda's voice, "My daughter, your trust has saved you; go in peace."

Tawa paged back to Revelation, as she loved reading prophecies about Christ's return, and her eyes fell on the last verses before Revelation. Jude 24 & 25: Now,

> To the one who can keep you from falling
> And set you without defect and full of joy
> In the presence of his Sh'kinah –
> 25   to God alone; our Deliverer,
> Through Yeshua the Messiah, our Lord –
> Be glory, majesty, power and authority
> Before all time, now and forever. *Amen*

When she returned the **Complete Jewish Bible** to Linda she said, "In case we do not see each other again, let me read you these verses. God will keep you and me from falling!" And she read her Jude 24 and 25.

"Ah, yes, sweet verses indeed!" exclaimed Linda. "And I can hear them in my beloved Rev. Weeks' voice in the King James Version which I also love: 'Now unto Him who is able to keep you from falling, and to present you faultless before the presence of his glory with exceeding joy, 25. To the only wise God our Savior, be glory and majesty, dominion and power, both now and ever. Amen.'

"The only wise God, Tawa. Remember, we worship and serve the only wise God, Who is able to keep us from falling, keep us from evil, and present us faultless, through Yeshua, our Messiah, our Lord, before the Presence of His Glory with exceeding joy. There's our word Glory again two times, Sh'kinah in Hebrew, Dear!

"I hope we will see each other again. But you are right. Life is uncertain. If we don't meet together again in this land, on this earth, we can meet in the air at the Second Coming of our Lord, like Pastor Pierre has been preaching."

Papua New Guinea Bible Church at Pabrabuk
The tree beside it is the evergreen with bougainvillea that
Susie Lorimer planted.